She should go back, spe... the truth, beg him to recon... would be given by her abs... resolve the situation. She kne... ...to be strong, but she didn't feel strong. She felt feeble, weak, miserable, and oh, so tired. Too tired to think straight.

Without thought or plan, Harriet mechanically walked toward the tube, running over and over different scenarios, each one becoming its own reality. The entrance to the station filled with the relentless ebb and flow of commuters. A fleeting gap. She stepped between, slowly traversing the internal echoing medley of tiled chambers and escalators. With each step, Harriet felt more anger, accompanied by guilt. She should never have kept pushing Nana to tell her about her family. She had been unwell. It was her fault Nana died. She didn't deserve a future. There could be no future. Not without Nana.

Harriet continued weaving through the sea of jostling, purposeful faces, colliding with a group of schoolchildren and tourists. Normally she would apologize, but she barged by. One of the regular buskers struck up loudly, acknowledging her presence and her usual generosity. He nodded, playing something for her, she didn't know what; she didn't hear. It was futile. Her mind was elsewhere.

She ended up on the platform with a plan, and a perfect sense of calm. She felt the telltale gust of wind from the ink-black cave. The train was coming.

A strand of hair came loose from her plait, flicking her face as debris skittered along the dais. The train was imminent. *People throw themselves in front of trains all the time.*

Secrets, Shame, and a Shoebox

by

L. B. Griffin

Prequel to
The Twenty-One-Year Contract

Secrets, Shame, and a Shoebox

Cover Art by *The Wild Rose Press, Inc.*

The Wild Rose Press, Inc.
PO Box 708
Adams Basin, NY 14410-0708
Visit us at www.thewildrosepress.com

Publishing History
First Edition, 2021
Trade Paperback ISBN 978-1-5092-3595-7
Digital ISBN 978-1-5092-3596-4

Prequel to The Twenty-One-Year Contract
Published in the United States of America

Dedication

For Dave, with much love,
… and yes, I'm still playing.

Acknowledgements

My thanks go to Nan Swanson, my editor, who has been a great support and guidance throughout this writing journey, and of course to The Wild Rose Press for taking me on, and to RJ Morris for front cover design.

Special thanks to my children—Sam and Kelly—who have been unwavering in their help, even when I haven't asked, and to Jac Forsyth and Chris Heywood, who gave me the final push to get it out there.

To writers and friends—most of whom have been there right from conception and have given their time, patience, and guidance—I couldn't have done it without you: Cindy Beadman, Barbara Compton, Peter Dixon, Paul Fines, June Foster, Jonny Griffiths, Jae Monroe, Dianne Preston, Davina Rungsamy, Katherine Tanko. I have listed you in alphabetical order because I see it as the fairest way of saying thank you with equal appreciation.

Chapter 1

London, 1957

Harriet Laws turned into Ham Street, a shabby string of two-up-two-downs where most considered the dregs of humanity lived. A riot waiting to happen. Not that the preconceptions of others bothered her, or her Nana. They loved their home, their neighbors, and anyone was welcome, any time of day.

Harriet spotted Mr. Oatley across the road, rooting through his pockets, drenched, looking lost. Angling her umbrella to stop it turning inside out, she waved.

"Everything all right?"

They talked over the jangle of a police siren a couple of streets away. London was rapidly becoming a city where everyone locked their doors, though there was nothing worth stealing in Ham Street.

"Can't find ma bloody keys!"

"Come round to ours if you get stuck."

Mr. Oatley raised his hand, dangling his keys triumphantly. She grinned; he was always searching for something.

Harriet had almost reached number nine when a sleek Jaguar screeched around the corner, slicing through the torrent, fishtailing toward her. It hit a blocked drain. Filthy water shot in all directions as a skinny youth leaned out the passenger window, drunkenly laughing his head off.

"Fancy a shag, darlin'? Plenty of room in the back."

Seconds later, a black police car came clanging around the same corner. Harriet didn't bother looking up, as the Jaguar was already gone. Ham Street was a shortcut to the low-cost, high-crime tower blocks. It would've been stranger if it hadn't happened.

Harriet kicked her shoes off and closed the front door. She wiped her rain-spattered glasses with the bottom of her dress and breathed in the rich, comforting smell of stew. Harriet loved food, especially her Nana's, plus, it was Thursday, her birthday. Nana promised she would make her favorite cheesy herb dumplings to go with yesterday's leftovers. She wandered into the tiny front room, turned her shoes upside down onto the hearth, and hung her coat across the dining chair. The room was spotless, with their two old armchairs angled by the fire to get the best of the heat. Picking up the coal scuttle, Harriet dropped more coal onto the dying embers, surprised Nana had let the fire get so low.

"Is that my birthday girl?" Molly called from the kitchen.

"Just topping up the fire, Nana."

"Did you get drenched?"

"Sort of."

"There's a fresh towel already laid out for you in the Posh Room. Off you go before you catch a death."

Harriet grinned, knowing she would freeze her knickers off in the new bathroom just as much as she had in the outside lavvy. She found Molly in the kitchen, sidled up next to her, and kissed her talcum-soft cheek.

"Did you have a nice day?"

"It was all right." She shrugged.

"Just all right?"

"Busy." Harriet forced a laugh as she unclipped her plaited halo and began to towel it dry. She'd never tell Nana she'd been one of the few girls considered smart enough to go to university. State subsidies covered only fees and accommodation; they didn't cover loss of income. Her grandmother was working two jobs already. Now their landlord had increased the rent, arguing his tenants should be grateful for the luxury of an inside lavvy, but everyone in the street was struggling to find the extra. Harriet pushed her glasses up her nose and began collecting the cutlery. University didn't come down to brains, it came down to money.

"Penny for your thoughts, dear heart?"

Harriet looked up. "I'm pinning my hopes on a position becoming vacant in the dress department. The girls seem happy enough there." Shocked at how easily the lie rolled off her tongue, she couldn't look her grandmother in the eye.

"And what will Miss Macy do without her best sales assistant?"

Harriet rarely told her grandmother anything bad about work. She *was* the best sales assistant, but her mean-minded supervisor never once recognized it. Instead, Miss Macy with her whale-boned corset limited managerial conversation to nasty little jibes about Harriet's weight.

"Muzz Laws"—Harriet mimicked her plummy supervisor—"Do not make eye contact with those disgusting men who wish to purchase fancy undergarments for mistresses, but *if* they want to know about potato sack bloomers or torpedo brassieres, send them straight to me."

Molly put the ladle on the saucer with a half-smile. "As I've said before my girl, you're lucky to have a job."

Nana was right, jobs were scarce; she was lucky to have one at all. Whilst her grandmother dished up, Harriet finished laying the table, then arranged the chess set by the fire, ready for afterward.

Harriet demolished her meal, while Molly moved her food around her plate with a fork.

"You all right, Nana? You look a bit pale."

"Stop your fussing," said Molly, fiddling with the tablecloth. "There's something I need to talk to you about."

Harriet watched her grandmother closely. She always tried to hide it when she was sick, but she couldn't hide the clammy, gray tinge creeping over her skin.

"Is it your job at the bakery?" If the whispers were true, they would never be able to find the rent.

"No, it's not about the bakery."

"Well, whatever it is, don't worry about it now. Tell me another time."

Molly put her hand up, and Harriet knew not to argue.

"No, I need to do this now. You've asked me more questions lately about your past, and you've probably guessed I've left some things out." She paused, seemingly apprehensive.

Harriet edged herself along her seat, curiosity getting the better of her.

"I've told you a lot about your mother but nothing of your father. I should have. He was such a lovely young man."

"You knew him?" It was a kind of vindication. She

always felt sure Nana was hiding something. Molly's hand shook as she took a sip of water. All Harriet felt was guilt.

"Nana, honestly, you don't have to tell me anything. Not today. Maybe tomo—"

But the glass was already falling from Nana's hand, the contents splashing out, shattering into tiny, sparkling splinters.

"Hattie…" The slow motion of events took only seconds. Her skin gray and lips inked purple, Molly clutched her chest. "Hattie?"

She tilted sideways and fell onto the cold, hard, unforgiving floor. Though her breath was weak, the faint rise of her chest gave Harriet a window of hope. Trembling, she bundled her cardigan into a makeshift pillow, silently praying, *Please don't die.*

"I'm going for help, Nana. I'll be back…really quickly."

The Donaldson's were the only people well off enough in Ham Street to have a telephone, and as she pounded on their door, freezing, soaked to the skin, all she could feel was fear. Fear held her heart. Icy blind with panic, she kept pounding. When Mr. Donaldson finally answered, Harriet burst into tears mixed with a rush of befuddled words.

"Jumpin' Jehosifat, come in, child," he said, hushing her to quieten down and calling out to his wife.

"Please. Get the doctor. It's Nana! Hurry!" She was jumping up and down on the balls of her feet, but Mr. Donaldson just looked at her like she was making no sense at all. She turned to run to the phone box two streets away.

"Harriet, wait!" Mrs. Donaldson peeled off her

pinny, grabbed her umbrella from the stand, and caught hold of her arm. "Edward, phone the doctor. Tell him to meet us at Molly's."

****

Mrs. Donaldson let out a cry and crossed herself. "Jesus, my sainted aunts! Molly? Harriet, be a good girl and fetch your grandmother a blanket." Crouching, she gently placed Molly's hands across her abdomen, then checked for the rise and fall of breath, but already knew it was too late.

Harriet grabbed the softest blanket she could find, holding it to her body, warming it as she ran back to the dining room. Harriet carefully wrapped her grandmother in the blanket, and cradling her in her arms, rocked back and forth, tears splashing down her face, not hearing, not listening, not believing.

Dr. Carwithen arrived at the same time as Father O'Leary. He placed a battered medical bag on the floor and leaned over Molly, lifting her limp wrist, listening for a heartbeat with his stethoscope. Mrs. Donaldson had her arm around Harriet, holding her steady. He shook his head sadly.

Harriet stared in disbelief. That was it? That was the sum of his expertise? She would not, could not believe his lack of effort. Nana was strong. Nana was her rock. Her life. She jumped up, slamming into the doctor, dragging him back toward her grandmother.

"No, you have to do something. You have to make her better!"

Doctor Carwithen hugged Harriet into the musky dampness of his Harris tweed suit, but she pulled away. As she choked on her own tears, she watched Father O'Leary kneeling next to Molly, looping a band of black ribbon between his fingers and black prayer book. Black clothes, black hat, black shoes, dripping black puddles on the bare floor. There was nothing but fury in Harriet's heart. Religion was a fake. Everyone in Ham Street knew Father O'Leary's compassion stretched only as far as the duty he performed. Once the priest was done, he excused himself and left.

Mrs. Donaldson took Harriet by the shoulders, talking to her kindly, gently, but all Harriet could hear was a high-pitched ringing in her ears. Then everything went black.

Chapter 2

When Harriet came around, she found herself in bed, her neighbor by her side.

"Harriet." Mrs. Donaldson sounded as if she'd just run a marathon. "You had us all worried. You fainted, dear. Hit your head on the table. You've a bit of a cut over the top of your eye, but the doctor's tended to it."

"Nana!" Harriet shot up. Her head exploded with pain.

"The doctor said you need to rest." Mrs. Donaldson reached out to comfort her, sitting on the side of the bed, shaking her head. "I'm so sorry."

"It can't be true. Tell me it's not true?" Harriet cried, burying her head into her neighbor, weeping uncontrollably.

"Hush now." Mrs. Donaldson gently patted her back. "I know. It's been such a shock." After a time, she eased Harriet from her.

"The doctor wants you to take these." She held out a glass of water and some white pills. "Please?"

****

Somber, respectful faces from the undertaker's met Mr. Donaldson whilst his wife sat in a small wicker chair next to Harriet's bed throughout the night. Muffled, muted, they came and went in their reverent, well-rehearsed dance without Harriet ever being aware. When Mrs. Donaldson did manage to drop off, Harriet's fitful sleep regularly broke her own.

By early morning, Mrs. Donaldson, rubbing her sore neck, softly tiptoed down the stairs. Though she made little sound, Harriet was startled awake by the singular click of the front door.

A painful throb above her left eye matched the feeling of inexplicable grief. Puzzled, she discovered a dressing, and the raw memory of last night washed over her. Burying her head in her pillow, trying to suffocate the awful truth away, a single sentence, spoken last night, rolled around until it became a nonsensical mantra.

"You're lucky to have a job."

Harriet forced herself out of bed and, in a complete daze, still wearing yesterday's damp clothes, readied for work.

"Harriet?" Mrs. Donaldson spluttered, meeting her at the gate with a fried egg sandwich and cup of tea. "Where are you going? I just popped out to sort Mr. Donaldson's breakfast. Come on, back to bed, my girl."

"Work," Harriet mumbled, pushing past. "Can't let my Nana down. Got to go to work."

To the outsider it would appear as if nothing happened. Harriet's actions were robotic, blind to the people around her. She had caught the same tube and walked the same fume-filled route with the ever-hopeful and growing tide of London's workforce since she began work in Dingham's Department Store.

****

Miss Macy, feeling pleased with herself, looked around her world of unmentionables. She would never admit it, but Fatty Hattie Laws' suggestions were paying off. Sales had increased month on month. A shiver of pleasure ran through her spine. Her ill-gained bonus this month would be even better than the last. Her lips snipped upward. Fatty Hattie, what a sap! Picking a stray piece of cotton from her two-piece and rolling it into a little ball, she flicked it into a waste bin and began her routine around the shop floor. Everything was neat and orderly. Fatty was indeed an excellent slave.

Miss Macy studied the functional lingerie, militarily folded into beautifully crafted drawers, waiting for the "more discerning clientele." But she felt irritated the regular dressing gowns remained unsold. They had been so popular in the past. Why, they even had an embroidered rose on the Peter Pan collar. But it was *Fatty* who brought the Chinese silk gowns to her attention, and she could not ignore their beauty. Fingering a robe greedily, she caressed it against her cheek, then checked her watch. Lifting the sample from the manikin, she walked swiftly over to the dressing room, Fatty Laws' concept, but she allowed everyone to think it was her idea.

Miss Macy dropped the robe over her two-piece, admiring herself in the mirror, smirking. She would easily be able to afford one with all the commission she creamed off the irritating Miss Laws. Tweaking her crisply lacquered marcel wave, she spied a tape measure, along with her slave's smartly written instructions on how to measure a brassiere. She scowled. How could such a young girl know so much? What riled her more was never thinking of it herself. Hateful Fatty Hattie was a natural saleswoman, and she hated her for all of it.

Standing in her usual position, at the front of the lingerie department, Miss Macy waited. When Harriet arrived, Miss Macy's pincushion lips quivered. Theatrically checking her watch against the large clock above the door, she entered the time on her notebook. Two minutes late.

"That will be fifteen minutes deducted from your pay, Miss Laws." She eyeballed Harriet disparagingly. "And I cannot possibly have you working on the shop floor looking like that." Harriet blinked, stunned.

"Your face, the state of your clothes? Most inappropriate!" Miss Macy scowled. "I don't wish to know your private circumstances, but for goodness' sake, clean yourself up."

In the ladies' room, Harriet found the wound above her eye had bled from under the plaster, leaving a small, dried rivulet, and a speckle of blue-black bruising peered out. Hurriedly she cleaned her face, knowing if she did not present herself soon, another fifteen minutes of pay would be deducted.

"About time," said Miss Macy, ready with a pencil and lined foolscap paper. "You can start by stock taking, in the storeroom."

Two days passed in similar fashion. By Friday evening, Mrs. Donaldson and Rosa, Harriet's friend, and neighbor, persuaded her to ask her supervisor for time off to attend the funeral.

Harriet arrived at Dingham's ten minutes early, requesting to speak with Miss Macy in private, doubting she would receive any support.

"Very well. Staff room, ten thirty, sharp. And as you're looking more acceptable, you may complete the dusting before opening."

Harriet struggled to focus on her work. To explain her circumstances meant once she said those awful words out loud, the terrible truth would be a reality, and there would be no going back. Watching the clock hands creep agonizingly toward the designated time, at precisely nine twenty-nine she arrived outside the staff room. Management did not encourage tea breaks or any kind of break. No one dared use the dingy staff room the size of a broom cupboard, only Miss Macy had that privilege. In a haze, feeling sick, stomach churning, she knocked on the door.

"Come!"

Harriet, shaking, adjusted her glasses and took a deep breath.

Her supervisor, not attempting to disguise her loathing, stared at her belly.

"If you've come to tell me you're pregnant, don't expect sympathy from me!"

"No."

"Well, you obviously aren't wearing the corset like I told you to." Miss Macy pointed to Harriet's mound triumphantly. "Well, spit it out." She continued making tea. "I don't successfully run this department on time wasters!"

Harriet gasped out her request. To her surprise, the woman said nothing untoward, only, "I see." Maybe she had been unkind and misjudged her after all.

"Thank you, Miss Macy. I will work extra, to make up for time lost, unpaid of course."

"Enough! Tidy yourself up, and no more putting customers off with your miserable face."

Harriet, feeling a modicum of relief at the marginal display of humanity, thanked her again and headed straight to the convenience. Trying to hold back a wail, she splashed cold water over her face.

What did she know about funerals? She had never attended a funeral, let alone arranged one, and she so wanted to do right by Nana. She did not want any part of this. All she wanted was her dear Nana back. Face blotchy, handkerchief wet, nothing would change facts. Harriet choked back a sob. If Miss Macy heard, she'd lose her job for sure.

She pinched her cheeks. Nana had taught her to be strong, to be positive. She had a job and had been given permission to attend her grandmother's funeral.

Harriet could not, would not, let Nana down.

Chapter 3

Every evening since Molly's death, Rosa arrived
with her brood, and pasta. Rosa had a baby almost every
year, and three years ago she gave birth to twins. Now
she had five pretty little Rosas, and one gorgeous little
boy, the dream of her husband. Rosa's children were like
her, wild, round, rosy-faced, black-haired, and brightly
funny. They were full of charm and packed with
ceaseless energy. They either hung in waves around her
skirt, tugged at her waist, or pattered in endless circles.
They pulled faces, played hide-and-seek, and screamed
delightedly when found. It helped Harriet to forget. For
a nanosecond.

"Come on, Harriet. Eat just a little bit, for me," Rosa
urged her gently.

"Later, I promise."

Rosa, defeated, scooped the smallest child into the
fold of her arms and took her perfect storm with her.
Once they were gone, everything came tumbling down,
and Harriet fell into a heap of shivering tears.

****

One week after Harriet's beloved Nana died, at nine
forty-five on the day of the funeral, Harriet braced
herself with supreme effort. The hearse arrived exactly
on time. With little interest in food, but with sedatives
floating around in her system, she felt punch drunk.

One of the funeral directors gently assisted Harriet

into the car. It came as no surprise to Harriet that neighbors quietly and respectfully lined the street despite the drizzle of rain. Acknowledging them all through glassy eyes, she smelt Lily of the Valley, her grandmother's favored scent, and felt the soft, simple touch of her comforting hand slipping into hers.

"Nana?" Harriet turned, only to find Mrs. Donaldson beside her. Stung with unimaginable grief, she heard the oiled purr of the engine, and they began the slow aching journey to the church.

Scent wafting, incense burning. The service vanished in a haze. Soon afterward Harriet found herself outside the stone-cold white building. Century-old trees and crumbling tombstones lined the gray gravel path. Beyond, more lavish monuments—solemn, stately, proud, and erect within the pruned grass. Amazingly, not one inch of the church grounds had been damaged during the war. She felt it a fitting respect for the dead.

Harriet shook hands with everyone, distractedly listening to respectful noises from mourners, many of whom she didn't even recognize. She considered the wake with embarrassment. Even with the prepaid funeral plan, her grandmother would have been mortified if she knew just how little it covered. With all the money Harriet had scraped together, she could only afford a few sardine-spread sandwiches and a cup of tea. The Christmas sherry found in the back of the kitchen cupboard would only serve five, at most. Even so, Harriet politely invited everyone, fervently hoping they wouldn't come.

Harriet's prayers went unanswered. People kept arriving, but with their arrival, they brought their own contributions. Overwhelmed by their generosity, she watched the procession. Mrs. Donaldson stood a full bottle of sherry on the mantelpiece with her best sherry glasses. Father O'Leary, never missing a wake, parked himself by its side. Others came with a variety of triangular sandwiches, jars of homemade piccalilli, pickled eggs, sweet, pickled onions, and quartered pork pies.

Harriet soon realized the extent of her grandmother's popularity as mourners were squeezed from the tiny front room and spilt into the kitchen. When there was not enough space there, others good-humoredly stood in the hallway or sat on the stairs. And as the sun began pushing its way through cotton-candy clouds, some made their way through to the back garden, to smoke a pipe or share a cigarette.

Not much later, a young man quietly introduced himself. Mrs. Donaldson swiftly relieved him of his packages, fussed around, rearranged the variety of cakes, and somehow managed to find a space.

"Just look," whispered Mrs. Donaldson to her husband. "Father O'Leary. The greedy blighter's already on his third sherry." Harriet overheard and, disappointed in the man, glanced over. He had been no help or support whatsoever.

Mr. and Mrs. Singh arrived with two large plates of samosas, followed closely by Rosa and a pasta mountain. And when Winston's wife proudly advised her Jamaican jerk chicken was her own special recipe, there were a few raised brows.

As the smell of a million spices vied for space in the tiny room, whispers between those less keen to try "foreign muck," became obvious. Mrs. Donaldson, considering herself a diplomat, hitched up her sleeves and took the first plate. Everyone watched keenly.

"This looks delicious," she said, smiling, and taking a portion of everything considered "foreign," and as she did, whispered bets were exchanged.

"She'll conk out for sure," said one.

"Two minutes, tops," said another.

"I'll give you a bob if she lasts five," said another.

Mrs. Donaldson, complimented Rosa, Mrs. Singh, and Winston's wife for their wonderful contributions, and nudged her husband in the ribs.

"Help me out, love." She handed him a filled plate.

Mr. Donaldson braced himself.

"Jumpin' Jehosifat, yessiree-Bob, you're right, Betty. I'd give a hunker hill of beans for these tasty treats!" Mrs. Singh, demurely lowered her eyes with evident pleasure, and Winston looked on proudly at his new, pretty, smiling wife.

"Ye daf' bugger, Donaldson, what kinda language is that?" Mr. Oatley, unable to contain himself, laughed loudly.

Mr. Donaldson continued eating with a deaf ear, and with hunger getting the better of empty stomachs, a queue quickly formed, with apprehensive minds turning to positive surprises agreeing, for "foreign muck," it was marvelous.

As mourners began sharing anecdotes and fond memories, it gladdened Harriet's heart. She knew just how different things could have been with such diversity of cultures and backgrounds shoehorned into one street. Her grandmother would help settle newcomers and introduce them to their neighbors. She would not tolerate an unkindness and could win an argument with just a look. As far as Nana was concerned, it didn't matter a hoot about background, shade, religion, disability, or political persuasion. Everyone, and that meant everyone, deserved to be treated equally.

With every generous word and new twist to a story, there was laughter at the way things were. Nana unobtrusively offering help, giving the last loaf of unsold bread from the bakery if she heard a family were struggling, or they would find one of her famous stews sitting on their front doorstep. She took care of the little ones when mothers were ill, arranging them in the kitchen on rainy days to draw or bake. On fine days they would pull herbs from the garden or prick out plants.

"I remember when Molly brought us some odd-looking stuff in a bottle," said a heavily pregnant Mrs. Dart, straddling a small, pale-faced child on her hip.

"My Danny here had the worst colic you could imagine. Up every night squawking his bloody head off." Mrs. Dart spotted Father O'Leary refilling his glass and attempted a deferential curtsey.

"Sorry, your worship, but it were true. When Molly said to give this stuff a try, I thought as nuffin' else were workin' I had nuffin' to lose. An' you know what? It were so good I tried it on me 'usband. I put it in his stout one night, and it shut his snoring up good and proper!"

Everyone roared. Mr. Oatley, renowned for being one for the whisky, began ruminating on when Molly found him at his doorstep soaking wet and unable to get in.

"Molly just took one look at I, rooted around in me jacket pocket, an' just like a magician, she produced tha' bloody key an' opened me front door! Ah swear she had tha' key in her own pocket all tha' bloody time!"

Someone from the other side of the room called out,

"It's more a surprise you ever managed to find your house, Ron Oatley! You were always rolling down the street, scratching your arse lookin' for it. Sure as eggs you would be there all night if it wasn't for her." And as an afterthought, "Oh, and by the way, thank you for your contribution to our Sylvia's wedding."

"How's that?" puzzled Ron from the other side of the room, with listening heads ping-ponging back and forth.

"Molly told me how good you were giving up your last bottle of whisky. One half went in the wedding cake, and the other half sat on the top table. The cake was fantastic! Even the wife gave us a kiss after having a slice." He winked at his wife. "And the whisky was not half bad." Everyone howled with laughter.

"Well, you owe I, John Digman, for I didna agree to her taking it, or it goin' to waste in a bloody cake, or in yer stomach!"

"Ah, be away with you, Oatley," another man retorted. "Molly did you a favor, and well you know it."

Mr. Donaldson lifted his glass, loudly interrupting the banter and possible ensuing tussle.

"A toast. To a woman who, I think everyone will agree, was dearly loved by all. Molly Laws."

"Molly Laws," the ensembled mourners murmured in return.

The voice of a male tenor started singing a gentle ballad, and everyone quietly, respectfully listened. As the heartfelt notes rang out, others who knew the words began to join in. A fiddler who needed no invitation started up with the next song, and someone with a harmonica swiftly joined in, and soon toes began tapping. Harriet strained to see who was initially responsible, vaguely remembering the same wonderful voice filtering through her grief in the church. As the group swayed, a tiny gap opened: it was Tom, the baker.

When at last the stragglers departed, Mrs. Donaldson began clearing the dishes. "You did your grandmother proud."

Harriet smiled weakly, following her lamb-like between the two rooms, helping to wash up. "Everyone has been so kind, Mrs. Donaldson. How can I ever begin to thank them?"

"Dear child, your grandmother was a lovely woman. She helped us all out in more ways than you can imagine. And you're no different."

Harriet briefly raised heavy lids.

"Yes, Harriet, you know—you heard them."

Chapter 4

Harriet arrived fifteen minutes early at Dingham's Department Store, a tidal wave of exhaustion and emotions enveloping her every move. But she knew Mr. Dingham himself would be visiting today to talk to staff about the new lines and innovative ideas. This might be her chance of promotion, a day to make Nana proud.

The Smithsonian clock ticked loudly on the wall, and the steel tube gleamed, ready to claim money, impatient to fly across the expansive gallery to Accounts. All garments were regimentally neat, color coded and sizes in order. The shelves and work surfaces still sparkled—everything filled and cleaned by Harriet two days earlier.

"Staff room. Five minutes." Miss Macy stepped out from the shadows, tapped her watch, turned on her heels, and disappeared. Worried, as requested, exactly five minutes later, Harriet knocked at the door.

"Come!" Miss Macy stood with notebook in hand, tapping it with a pencil, and pounced the moment she entered.

"Miss Laws, have I not taught you the intricacies of this job? Have I not spent time and patience to ensure you do the finest work possible for our esteemed employer? Have I not painstakingly taken you through your contractual obligations?"

"No, Miss Macy? I mean, yes, Miss Macy."

Puzzled, knowing she wasn't late, Harriet nervously pushed her glasses back up her nose, desperately trying to work out what could possibly be coming next.

"Very well, you understand I have done everything in my power to help you out."

Harriet was sure she could hear a hint of glee in her supervisor's voice as she handed over a small brown envelope. Harriet accepted it with quiet discomfort. Miss Macy indicated she open it, then waited, her hands folded and pressed against her midriff.

Harriet's delicate fingers prized the glued paper open and counted three days' pay. Baffled, she stared at Miss Macy, who held a look of smug superiority, and with the door open, her voice carried to arriving staff hanging up their coats.

"You will be aware you are not entitled to any pay at all. Be grateful I am a kindly sort."

For a second, Harriet believed Miss Macy had spoken to their "esteemed employer" and he had provided her with an advance at this awful time. Harriet began thanking her, but Miss Macy held up a talon, insisting silence.

"No, Miss Laws. Considering everything, I believe our esteemed employer has been extremely generous. Three days' severance pay is more than fair."

In hushed whispers, staff gathered. Harriet blinked, bewildered. Miss Macy had said she could take the time off, hadn't she?

"Severance? I'm sorry, Miss Macy," she faltered. "Did I hear you correctly? There must be a mistake. You do remember I went to my grandmother's funeral yesterday. You agreed."

Her supervisor gave a slow, sly smile. Harriet's

confusion turned to instant clarity and fury. Macy hadn't agreed or disagreed. She'd implied but didn't state Harriet could have time off.

How could she have been so gullible? How could the woman be so dishonest, so mean?

"Miss Macy? I distinctly recall offering to work overtime and not receive pay so I might go to my grandmother's funeral."

The Vulture held a look of astonishment that her seniority dare be challenged. Harriet paled, holding the envelope so tightly the coins cut into her palm. She didn't deserve this. She wanted to strike her. Miss Macy made for the door, but Harriet stood in her way, drawing up all her five feet five inches, head high.

"Miss Macy, you clearly have issue with me, though I don't know what I've done." Her heart beat so hard it hurt. "It cannot possibly be the quality of my work or going to my grandmother's funeral. And, as you well know, I've made more suggestions and completed more sales than anyone. Including you!" Harriet surprised even herself, having never dared speak out before.

"I have Raymond waiting," Miss Macy squawked. Raymond, the only strong-looking male in the whole of the store, used on rare occasions to eject unwanted riffraff out.

"Very well, I hope you sleep well with your conscience. And as my dear grandmother would say…" Harriet raised her frame a little higher. "The green-eyed monster of jealousy makes for a very sad and lonely child."

Turning toward the door, she spotted a framed certificate hung on the back wall. Emboldened in black ink, the words read:

Miss Mavis Macy Best Saleswoman 1957

Harriet froze. Everything began clicking into place. She could not believe it. If it had not been for her breathing life into the department with innovative ideas, they would still be in the dark ages. But more importantly, Mr. Dingham was visiting today, and her supervisor had never allowed Harriet to sign a sales docket or use the jet-propelled tube for monetary purposes. In fact, Harriet had never received one single bonus from her sales or recognition for her hard work. Seeing Harriet studying the certificate, Miss Macy's voice pitched stratospherically.

"Raymond!"

"You are not only a thief, but a liar. In fact, I've more time for the cockroach foolishly about to climb your leg. And rest assured, you will be found out!"

Miss Macy screamed as the bug scuttled across the floor. Harriet had never felt so mean or hated herself more. She passed the small congregation outside the staffroom. Her face, dark with shame and shock. Harriet half expected to be frog-marched out of the building. Instead, with each step Harriet took toward the main entrance, a small ripple of applause grew, with murmurs of support. To her surprise, Raymond held the door open as if she were royalty, his eyes sympathetically meeting hers.

"Take care, Miss Harriet. I am so sorry."

Harriet stepped outside the store, her head in turmoil. White noise deafened her, filling her mind. She would surely pass out. Traffic poured past, horns honked, smells oozed, grates steamed, footfalls crowded in. She tried pulling herself together. The job had never been what she wanted. But the landlord would expect payment by the end of the month. They were already short of cash. Nana would be furious. Harriet gulped. Translucent tears fell as the awful truth came back to her. She would have given anything to have her grandmother scold her!

Harried shoppers and bowler-hatted businessmen passed by like oil waltzing through water. No one stopped or showed concern. The only effort made was to avoid eye contact or touch at any cost. Harriet pulled out a crumpled handkerchief from her handbag and blew her nose. The results showed London's pollutants, reminding her of the filthy, stinking, rotten Macy.

She should go back, speak to her employer, explain the truth, beg him to reconsider. No, the only proof would be given in her absence, though it wouldn't resolve the situation. She knew she needed to be strong, but she didn't feel strong. She felt feeble, weak, miserable, and oh, so tired. Too tired to think straight.

Without thought or plan, Harriet mechanically walked toward the tube, running over and over different scenarios, each one becoming its own reality. The entrance to the station filled with the relentless ebb and flow of commuters. A fleeting gap. She stepped between, slowly traversing the internal echoing medley of tiled chambers and escalators. With each step, ever downward, deep into the earth, Harriet felt more anger, accompanied by guilt. She should never have kept pushing Nana to tell her about her family. She had been unwell. It was her fault Nana died. She didn't deserve a future. There could be no future. Not without Nana.

Harriet continued weaving through the sea of jostling, purposeful faces and collided with a group of schoolchildren and tourists. Normally she would apologize, but she barged by. One of the regular buskers struck up loudly, acknowledging her presence and her usual generosity. He nodded, playing something for her, she didn't know what; she didn't hear. It was futile. Her mind was elsewhere.

She ended up on the platform with a plan, and a perfect sense of calm. She felt the telltale gust of wind from the ink-black cave. The train was coming.

A strand of hair came loose from her plait, flicking at her face as debris skittered along the dais. The train was imminent. *People throw themselves in front of trains all the time.*

Chapter 5

"Miss Laws?" Harriet didn't move. "It's me, Tom Fletcher?"

"I'm coming, Nana," Harriet whispered over and over, planting herself closer toward the lip of the platform, fixated, cold thoughts biting her heart. Seconds later, headlights streaked within the darkness and the train hurtled from the ink-black tunnel. Harriet was prepared. Only a step away. Silver slicked lines beckoned. Just one more step. People began moving forward, bidding for prime position. Crossing herself, she closed her eyes tight.

"I'm coming, Nana."

It all happened so quickly. Brakes squealing. Train slowing. People surging forward. The rush of noise filling her ears. As she began falling, a sense of peace enveloped her, soft as a warm blanket.

"Miss Laws!"

"Nana."

"Miss Laws?"

Harriet's eyes snapped open as strong arms wrapped around her, pulling her back to safety.

"Let me go!" she cried over the squealing of metal on steel; try as she might to free herself, his arms continued to hold her. They were so close that if they'd been the same height their noses would have touched. As the train hissed to a standstill, he murmured something in her ear, holding on to her as if they were lovers.

The crowd shuffled past in air force formation, sandwiched commuters avoiding eye contact. Tom held her more gently as the train whisked away and the rumble became no more than the sound of a distant, beating heart. Harriet looked wildly about the station, an empty tomb, yesterday's news, hinting at a previous life, shredded, spiraling above the silver tracks of death, her eyes drawn to the billboard. There was an image of a happy family gathered around a fire.

Her legs buckled. Just one more glance at Tom's kind, worried face and she burst into tears. What the hell was she thinking? How could she? It was total madness. A sin.

Gently, Tom guided Harriet to a nearby bench and offered a clean hanky. Passengers began filling the catacomb as they sat side by side, quietly, until at last her painful sobs turned to gulps. Even when she managed to gather control, he sat silently by her side, as if it were the most natural thing in the world. There was a comforting air about him. A patient gentleness she'd never experienced from anyone other than Nana. Tom smiled as she wiped the last tears away, words thick in her throat, mumbling something incoherent.

"How are you feeling?"

It was extraordinary to think, but it was as if those few words gave her permission to talk, and once she started, she couldn't stop. Just as the platform continued to fill and empty, as trains came and went, her words ebbed and flowed. Tom listened, really listened, not interrupting, or giving his view.

Harriet realized she had not spoken to anyone since Nana's death, not properly. There were snatched conversations with Mrs. Donaldson, and the pained expression of Father O'Leary when she tried to seek his guidance, so she'd bottled it all up. By the time she finished talking, between gulps of air, she felt drained. The platform had filled with new strangers, averting eyes, vacant looks, checking watches, clocking boards, bodies pressing against the unknown they would never normally allow in polite society. The next train was on its way. Tom waited a while, then gently nudged her.

"I know it's a bit of an understatement, but you've had a helluva time lately." Her bottom lip quivered. "How about coming for a coffee?"

Harriet, still looking to her lap, raised a concerned brow.

He apologized, seeing her reaction. "I'm not inviting you to my home. I meant we could go to a café, or something?"

Harriet hesitated, she'd never known any men, not properly. She kept her distance deliberately. Nana's warnings were clear, strict, Victorian, but for good reason. She had no idea about men. She flushed, her thought processes racing in directions she'd never dared think or challenge before.

"Of course, you won't want to come. I understand." His voice trailed off. Then, as if he had a memory of her beloved Nana flash through his head, "You know, your grandmother was a helluva cook."

Harriet, surprised at this, found herself shakily laughing. She glanced up shyly.

He smiled a hopeful, lopsided smile.

"She was, wasn't she?"

Tom's face was warm, gentle. It was true she didn't really feel like socializing at all, but thoughts parried in her head. How could she throw the gesture back in his face without offending him? She should continue to obey Nana, keep a safe, respectful distance.

Harriet dabbed her eyes. Tom had just saved her life. He was being thoughtful. He knew her grandmother, the offer made from kindness. What would be the harm? When she agreed, she could not help but notice his look of relief. Tom placed her hand on his arm and, keeping it there, guided her from the bowels of the earth and out into bright, crisp, spring sunlight.

They walked along busy streets filled with the cacophony of life surrounding them. Harriet found Tom's lack of conversation welcome, easy to be with. When they came across one of the new espresso bars, they peered in. Music by The Crickets, "That'll Be the Day" poured out. The café overflowed with duffel-coated academics, lit cigarettes in one hand, coffee cups in the other, noisily debating their last lecture. Those not involved with the lively banter sat, fringes flopping, coffees suspended mid-air, immersed in books piled high on small round tables.

"It's a bit busy. We could wait for a space. What do you think?" The beat of music, the smell of freshly percolated coffee, and the fever of academia would normally rouse Harriet to be part of that scene, but her heart held no light. She shrugged.

"Let's try somewhere else," said Tom, taking the cue.

Two streets along, they found a café closed to business, a pile of unopened mail strewn in the doorway. An agent's "To Let" sign filled the grimy window, a collection of black flies heaped in death's sleep on the dusty sill. With an unspoken agreement, they walked on, their footsteps becoming one, moving in unison between footfalls and belching traffic fumes. Eventually they came to a small suburb, a compact road full of parked cars, restaurants, and grocery shops.

Tom was talking, not paying attention, until they turned the corner. Two shops down, they found themselves at the entrance of Daisy Baker's. Harriet's heart stopped. It was as if fate guided them there. She studied her grandmother's place of work as if she had never seen the lovely pink candy stripe canopy and sparkling glass shop window. Inside, two middle-aged women were busily serving a growing queue. The window displayed a wonderful array of breads and cakes, the centerpiece a beautiful three-tiered wedding cake. Viewing it up close, Harriet was surprised to find it was made not from cake at all, but from cardboard. A customer exited with a loaf of bread, and its glorious aroma, like a warm sunny day in the park, drifted out. She noticed a postcard placed in the right-hand corner of the window:

"S*hop assistant required. Apply within.*"

"I'm sorry." Tom's face cast a shadow. Harriet, recognizing his discomfort, put her hand lightly on his arm.

"Please, don't feel bad."

Tom nodded, mumbling, "No one could ever replace your grandmother." He looked bothered. "We could have coffee out the back. I have cakes you could sample. Your grandmother was my trusted critic, you know."

"Really?" Harriet, readjusting her specs, looked properly at him for the first time. "*Your* critic?"

"Yup, most definitely, and nothing would please me more if you would try out my new recipe. Maybe give me your view?" His eyes darted to the floor, embarrassed. "Sorry, I wasn't thinking. How selfish."

"No, it's not selfish at all, and yes, thank you. I would love to."

"Great!" There was a sense of relief in his voice. "I just hope you won't be disappointed."

"Fishing for compliments already?" Startling herself by the flippant comeback, Harriet flushed pink. Tom flashed a lopsided smile, eyes twinkled amusement.

Harriet had never been in the back of the bakery before. In her head it was where only bakers were allowed. A small gravel back yard gave way to a crumbling outhouse. Propped against the side wall were three delivery bikes fitted with large wicker baskets strapped to rusting handlebars. Tom tapped the wheel of one of them with his toe.

"That was mine once," he said, fondly adding, "the wonky chain damn well knocked me off a few times, I can tell you," and he led her into the heart of the bakery.

The room was sparse, made for work, not relaxing. Rough, uneven flagstones covered the entire floor. Towers of empty crates were stacked neatly next to hooped breadbaskets. Two sturdy tables sat centered along the back, and a countertop stretched between the sink and three gas rings. Five autumnal gold wooden paddles, their tips burnt to umber, filled a huge, wide-brimmed wicker basket. And ovens, set inside impenetrable walls, even though cold, gave a delicious, lingering smell of freshly baked bread.

Tom, humming quietly to himself, lifted three of the crates from the tower, and arranged them on the floor, two as seats, one as a table.

"This is how we do things here." He smiled,

reaching into a drawer before placing two tea towels across the middle crate. "I lied when I said coffee and cakes." He looked a little awkward. "I can only offer tea."

"Tea sounds perfect." Unsure why she agreed to be there, Harriet polished her glasses. Tom put an enormous, dented kettle on blue flames that grew and licked the outside, adding more black soot. Collecting two mugs and a tin of loose-leaf tea from a cupboard, Tom absently ran his hand through his floppy black hair.

Harriet considered his wiry frame. Tom didn't come close to the gorgeous American king of Rock, but his features were good, balanced, kind. Harriet noted how knotted muscles displayed themselves from under rolled-up shirtsleeves and found herself trying to guess his age. He turned to find her looking at him and smiled his lopsided smile. She averted her eyes with embarrassment and saw the bright white bakers' aprons and hats hanging on the shop door's hooks.

"How long have you been working here, Tom?"

He drew a deep breath. "Oh, I started here when I was around ten."

"Ten?"

"Yes." He set out the mugs.

"What about your parents? Didn't they mind?"

Tom swallowed before speaking, lifting his shoulders, and she got the sense of hurt.

"My parents and sisters were killed in a bombing raid. Our home was razed to the ground, like most in the road."

"I'm so sorry."

Tom shrugged, but his kind calm composure detailed sorrow. "I was the lucky one, out playing footie with my mates in the next street. Ended up like so many waifs and strays."

"Oh, my goodness! And here's me, being all pathetic."

"No, not at all. Funny thing. How life turns out, I mean. I always had a hankering for baking." His eyebrows rose with a smile. "Guess I was always hungry. When I found this place…well, the smell of bread, you know. I hung around and asked loads of silly questions." He grinned. "John, Daisy's husband, got fed up with me pestering. When they found out I had nowhere, they took me in."

A well-worn smile crossed his face. "I really was one of the lucky ones. John gave me my first lesson in kneading dough. His sons were great, too. They were like the brothers I never had." Tom paused as if they were there standing right in front of him. He turned away for a second, before forcing himself to speak again.

Harriet knew Daisy's husband and three sons never came home from the war. She could only guess it must have been hard to adjust, like so many, trying to get on with life after the war. Her grandmother remarked once that Tom took great care of Daisy, and she in turn treated him like a son.

"Anyway," his voice went on, deep in his throat, "I plan to have my own string of shops one day. I want to make Daisy proud. Make sure she's taken care of." His eyes twinkled. "Hence my quest for compliments! In fact, did you know it was your grandmother, Molly, who suggested I make a business plan?" He looked at her square-on. "If it wasn't for her, I would never have had the confidence."

It pleased Harriet. She liked the look of Tom, and

knew Nana liked him. She quietly studied the dark-haired baker again; he had literally saved her life. How could she ever repay him? Harriet turned to the fresh white aprons, her mind working over the day. No job, no money, no beautiful Nana, but here she could possibly continue life, be a part of her history. Taking a deep controlled breath, she said, "The job in the window…do you think I might have a chance?"

Chapter 6

As Harriet left Daisy Baker's, Tom gave her a small white paper bag.

"I just need an unbiased opinion." She peeked inside. Two perfectly formed clotted cream meringues were nestled at the bottom.

"I couldn't possibly," she murmured, doubtfully patting her stomach, instantly recalling Miss Macy's vile insinuations.

"They're light, and different from the norm," Tom persisted. "Tell me what you think, tomorrow."

She looked bemused.

"When you come to see Daisy for the job?" He sounded worried. "You will?"

She gave him a weak smile.

"Yes, of course."

"Promise?"

Harriet's eyes watered, truly humbled by Tom's concern.

"I promise. Thank you for being so kind."

****

Harriet retraced the same chaotic route taken earlier, and like most Londoners, she was desensitized to the regular infusion of nicotine and smoke. With her mind set elsewhere, gathering fear, even the hustle and the market traders bawling in her ear had no effect. Soon the entrance to the underground loomed, and she heard the newspaper vendor's hypnotic chant. As she dipped her hand into her purse, she caught her breath at the distant rumble of a train. Her heart pounded, and her hands went clammy.

"You all right, miss?" asked the old man, folding the *Evening Standard* and handing it over.

"What? Yes. Thank you."

A red double-decker pulled up at the bus stop with a huge yellow soap advert splashed across its side. It was going her way. She couldn't face the underground, not today. Passing the peak-capped conductor, Harriet climbed the spiral staircase to the top deck and found a solitary seat by the window. Clutching the gift from Tom in one hand and the newspaper in the other, she felt complete and utter shame. Nana would have been ashamed of her. She always taught her life was precious, not to be abused or treated lightly. Harriet knew how wrong her actions were. What the hell had she been thinking? She would go to confession. Do penance. No doubt Father O'Leary would make her do a million Hail Mary's, but she knew with absolute clarity just how lucky she was to be alive.

Harriet found the ticket collector standing in front of her with an odd expression. Had she spoken out loud? She passed him a thruppenny bit, he gave her change, and he whizzed the little handle on his machine. It spat an ochre ticket, and he moved on. "Fares, please."

Wiping the windowpane in confusion, she smeared a breath of condensation with her hand. But with the bus journey being slow, it gave her time to think. She caught a glimpse of a square of grass surrounded by crocuses nudging their way through dark earth, reminding her of precious moments shared with Nana in their garden.

They would always marvel at their tiny shoots.

A new life. A new beginning. How lucky Tom had been there. He'd provided her with a chance to see it.

****

Closing the front door, Harriet instinctively called out. Her heart sank. Her entrenched routines had changed forever. She kicked off her shoes and walked into the kitchen, wishing Nana were cooking up a pot of something, that all was as it had been before everything became a nightmare. This was home, where so much love and laughter had been shared. Attempting a speck of normality, Harriet put the kettle on and, out of habit, collected two teacups and saucers. How she wanted to talk to Nana about her day. Taking a breath, she whispered a one-sided conversation, trying it for size.

"I went to Daisy Baker's today, Nana." It felt right. She would tell her what happened. Well, maybe not everything.

"Tom gave me this to try." Tearing open the bag, Harriet displayed its contents. The kettle shrilled, and she jumped, her heart thudding wildly.

"I knew you were here, Nana!" Shakily laughing, convinced she caught a movement, she turned, but found nothing. She took the meringues from the bag, and cream stuck to the sides, leaving a sticky residue.

"Toffee and coffee?" She licked the tips of her fingers clean. "You're right, Nana, Tom is an excellent baker, and I'm going to apply for the job at Daisy's because the not-so-marvelous Macy has sacked me!"

****

That night, like every other night before and those to follow for some time to come, Harriet barely slept. Nightmares of Miss Macy, trains hurtling from tunnels, and visions of Nana's last moments on earth woke her sweating, shaking, and weeping, long into the night.

Harriet rose much earlier than usual the next day. It would be a long walk to Daisy's Bakery. Harriet grimaced, hating the thought of any kind of exercise, but with dwindling finances there was no other option.

She stepped out into the dark that blanketed most homes and discovered suburbs, dotted with little iron-fenced parks, locked off in relative peace before the hustle of London sprang boisterously to life. She felt privileged to experience the dawning of the new day, from the beautiful clarity of a solitary blackbird filling the air with so many breath-taking notes, and the distant call of "coo..ee" from the cockle lady cutting across the quiet air, to the simple clink of milk bottles placed on doorsteps. By the time Harriet arrived at Daisy's, even though the cold clipped her ears, and her toes were frozen, she felt an unfamiliar but pleasant glow.

At five forty-five, checking her watch, pleased to be early, she stood outside the locked door with its sign turned to Closed. Harriet investigated the shop front's soft lighting, watching the progress of a buxom shop assistant arranging a display of cakes inside. She disappeared, only to return with another basket. Harriet wondered about Tom, and gingerly tapped on the window. The woman, flushed pink with exertion, shook her head, mouthing "closed," and pointed toward the sign. Harriet persisted, and as the woman opened the door a little bell attached to a string tinkled above her head.

"Sorry, luv, we're closed—come back at seven?"

"My name's Harriet Laws. I've come to see...."

"Oh, my lor', 'course 'tis. Sorry, luv, haven't got my

specs on. They steam up so. Come on in. I'm Mrs. Turpin." Immediately she gave her condolences and gently squeezed Harriet's shoulder.

"Make sure you lock the door behind you, luv. Tom said you'd be coming. Daisy's already out the back. But it's a really busy time. Give me a hand, will you?"

Harriet promptly took off her coat, placed a package on the counter, and began stacking the bread until the last basket was empty.

"Is Tom here?" she asked Mrs. Turpin shyly as they worked.

"No, he'll be back for his second shift around two." Disappointed, Harriet sighed. She wanted to see him, thank him for everything, and perhaps give him her thoughts on his meringues. Instead, Harriet presented Mrs. Turpin with the small package with his name printed on the front and asked if she would mind passing it on. Mrs. Turpin, giving her a quizzical look, nodded, and sent her to see Mrs. Baker.

The heat from the kitchen, where she and Tom were only yesterday, caught Harriet by surprise. The unmistakable smell of yeast and freshly baked bread hung heavy, fresh, and enticing. She found Mrs. Baker perched on a high stool, and in front of her a neat row of tiny cupid pink roses lay on greaseproof paper. Mrs. Baker, poised to make another flower with a slither of paste between bent forefinger and crooked thumb, stopped her work as Harriet arrived.

"Good morning, dear." Mrs. Baker immediately offered her condolences, dabbing at tears with a tiny lace handkerchief. Harriet nodded, unable to speak, trying to control her own emotions.

"It was so kind of you to come to the church, Mrs.

Baker," said Harriet eventually, vaguely remembering a wheelchair, now appreciating the lengths she must have gone to. Mrs. Baker was a picture painted in two halves, her top half a warm soft, round, gentle bunny of a woman. She wore a string of pearls that peeped through the open neck of her baker's jacket. Lavender-blue curls spun softly around her head; rosy cheeks and intelligent, bright, black-currant eyes smiled.

"Those are lovely," she commented on the little row of icing flowers, attempting to relieve them of their shared grief.

"I wish they were as good as your grandma's, Harriet. I find it so difficult these days to do anything intricate. My fingers don't work so well. Not as bad as my legs, though! Blasted knees." She tapped at them crossly. "Poor Tom," she exhaled.

Harriet gave a puzzled look but received no explanation.

"The doctor offered me calipers. I should be grateful for small mercies."

Harriet, chewing the inside of her lip, indicated the sugar paste.

"I quite like fiddling with things. Can I?"

Mrs. Baker pushed a white ceramic bowl her way, and Harriet began to mold a delicate rosebud into shape.

"Do you really want to work here, Harriet? Won't it upset you?"

"I want to work here for lots of reasons, Mrs. Baker. I need a job, for one, and it would make me feel close to Nana. I know how much she loved it here. And I promise I will work hard and won't let you—or her memory—down."

Harriet's stomach gurgled. Mrs. Baker laughed,

delighted, a bubbly rumble of infectiousness, and offered her a cake and a cup of tea.

"I've always known you're a good girl, Harriet. If you're sure, the sooner you can start, the better," and though at least forty years her senior, Mrs. Baker insisted she be called by her first name.

"Oh, thank you, Daisy, thank you so much." Harriet showed her the rosebud before placing her effort on the greaseproof paper. "Will this do?"

"Yes, most definitely. It's perfect."

****

Tom had not slept, worrying, wishing he'd walked Harriet home yesterday to make sure she was safe. After his first shift, he decided to hang about. He found a doorway opposite the bakery, deciding if she didn't turn up, he would go to her house straight away. When Harriet arrived, Tom smiled with relief, unable to take his eyes off her. She looked so young, a little flustered and vulnerable.

He watched her adjust her clothes and smooth down her hair and coat before she knocked at the shop door. He grinned contentedly as she began waving her arms at Mrs. Turpin. He felt tempted to make himself known but thought better of it. She might think him creepy. All the same, he was glad to see her again.

He watched Mrs. Turpin open the door, the light from inside the shop flooding out onto the pavement along with her voice. He just caught Harriet's voice, and she was instantly welcomed in. He laughed when he saw her being put straight to work. He knew she was safe. Mrs. Turpin would take care of her, and so would Daisy.

Chapter 7

Daisy could not offer a full-time position, but Harriet was keen to take whatever was on offer. She checked her watch—just after six fifteen. Perhaps she could find something else to fit in with the bakery? Maybe a typing job. She could learn easily enough. Every woman seemed to be doing secretarial work these days.

Two miles later, scouring every shop window for adverts, Harriet crossed the road. The bustle of impatient traffic forced her to dodge between vehicles with jeering horns. Eventually, she came across a news agent and studied the positions vacant in the shop window. She screwed up her face. None of them would work for her, timewise, and reluctantly she bought the local paper, hoping it would offer more jobs and places to let. Not long after, Harriet came upon another row of businesses. In the window of a small but smart Italian restaurant, there was a postcard offering a position of waiter. She pondered. A waiter—perhaps they might consider a waitress? With no evidence of life in the restaurant, Harriet noticed a greasy spoon, open, across the road. A perfect place to wait. Checking her purse and deciding she could just afford a cuppa, she thought it might pay to sit a while and maybe get some information.

The bell strung across the top of the door rang loudly as she entered, and the smell of fried onions greeted her.

A twisted dirt-brown cord hung in the center of the room, and attached to the cord, a black wig of dust coated the bulb. She stood at the counter politely waiting. Eventually a pock-faced male arrived. Stale cigarettes and fatty sausages wafted her way. He had a tea towel tied around his skinny waist, blotted with a multitude of aging stains she would rather not think about. Her discomfort increased as his gaze lingered over her breast line.

"Well?"

"A cup of tea, please." She adjusted her coat, embarrassed.

"Mugs only, in this establishment. Been busy all morning. You're lucky to find a seat." Harriet's eyebrow rose, seriously doubting he had a run of customers. Tea Towel slapped a chipped mug on the counter and poured tea pale as white sand.

"Want anything else?"

"No, thank you." Discouraged by the grubbiness of her surroundings, she still forged on. "I'm looking for a job." She pointed. "I'm hoping to apply for the one advertised in Luigi's."

Tea Towel walked from behind the counter and folded his arms. They both looked at the restaurant.

"I don't suppose you know the owner, do you?"

Snickering, he pulled the tea towel from around his waist and flicked crumbs from a table onto the floor.

"Kinda. The greasy Eye-talian's always sniffing around skirts." The man wiggled his brows, his eyes again freely wandering to her breasts. "He'll like you."

Harriet prickled and her dislike grew, but it was cold outside, so she resolved to stay.

"I guess he's okay once you get to know him." He

paused, then grumbled to himself, "For a greasy…" The rest of his words, as he scratched a dirty fingernail around the inside of a mug, removing a lump of crud, were so low she didn't catch them.

"Do you know what time they open?"

Tea Towel wiped his nose across the back of his shirt sleeve, shrugged, and disappeared out the back.

****

Harriet selected one of the five tables crammed tightly into the small space. After studying the tarred, stained walls and checking the chair for cleanliness, she turned her attention to the newspaper, where an article briefly touched upon Ghana's independence of the United Kingdom. The mug of tea offered little heat, and no way would she take a sip.

Moments later, a man ducked under the doorframe, just missing his head. An ill-fitting uniform gave away he worked on the trains. Harriet shivered involuntarily, a cold reminder it could have been all so very different. He glanced over, and she acknowledged him with a small smile and a nod. He politely averted his eyes. She knew the rules but had never truly understood them. Black men were not supposed to talk to white women. She always thought the unwritten rules were born out of poor education and stupidity. But riots were not unheard of when rules were broken and ignorance stepped in.

As he crossed the floor, Harriet noticed the lino covered in black spots and, trying to ignore the grime, surreptitiously studied him instead. She noted with interest how his skin was darker than that of Winston, her neighbor. His frame was not as soft or rounded either. He was longer-limbed. His movements hinted at fluidity, strength, power. He sat down several tables away, knees sticking out, unable to fit comfortably underneath. He waited in affable silence until Tea Towel came out from the back.

"Not you again!" Tea Towel groaned. "I told you not to infect my place with your filth!"

Harriet nearly choked.

"I would like a cup of tea, if you would be so kind," the tall man replied reasonably.

Harriet felt surprised, not only at the response, but comparing his voice to Winston's wonderful rich round lilt, by contrast he sounded as if he were royalty. Looking at her this time square in the eye, the man smiled politely.

"I have no wish to argue."

Harriet hated confrontation at the best of times, but something about him captured her imagination. Why shouldn't he have a cup of tea in this grotty establishment and be treated with respect? Wishing she possessed just one ounce of her Nana's diplomacy, she considered how they often discussed all things, home and abroad. Martin Luther King, a Civil Rights activist, was already gathering waves of support, and she'd heard about Rosa Parks, an African-American arrested for civil disobedience, standing up for, or rather, sitting down for what she believed. Harriet had nothing but complete admiration. In her view, segregation was as insulting as it was inhuman—it should never have come to that in the first place. Yes, she could be polite, and bold.

"Excuse me." Her chin jutted out ever so slightly, her heart fluttering crazily. "I would be pleased if you are courteous to my friend and arrange his order—and replace my cold tea with a hot, fresh one." She paused, hoping she provided a "don't mess with me or else" look on her face.

"And in a clean mug this time. If you would be so kind?"

Tea Towel glared. The tall man's expression displayed a mix of quiet humor and surprise. To Harriet's amazement, and with only a momentary standoff, Tea Towel huffed and began brewing a new pot. Once done, making his point, he slapped the enamel teapot on the counter, and tea sloshed out the spout.

"There. Wasn't so difficult, was it?" She smiled, ignoring the unnecessary show.

"I want payin' now."

But as Harriet briefly thought about paying, the tall man rifled through his pockets, checked the coins in his palm, and placed them on the counter.

"Thank you for the offer, ma'am, but I always pay my own way, and if you would be so kind, please allow me to pay for yours." He held out his hand. "George Henry Windsor." He gave her the brightest, whitest smile she had ever seen.

"Miss Harriet Laws." As her hand was completely swallowed by his, she smiled. "But my tea should be free. The first one was barely warm and with hardly a lick of color."

Whilst the odd couple sat at different tables, with Tea Towel glowering from behind the counter, Mr. Windsor struck up polite conversation.

"I only come in here to stay warm. The tea is disgusting, much like the place, but it serves its purpose." Harriet looked quizzical.

"My wife's expecting our first child. The midwife says she needs as much rest as possible, so I wait here a while after my shift, to give her a little more time."

"How thoughtful. When is she due?"

47

"One more month."

"How exciting."

"Yes, we're really happy."

They chatted a while, until Mr. Windsor, spotting a white van with a "Luigi's" logo on its side, pointed it out.

"Well, I think that's my cue," said Harriet, leaving the mug still full, but her hands a little warmer. Mr. Windsor opened the door, and they parted company, each wishing the other good luck for the future.

Chapter 8

Harriet spied a sign on the wall inviting trade around the back. The kitchen door was ajar. A short, round man bobbed around the shiny kitchen, singing instructions to his staff while holding a balloon whisk as if he were conducting an orchestra. Harriet, having never seen anything quite so funny, watched mesmerized. Eventually one of the staff interrupted him, and Harriet, introducing herself, explained her purpose.

Luigi beamed widely. "You speak to my darling Sofia, no? She is in the restaurant." He indicated she should follow him, and as he made the introductions Harriet considered Sofia more beautiful than any classic Italian film star.

"Do you know anything about Italian cuisine, Harriet?" Sofia smiled, her dark fathomless eyes studying her.

"A little. I have a friend…" She hesitated. "Rosa has Italian blood and makes the most wonderful pasta dishes."

"Good. You will find my papa runs the best Italian restaurant in all of London. If you please the customers, the tips will be better than the pay." And as Sofia eagerly began discussing their exclusive clientele and outlining expectations, Harriet looked around the small but select restaurant.

Exotic paraphernalia boasted the Italian experience

with signed photographs of film stars pinned tastefully over the bar area. Booths offered intimacy, and tables were snugly covered with little red-and-white-checked tablecloths. Upon them wine bottles turned candle holders hung thickly with years of spent candle wax. At the back, a long table was set for ten, cleverly separated from the rest by trelliswork, provided privacy. It was altogether incredibly charming, and Harriet felt a tingle of anticipation. The hours would work out beautifully with Daisy's. If she were offered the job, it might be the answer to her prayers. Whilst continuing to describe the work, Sofia started preparing for the lunch time trade. Harriet followed suit, collecting fresh table linen, quickly folding used tablecloths into piles ready for laundering. Instinctively Harriet laid out the silverware and glanced over the prices.

"Is the menu changed at all?"

"Absolutely." Sofia was clearly pleased with Harriet's initiative and question. "Whilst the basics are always available, Papa is innovative and enjoys creating a varied menu. He will talk through the ingredients, and you will taste, so you can confidently describe each dish in detail."

Harriet raised a brow.

"You must also be aware if customers do not wish paparazzi. We politely discourage them, though of course some of our famous customers appreciate the attention, and it's good publicity for us. Why, even last night we had film royalty here." Sofia pointed to a signed black-and-white photograph of a young man and woman.

Harriet, intrigued, glanced at the signed photographs, previously not really believing their authenticity.

"Haven't they just finished making a film together?"

"Yes." Sofia glowed with pride, smoothing out a tablecloth, then suddenly turned ash pale.

"Are you all right?"

"I still get sick. That's why Papa wants cover."

"How long do you have left?"

"Oh, goodness, too long."

"I believe ginger or dry toast is good for sickness. Or maybe ginger ale. If you haven't tried it before?" Harriet offered.

"Are you a midwife as well as a waitress?" Sofia asked upon her return, carrying a glass of ginger ale and a cracker.

"No. But when you've been around as many mothers as I have, you get to hear all sorts. Most of which I'd rather not know and won't tell you about until I know you better!" They both laughed.

"I have a confession, Harriet. I doubted you would fit in, but now I know different." Sofia pulled a face. "But there's one little thing. May I ask you, when you work here, to pull your hair into the nape of your neck, like mine?" She winked.

"Less Austrian, more Italian."

Luigi's face lit up when they walked back into the kitchen.

"Now, Papa, I don't want you taking advantage of Harriet's good nature."

Luigi ruffled her hair. "Bella? When I taking the advantage?"

"Papa." Sofia sighed, blissfully aware of his adoration. "All the time, Papa, all the time!" She flashed a look at Harriet. "My Papa, he's a pussycat, really."

****

Harriet walked out of Luigi's hardly able to comprehend she'd had two job offers in one day. She glanced across at the greasy spoon. Tea Towel stood in the middle of the café in a fog of nicotine, but George Henry Windsor was nowhere in sight. Crossing her fingers, she hoped he and his wife would be all right, and her own small amount of luck would hold out. All she needed now was to find somewhere to live.

Chapter 9

Harriet sat at the dining table, gingerly rubbing sore heels, studying rents available. Turning the pages over, she talked through her day, imagining Nana sitting opposite and asking her opinion. She circled a couple of possibilities. Picking up a small piece of leftover pie, doubts began clouding her mind. The morsel dropped onto the plate. Crumbs sprinkled across the table. What if she couldn't find somewhere to live? What if she couldn't pay her way? Rubbing the dents in her nose from her glasses, steeling herself to her new task, she told herself to pull herself together.

****

She'd found five rooms to let, in roughly the same area as Daisy Baker's, and to her relief, Harriet found they were much cheaper than bedsits. A telephone box beckoned two streets down, but the pennies in her purse vanished as quickly as the rooms to let. Now, with the last two rooms gone, she would need to look farther afield.

Success! A room still vacant. Yes, she could view it. After checking her funds, Harriet decided she must walk. Even though it was against her moral compass, it was a financial necessity.

Dusk turned to dark, and by the time she arrived, the newspaper strips in her shoes had mashed into stony lumps, and her feet were a blistered, painful mess.

Checking the time, she found it nearing six, late enough, especially in an area she didn't know. Tentatively knocking the brass lion-head door-knocker, Harriet waited.

"I'm comin'!" a female shouted irritably. Moments later, the door flew open. A woman confronted her, grips forcing bleached blonde hair into curled snails. A cigarette stuck to her bottom lip.

"Yes?" The cigarette magically stayed put.

"Good evening, I believe you have a room to let?"

"Nope. You believe wrong. It's gone." Harriet's head dropped. The woman looked her over.

"I heard there's a room goin' beggin' in Calvert. If you hurry, you might get it before them furriners do." Harriet cringed. The door slammed in her face. Arguing started up inside. She decided against knocking again. Her heart thumped dully. Was this going to be it, a fight for somewhere to live? A woman scurried past. She couldn't give up, not now. She called out, "Please, miss?"

The woman stopped. "Yes?" She sounded breathless.

"Do you know where Calvert is?"

"Calvert Street. Yes, love. I live there. If you want, you can walk with me."

"Thank you," said Harriet, relieved to have company. Even though blisters tortured her every step, she hobbled along, trying to keep up with the woman's pace, and other than briefly introducing themselves, they didn't speak. After about ten minutes, Mrs. Gaffney stopped.

"Well, this is mine." Mrs. Gaffney pointed toward steps leading to an arched doorway with a large black number two etched into the glass above. The door had a huge gash in its frame. The side panel exposed splinters of fresh wood.

"What number do you want?"

"To be truthful, I'm not sure." Harriet felt foolish. "Someone told me there is a room to rent."

"Well, I never! I don't know of any others, but I've got a spare room. I've just put an ad in the news agent's. Could have saved myself a pretty penny, I can tell you."

The streetlight gave Mrs. Gaffney's face an eerie look. "Come in. See what you think."

Harriet, not believing her luck, gratefully accepted. Mrs. Gaffney muttered under her breath about the damage to her door, and as she put the key in the lock, a man spoke from behind. Mrs. Gaffney turned. "Hello, Albert."

"Mrs. Gaffney." A potbellied man nodded, lifting his trilby.

"Go on in, Albert."

"Ta," he said, tottering past and down the dimly lit hallway, vanishing out of sight.

"Mr. Noble is one of my lodgers," said Mrs. Gaffney.

Suddenly Harriet felt trapped, but Mrs. Gaffney, still talking, began walking up the creaking stairway, encouraging her to follow.

"I haven't had the chance to check the room," she said, with obvious embarrassment, flicking on a light on the next landing. "So, I apologize in advance. My lodger was carted off to Her Majesty's Hotel this morning. If Jim hadn't been on the way out when the police arrived, the whole bloody door would have been bashed off its hinges." Mrs. Gaffney didn't pause for breath.

"Jim's one of my other lodgers. Saved me a fortune." She stopped on the third turn of the staircase.

"Doors don't come cheap, you know, and the police have no care at all. They won't pay damages."

Harriet gave a half smile.

"Now, don't go thinking I've a houseful of criminals. I had no idea what he was up to. And he always paid his rent on time."

They arrived at the top of the house.

"Anyway. Here we go."

The only door on the landing was ajar. Mrs. Gaffney pushed the door open farther and beckoned her to look.

"Good God. Look at the state of it! I'm so sorry. What did I tell you? The police are a law unto themselves!" The landlady sniffed the stale air disdainfully. The smell reminded Harriet of the greasy spoon café, and she tried not to gag.

"I'll air it out and clean it up, of course." Mrs. Gaffney opened the skylight a tad, allowing the cold night breeze to touch the room.

The room was pokey. It looked as if a fight had taken place. Grubby clothes were strewn across the floor. A stained, lumpy mattress spewed its guts, and an upturned chest of drawers lay in pieces.

Mrs. Gaffney looked at Harriet in the tobacco-stained light of a forty-watt bulb. "The rent's fair."

Harriet tried not to gasp when she heard how much. But she agreed she would call back with the deposit by twelve thirty latest, the next day, or lose the room.

Harriet left, wincing. It wasn't the room was tiny, or it needed a good clean. The pressing issue of the deposit concerned her more. Two roads on, she came to a zebra crossing. The Belisha beacons pulsated in time with her throbbing heels. Her heart felt like lead. Tears dripped unchecked. She caught a sob in her throat. A lone passerby looked at her sideways. This would never do. She had to stop moping. She had to be strong.

Wondering how she could raise the cash, Harriet's mind drifted to the painting in Nana's bedroom. She felt it must have some value. They both loved it. Her grandmother said it'd been a gift, but never said who it was from, only that one day it would be hers. Harriet hated the thought of selling or putting it on hock. Sick at the thought, she swallowed, willing herself to be tough. She could see no other way.

****

Detesting the silence when she opened the door, Harriet stood a while, angry and frustrated, in the dark. Her heels were killing her. She flicked the light on before gingerly taking her shoes off and flinging them down the hallway. More pain followed, oozing translucent blood. She pummeled the wall furiously with her fists, crying over and over, "I'm sorry, Nana!"

Lifting her glasses, wiping tears away with the back of her hand, Harriet noticed a piece of paper trapped in the letterbox. She pulled it out, and the letterbox clattered shut. Through misted eyes she read the note, from Mrs. Donaldson, simply written. No nonsense, just like the lady herself.

"Harriet, come and see me as soon as you get this message. Mrs. Donaldson." Harriet, though thoroughly ready for bed, was worried. She briefly tended her wounds, pushed her heels back down into her shoes, and did as requested. Mrs. Donaldson answered the door.

"Quick, Harriet, come on in, before you let all the heat out."

It occurred to Harriet that even though they were neighbors, she had never stepped farther than the front door before. Mr. Donaldson was sitting in a wing-backed chair, reading a broadsheet. Smiling, he made himself scarce, taking the paper with him.

"Sit down, love," said Mrs. Donaldson indicating a pale pink two-seater settee. "I need to get something."

Harriet's eyes were instantly drawn to the television set, the screen the size of a biscuit tin, and wondered what it might be like to watch one.

"Here." Mrs. Donaldson presented Harriet with a small brown envelope. Her stomach flipped. It reminded of the severance pay.

Mrs. Donaldson proffered the envelope again. Puzzled, Harriet took it from her as if it were on fire, but her neighbor looked genuinely pleased with herself, and, for once, spoke at length.

"I'm sure you won't mind, what with our conversation and all?" Harriet couldn't remember having a full-blown conversation but listened without interruption.

"I've spoken to Rosa and Mrs. Singh, but you know they're fit to bursting. And I would offer you a room in a heartbeat, especially with the landlord almost doubling the rent—all because of a blasted inside bathroom!" Her gaze briefly rose to the heavens.

"But we get the lovely news our Frederick's expecting their first, so exciting. Like I said before, they've moved to Somerset for his job. Frederick's found a lovely house there. It's huge! And what with Mr. Donaldson retiring from the Ministry next month, Frederick's asked us to move in with them." She looked at Harriet.

"Well, go on, open it!" She was unable to contain her excitement.

Mr. Donaldson peered around the door. "I'm sorry, Betty, but you haven't actually explained what the envelope is for, or how you came by it."

"I did!" said Mrs. Donaldson.

"Nosiree-bob, you just think you did." Mr. Donaldson winked at Harriet. "What my wife is trying to tell you is that everyone in the street has clubbed together. To help you on your way."

He laughed at Harriet's obvious confusion, smiling warmly. Harriet adjusted her glasses and, turning the small but bulging envelope over in her hand, found it covered in signatures.

"You better open it up quickly, or my Betty might explode into a million pieces."

Harriet, still surprised, found tucked inside the envelope a huge sum of money.

"But..." she stammered, "what do you mean *they clubbed together*?"

Mr. Donaldson put his pipe into his mouth and began fiddling with tobacco in the bowl.

"It doesn't take a genius to work it out, love," said Mrs. Donaldson. "Everyone wanted to show how much we care. This was one small way we could help in return for everything you and Molly did for us."

The envelope's contents briefly filled Harriet's desperate mind with hope, and instantly she knew it was far more than she ever earned in a week at Dingham's.

"No, I couldn't. Really." Her throat constricted so that her voice squeaked. "Thank you. It's incredibly generous, but I just couldn't." She tried handing it back. Every penny counted to her friends in Ham Street.

"Yes, you can. Accept it or offend everyone." Mrs. Donaldson nodded.

"You look shattered, love. Go on, take yourself home and get to bed, and put that somewhere safe."

Harriet, trembling, clasped the envelope, her mind gathering possibilities. The money would cover the deposit. A huge weight lifted, and with painful blisters momentarily forgotten, she flung herself at the couple, burying her head against Mr. Donaldson's broad chest.

"Jumpin' Jehosifat," he said, patting Harriet's back.

"How can I ever repay you?"

"No need, love. It's the very least we could do."

"Everyone has been so very, very kind." Harriet hugged Mrs. Donaldson. "I will never forget. Not ever."

"When you've found somewhere to live, let me know. We'll all help as much as possible. Off you go now, before you fall asleep right in front of us," said Mrs. Donaldson, ushering her out of the house.

****

Harriet knelt at her bed and blessed everyone for their amazing generosity, which she truly felt undeserved. But above all, she felt an overwhelming sense of gratitude toward her neighbors as they continued to extend their friendship. Putting the treasured kindness into her handbag, she snuggled down with Nana's favorite cardigan, breathing in the last hints of Lily of the Valley, but as she did, her head began thumping with fear. Fear of new beginnings and the unknown.

Chapter 10

Stepping into the dark, damp, early morning air, Harriet found comfort in the drizzle and solitude. She walked three streets purposefully, head down. She heard the familiar chink of milk bottles, and a gentle swoosh as the milk-float passed by. Harriet could just make out the milkman's cheery wave. He stopped.

"Hello, love, fancy a gold top?" The crate swung around in his hand with the bottle beckoning. Harriet declined, though a pint of creamy gold top sounded wonderful.

"I haven't seen you around before." He sized her up in the gloom.

"No, I've just got a job at the bakery, mustn't be late." She tried to move on.

"Here. You'll be doing me a favor. Old Mrs. Fisher's in hospital. She won't need it. Pay me when you can." Harriet peered at the older man with his little white peaked cap, guessing he would be around her grandmother's age. He would lose money if he didn't sell all his milk.

"Are you going to Ham Street?"

"Yes."

She dipped her hand into her purse. "Here you are." She gave him tuppence. "Pop it on number six's doorstep. Mrs. Dart's. She's just had another baby, her fifth and their first girl."

"Right-e-oh. Will do." The milkman smiled, dropping the money into a deep overall pocket. Resettling his crates, he climbed back into his float and hushed away down the street.

A dustcart clanked toward the crossroads, pouring smoke along with an obnoxious odor of rotten eggs. The cart parked right in the middle of the junction, stopping any would-be traffic. Two dustmen jumped from the wagon. Both wore battered leather caps and waistcoats. One had horse rope tied around his waist to hold up his trousers. Without care, they clattered metal lids to the ground and hurled bins onto their backs. Some of the contents spilled out onto the road, but they ignored the stinking glue ladling itself to the ground and the paper debris slip-sliding away.

From opposite sides of the road, they embarrassed themselves expounding pornographic detail of their last night's escapades, loud enough for Harriet to hear every filthy word, and bursting into peals of laughter, insinuated she was a lady of the night. Harriet refused to lower herself by responding. A rat darted its head up from a nearby drain, quickly followed by another, and she sidestepped them, shuddering. The dustmen jumped back into their wagon, but one hung out the window, making suggestive hand gestures as they pulled away.

Dark still prevailed when Harriet arrived at Daisy Baker's in good time. Hanging up her coat and quickly changing into the whites provided, she began helping Mrs. Turpin. As the older woman gave directions, she imagined standing in the same place Nana once did, and somehow it gave her a small measure of comfort.

Daisy and Mrs. Turpin were nothing like her previous employer. They were kind and checked Harriet was okay with the first job before issuing her with another. The work was simple, methodical, and, for the moment, its simplicity suited her. By six thirty, all the goods were displayed in neat, ordered rows and the kettle was whistling away out the back.

"Come on, love. While the pay isn't brilliant, Daisy's very generous in other ways. You're entitled to two cups of tea and a filled roll or cake, and you can take home a share of any leftovers."

Harriet welcomed the break and found Daisy rolling out marzipan for the bottom tier of a wedding cake, but she looked awkward and uncomfortable perched on the stool. Whilst the two women chatted and sipped hot, tangy sweet tea, Harriet soaked up the atmosphere, remembering it was only two days ago when she first sat in this very room. With a slight bow of the head and a prayer, she silently thanked Tom.

****

Harriet surveyed Calvert Street with its regimented army of arched doorways. She knew Mrs. Gaffney's room was a Hobson's choice, but she had to live somewhere. A man exited Mrs. Gaffney's, and with it an idea sprang to mind. With sweaty palms, Harriet matched the man's pace and engaged the stranger in conversation. Five minutes later, Harriet shook his hand, and he went on his way.

Mrs. Gaffney held a slim cigarette holder as if she were a film star, but the cigarette remained unlit. Her loose voluminous wave, makeup, and modern clothes suggested she took pride in her looks.

"You're younger than I first thought," said Mrs. Gaffney doubtfully. "How are you going to manage the rent? I'm not a charity."

"I wonder if we could discuss the details inside?" The landlady nodded a thin, small smile, but her tone softened.

"I suppose you'll want a cuppa?"

"Thank you, that would be lovely."

Mrs. Gaffney lit up and inhaled. Harriet followed the lazy blue-gray smoke trail along a tiled herringbone hallway, ending up in a good-sized kitchen. A dining table with six chairs stood in one corner, and on the opposite side, an up-to-the-minute, pale green kitchen unit with little cupboards and glass windows. At the end of the room, a double door led to the outside garden, providing welcome light. To be fair, the room was sparkling clean, unlike the upstairs room Harriet viewed the night before.

"Mrs. Gaffney, how many bedrooms do you rent?" She made it a polite question, already knowing the answer.

"Three, four when we're full," Mrs. Gaffney replied, filling the kettle. "My husband was killed in the war. I have to make ends meet somehow." She blinked a tear away. Harriet nodded sympathetically.

"I don't take any nonsense. The room is for the person who pays for it. No extras. Like boyfriends." She tapped an inch-long column of ash into a saucer, though an ugly china ashtray sat right next to it.

"Do you have a beau?" Mrs. Gaffney remained standing, a spiral of smoke rising into the air as she stirred the teapot.

"No." Harriet took a deep breath; it was now or never. By the time the landlady finished her tea, Mrs. Gaffney was laughing and had agreed to Harriet's terms without considering an option.

****

Pleased with her day's work, Harriet immediately went to Nana's bedroom upon arrival at home. Sitting on the edge of Nana's bed, she stroked her hands across the soft coverlet, her gaze resting on the oil painting. The frame always felt at odds with the quality of the artist, but Harriet loved it and often came into Nana's bedroom just to lose herself in it. The artist's strokes were so lifelike she felt she could dip her toes into the trickling water, hear the geese waddling toward the stream, and feel the wind in the trees, caught in dappled sunlight. The countryside seemed idyllic. With sudden alarm, Harriet realized she would need to pack, to go through Nana's belongings, maybe forced to give most of it away. All at once, Harriet began to retch. Running down the stairs, she flew into the remodeled bathroom and emptied her soul into the pan.

Chapter 11

The next day Harriet would move into her new lodgings. Her neighbors kindly offered to finish off the house clearance whilst she worked. She would have laughed at the spectacle. Three men valiantly filled the rag-and-bone cart whilst containing the blasphemous roars of Ron Oatley in and outside the house. But by the time Harriet returned home, as promised, the job was done.

Harriet felt like a trespasser in the empty rooms echoing her final steps. Sunlight drifted through the windows as she made her goodbyes remembering the good times, touching each wall, thanking them for their warm comfort on cold wintry nights and welcome shade in the summer. Every room held a story, a memory box of emotions printed in indelible ink.

In the kitchen her most vivid recollections were conjured. Nana teaching children to bake cakes, their little faces wide-eyed, fingers sticky, laughter excited. Creamy mixtures turning from pale cream to gold, swelling in the oven into hot, sweet, rounded hills. Mums chatting, shelling peas, peeling potatoes. The pleasure of seeing new, precious lives born in their street. Harriet unpinned a slice of reversed wallpaper stuck to the wall, with Nana's beautiful handwriting on it, and studied the verse passed down by her great-grandmother. On wet days, children were encouraged to make one of their own.

She smiled, recalling the effort of little Alice, valiantly attempting to color in the similar border of looping, curling, fancied drawings of butterflies and bees, her big brother Arthur praising her for her efforts as orange crayon fell outside the lines. The verse's meaning was clear to all. She read it aloud, just as she had done so many times to a demanding audience, darling little cherubs patiently sitting cross-legged, lying on the floor, twiddling hair, or pushing wooden cars:

"If a child lives with blame they learn to condemn.

If a child lives with violence they learn hatred and anger.

If a child lives with scorn they learn to be shy.

If a child lives with tolerance they learn respect.

If a child lives with encouragement they learn to develop and encourage others.

If a child lives with praise they learn to appreciate and praise others.

If a child lives with fairness they learn to treat everyone fairly.

If a child lives with security they learn to trust.

If a child lives with approval they learn to like themselves.

If a child lives with acceptance and friendship they learn to find love in the world."

Harriet bit back tears, rolled the verse slowly into a tube, and tied a little string around its middle.

Upstairs, still unable to comprehend the sum of two whole lifetimes were contained within one tea chest, she stared at a bright rectangle of yellow paint where the painting once hung. The tea chest sat on the floor, the painting propped against it, and on top, a shoebox, the box unremarkable, no markings other than the size, a three. She knew it well. The label was beginning to peel away, the lid dented and concertinaed in at the corner. She only once dared try on her mother's satin pointes, wishing she were as dainty and talented, wishing she had known her mother. It was a wonderful keepsake, now a vivid memory of the day Nana died. A deep well of guilt pulsed through her veins. Her grandmother was about to tell her something important. Whatever it was, Nana had seemed worried, and Harriet hated herself. She should never have kept asking, pushing for answers, wanting to know about her father. Harriet knelt, placed her hands together to pray, just as a loud report reverberated around the empty house. When she looked out the window, pigeons were flying air-force style over rooftops. She spied Ron Oatley lolling at the bottom of the path and Mr. Donaldson by the gate. When she opened the front door, Mr. Singh welcomed her with his broad smile and endearing wobble-headed speech.

"It is time we are going to the bedroom. We are finding your big chest, no?"

"Ya daft bugger, Singey! Watch what yer sayin' ta the lady." Ron was laughing his head off. Mr. Singh remained blissfully ignorant, whilst Mr. Donaldson looked on mightily embarrassed.

"Yes, it is time, Mr. Singh." Harriet wanted to laugh despite herself. "You have all been so very kind."

"Yes, yes. It is your pleasure. Your bed is being in the van waiting for the sleeping." Mr. Singh looked over his shoulder.

"Mr. Ron is here. Mr. Donaldson is also returning from the work to be helping." Mr. Donaldson stepped forward, winking at her. A no-nonsense air, like his wife.

"Mrs. Donaldson says sorry. She's gone to our Frederick's on the train. Somerset's a way from London, what with all the stops. You must come and visit once we've moved, and you're settled?"

"That would be lovely, Mr. Donaldson." Hugging him, she bit back tears. "You've been such good friends." She handed over a paper bag filled with Chelsea buns as she thanked them.

"Shame ta kettle's not on," said Ron wistfully, around a mouthful. "Would go down ta treat with a cuppa."

Chapter 12

Harriet hated any form of exercise, but with public transport an unaffordable luxury, walking remained her only option. Yet, by the end of her first week she felt amazed at how much better she felt.

Tom's gift of meringue and the surprising twist in flavor had inspired Harriet to make a few suggestions. She had hoped she might bump into him, but their paths never crossed, his shift being over before hers began. As the days passed and, with no word, she worried Tom may have been offended. Another week on, and there were two small white cake boxes waiting for her, along with Mrs. Turpin's unmasked curiosity.

"I've never seen Tom so excited. I thought he was fit to burst when he handed me these."

Harriet shyly peeked inside a box. It held three-inch rectangular cakes with a creamy whipped topping and the tiniest of fondant carrots on top. She gasped, delighted.

Mrs. Turpin shuffled closer, her huge breasts edging Harriet out the way so she could eye the contents doubtfully.

"What on earth have carrots got to do with cake?"

Harriet grinned, relieved. Tom had not been offended after all. The second box felt so light she thought it empty. Instead, inside, there were eight miniature meringues with flecks of lilac running through.

"What do we have here?"

"Smell them, Mrs. Turpin." She lifted the box toward her.

"Reminds me of them Parma violets. I think it's time for a taste test and tea." Mrs. Turpin bustled out the back before the next raft of regulars arrived.

"At long last," said Daisy, already pouring tea when Harriet offered the fancies around. "I thought Tom would never be satisfied. He's been working his socks off trying to get the ingredients right. Why, he wouldn't even let me have a nibble!"

"I have one problem," said Mrs. Turpin, having wolfed down her meringue in one go, and a carrot cake in the same manner. "They're just not big enough!" They were still laughing when the shop bell alerted them to custom. Harriet peeked through the curtain of colorful plastic strips, and just as Mrs. Turpin was about to help herself to another fancy, she whipped the samples right from under her nose.

"Good morning, Madam. How can I help?" Harriet strategically arranged the fancies on the countertop. Mrs. Turpin arrived, blinking in disbelief.

"My good friend Mrs. Shan-Kydd tells me this bakery is something special." The woman gestured toward the miniature cakes. "I think she may be right. They, I believe, are exactly what I am looking for." Harriet immediately offered a sample.

"It's a little early. But thank you." She paused for the briefest of moments. "Our usual suppliers have let us down." The woman's eyes were masked by dark glasses. "I'm hosting a charitable event, for two hundred, this Saturday." Her cheek twitched. "Could you possibly cope with the order?" Mrs. Turpin, agog, nudged Harriet.

"Absolutely, of course we could!" Mrs. Turpin remained mute. "Perhaps you would like to speak to the proprietor, Madam?" Harriet was uncomfortable with Mrs. Turpin's odd behavior.

"Could you ask your employer to telephone me, say, after two this afternoon?" Harriet took a card from the gloved hand and read the name.

"Certainly, Lady Carmichael. I will inform Mrs. Baker straight away, and if you would like to take these samples? To try later?" Lady Carmichael smiled enigmatically.

"I like your enthusiasm, young lady."

As Harriet boxed the fancies, she sensed there was more than just the issue of her suppliers. Harriet's fertile imagination ran wild. She'd heard about smokescreens, women covering blackened eyes or—just as bad—trying to laugh off their stupidity with feeble excuses, like walking into a door or falling over fresh air. Placing the boxed cakes on the counter, she spotted a bruise barely hidden under heavy makeup. Rich people didn't experience that. Did they?

Mrs. Turpin, gathering her wits, raced from behind the counter and held the door open, curtseying. "Well, bless my soul!" Puffing, pressing herself against the closed door, stopping regulars from coming in, she asked, "Do you know who you've been speaking to?"

Harriet laughed, looking out into the street, watching the peak-capped chauffeur assist their latest customer into her limousine. A gaggle of fascinated children were looking on in awe, marveling at it. Some older lads stood back ignoring their own scuffed shoes and long stockings, hands stuffed into shorts, attempting nonchalance as if they already owned such a vehicle, or planned to, one day.

"Oh, my goodness," said Mrs. Turpin, panicked, releasing the door and letting in an annoyed Mrs. Crouch.

"Too posh for your regulars now, Mrs. Turpin?" she cackled, pointing to the fancy car.

"No, no, dear, sorry, Mrs. Crouch." Mrs. Turpin quickly resumed her position behind the counter. "Just had a bit of a shock is all."

"Will Daisy be cross?" whispered Harriet.

"Mark my words, Daisy will be glad not to have had the difficult walk through to the shop, and Tom? This is just what he has dreamed of!" Swishing out the back, she called, "Daisy! Daisy! Just you wait to hear what our Harriet's gone an' done!"

"Sorry, Mrs. Crouch." Harriet smiled, with a feeling of excitement rising in her chest. "What can I get you today?"

Chapter 13

The cold early morning air reddened Harriet's cheeks, and the hour was so dark it allowed stars to glisten from the heavens. Anticipation pulsed through her veins. She was part of the team preparing for the garden party. The prospect of seeing Tom thrilled her.

Harriet arrived at the bakery at precisely four o'clock. She could feel the heat from the ovens oozing the scent of gorgeous hot bread into the air. Mrs. Turpin bustled across the room, hung up her coat, and grabbed aprons, handing one to Harriet. Two older bakers, though extremely busy, acknowledged them with a wave. Marjorie and Dorothy arrived minutes later, exchanging pleasantries.

"Well, well," said Tom, turning to smile brightly and wink at Harriet. "Good morning, and a special good morning to Harriet, the best saleswoman in all the world." She flushed at the compliment.

Tom's face was unshaven, the dark stubble giving him the look of a ruffian, but in the pit of her stomach butterflies fluttered, and she tried desperately not to show her sense of pleasure.

"Well, as everyone is here," he began, "firstly, thank you for getting here so early. I have a plan of action."

Tom quickly issued instructions, and the moment they were organized, he disappeared through the side door, the entrance to Daisy's flat over the shop.

Five minutes later, he returned, carrying Daisy, carefully, gently, cradling her in his arms as if she were a small child. Harriet couldn't stop staring. As Tom eased Daisy onto her stool, a small cry of pain escaped her lips.

"Sorry, did I hurt you?" He looked on anxiously, but Daisy patted his arm.

"I'm fine, thank you, Tom." Daisy smiled, her string of pearls in place as usual, peeking out behind her unbuttoned baker's coat. Adjusting her glasses, she hitched the cord over her neck and called to everyone.

"Morning, everyone. Thank you so much for helping out today." She whispered to Harriet, "Without Tom's help, where would I be?" Harriet glanced at Tom, his actions confirming his quiet strength of character and her strong confidence in him.

Under Tom's guidance, there were two clear agendas. First, the usual front of shop provisions and general deliveries, and then the order for Lady Carmichael. Throughout the next few hours, Harriet found herself frequently glancing over at Tom, watching his broad back moving swiftly between jobs, whipping up a variety of cake mixtures, piping choux pastry, checking for the perfect shiny-smooth consistency of icing. He measured the size of cakes and fancies for perfection, and around six thirty all the regular orders were complete.

Breads, rolls, cakes, and fondants began to pile high in the shop front. Along the right-hand side of the kitchen, set specifically for the garden party, another fantastic display began to mount. The extra bakers, drafted in from retirement, were clearly happy in their work, their camaraderie evident, joking, laughing, all helping to make a great team effort.

Whilst Daisy checked the order and prepared boxes in readiness, Harriet worked on an array of sugar paste decorations and anything else asked of her. And, as time ticked by, a sense of urgency swept in, and Tom began singing. Harriet didn't recognize the song, but the melody had an uplifting rhythm which seemed to make them work even faster and, if possible, enhanced their teamwork.

As the garden party order cooled, Daisy ticked off the list. From there, the delivery boys took them to the drivers, experienced in arranging their load. Just once, Harriet caught Tom glance over, his concentration lost for a moment, wiping his brow, leaving a dusting of flour on it. He grinned, a lopsided grin, before returning his attention to the job in hand. That one small look was all she needed.

By the end of the shift, tea, stacks of hot buttery toast, and a pyramid of currant buns with kernels of sugar on top sat on the work surface. The workforce took their cue, perching on empty crates or leaning against the walls, steaming mugs in one hand, food in the other. Though exhausted from their efforts, there was an animated buzz, and laughter continued to fill the air. After a few moments, Daisy looked over at Tom. He nodded, and as she began to speak, the room fell silent.

"I want to say a huge thank you. Without you, we would never have achieved what we have today. I'm sure you will agree it is nothing short of a miracle. So, there's something extra in your pay packets. Not only for your loyalty and hard work, but for being such good friends."

A roar of approval erupted, with a chinking of mugs. Adjusting herself on her stool, Daisy smiled and took a deep breath.

"You have been marvelous to work with over the years." She looked around the room, all eyes upon her. "I know we all miss Molly." Mugs were raised again, this time with murmuring assent. Harriet gulped back a lump in her throat.

"But I miss Molly more than you'll ever know. Her intuition, her patience, her wise ways, kept me on track long after John and the boys..." Daisy held her composure. "And of course there is our Tom." She looked at him and beamed. "He's been steadfast throughout. Without him, the business would have failed long ago." Daisy patted her legs. "I'm not as nimble or as young as I used to be."

There was a ripple of consolatory understanding.

"And poor Tom, here, hauls me up and down those blasted stairs every day." Her face crinkled around her bright smiling eyes.

"So I've come to a decision. If you haven't heard the whispers already, it's about time I retire, let someone younger take over." Daisy raised her hand to quieten the dismayed surprise.

"Before you start worrying, all your jobs are safe, and with this new order it may be the start of a whole new venture." She looked toward Tom.

"Tom has agreed to run things from now on. And I know I can leave things safely in his capable hands. I will be here, but as a silent partner." She ran her fingers over her pearls. "Though I don't know how silent."

Tom shared the joke, encouraging her to be as vocal as she wanted. There were whirrs of support, mixed with hugs, shaking of hands, and pats on Tom's back. Daisy's choice clearly met everyone's approval, and Harriet, though equally pleased for him, sat there remembering her grandmother's last moments on earth, and the beginnings of a conversation never finished. Why had she kept the knowledge of her father a secret? What was it she had been about to say?

****

Tom decided he would travel with one of the drivers and make sure Lady Carmichael was happy with the order. To Harriet's complete surprise, Daisy instructed her to go with Norman in the other van. Harriet could not have been more pleased. Ten minutes later, she slipped into the front seat. Specially designed racks closed off the cab. Norman, a small, wiry man in his late forties, nodded as he plonked himself comfortably beside her in the driver's side. Chomping on the last piece of toast, twisting his flat cap askew like a naughty schoolboy, he winked cheekily, his face creasing into a million tramlines.

"Hold tight, girl, we've gotta mission to get there on time." He revved the engine loudly. Harriet's eyes widened. Norman laughed. She quickly realized he was just horsing around, as Norman drove with care but happily yelled at other road users as he weaved skillfully in and out of London's traffic.

Eventually, they slowed, no longer in central London, the noise of harried traffic so far behind birds could be heard sharp against the air. How silence stilled suburbia. Mulling over the day Harriet met Lady Carmichael, she could not quite put her suspicions aside. Harriet shook herself. Probably what posh folk did, wear sunglasses all the time. Besides, it was quite the compliment to have the business, and Daisy's good name was indeed growing.

Harriet's thoughts turned to the straight road lined with trees, wondering at the glory of their new leaves peeking out in fluffy lime green. The pavements looked newly surfaced, weed free, not a pothole in sight, so unlike Ham Street. High white-stone walls ran along the paths, hiding the properties from view, and huge gates were flanked by pillars with colossal ornaments. Norman grunted, looking for a clue.

"Over there?" Harriet pointed toward a wide-open driveway sentried by a male wearing a smart dark gray suit. They pulled up alongside. After a brief discussion, the man, checking his list, directed them down a long meandering drive.

"Bloody hell. Butlers, guards. This place is enormous!" said Norman once out of his earshot. "What it is to be a lord of the manor, eh?"

The view took Harriet's breath away. Neatly manicured lawns stretched either side, leading them toward a mansion. Staff busily milled between two cream-colored marquees as Norman pulled on the brake and checked his watch.

"Well, m'lady, we've made good time. Now all we have to do is get this lot unloaded, double quick."

"Shall we get on with it then, Sir Norman?"

As she stepped out the van, she viewed a dusting of pink light cast across the early morning's powder blue, and the air greeted them—fresh, sweet, and new, a beautiful reminder of life as it should be. "It's going to be a glorious day."

Norman got to business identifying where to place the delivery, and not five minutes later Tom arrived with Frank. Norman swiftly introduced them to the housekeeper, a smartly dressed woman in sensible flat black shoes, her hair pulled back into a tight bun, giving her a look of severity not matching her personality at all. As she ran her finger down her list, she looked pleased.

"Wonderful. The tables are all laid out ready and waiting." A broad smile crossed her face. "Ask for Philip. He'll direct you." She pointed toward the marquee on the left.

Within the hour they were finished.

"Well, I'm for the off, m'lady!" said Norman. "Don't want me missus on the warpath."

"Come on, Tom," Frank agreed, winking. "We've done all we can. Let's leave it to the toffs. Sir Philip can take over now."

"I just had a thought," said Tom. "Would you mind if I drove you to Luigi's, Harriet? I know you start in an hour. Plus, I've a couple of things I'd like to discuss." Surprised, confused, Harriet just nodded.

"The keys are in the ignition," said Frank, nudging Norman. "Come on, you old bugger. I thought you were in a hurry." Norman doffed his cap.

"Bye, m'lady!"

"Bye, Sir Norman." She playfully curtseyed and waved them off.

Tom walked with Harriet toward the van, a look of concern on his face.

"You don't mind coming back with me?"

Harriet's heart skipped a beat. How could she possibly mind? Tom had turned his back against the rising sun. She could feel the warmth on her face and see the outline of his torso through his shirt.

"It's been hectic. But well worth every minute, don't you think?"

"Absolutely."

"So how are things?"

Harriet blinked in the facing sunlight, her heart pounding at the question.

"I'm sorry. I've upset you."

"No. Really. I'm doing much better." She touched his arm. "Thank you for asking."

There were the briefest of moments when she forgot. She had not cried in two days. She was doing better.

Tom opened the passenger door in contemplative silence.

Harriet pushed her feelings away, still sensing his warmth and masculinity.

"I would like to think we could become good friends, Harriet."

She turned toward him in surprise. "I thought we were friends."

"Yes. We are? Good. What I mean is… Well. How would you feel if I asked you to celebrate my new role at the bakery? Not a date. I know I'm too old. But as friends? Nothing more?"

"Are you digging for compliments, Tom?"

"No! Sorry." He groaned. "I'm messing this up, aren't I?"

"Let me get this right." She was trying hard to disguise her delight. "You're asking me out. Not a date, but to celebrate your new job. As friends, because you're too old for anything else?"

"Yes."

"I have one condition and one question."

"Oh?"

"Because we're friends, we'll go Dutch."

Tom shook his head, defeated.

Her laughter filled the air, warm as the sun caressing

his skin.

"And the question?"

"Just exactly how old are you? A hundred, or a hundred and two?"

Tom grinned, shrugging, pushing his dark floppy fringe back off his face. "Let's just say too old."

Tilting her head to one side, she studied him. "Yup, ancient. Why, you're almost old enough to be my grandfather."

"Hey!" He laughed, putting the van into gear.

"Tom. Seriously. Thank you. You know. For being there. You will never know just how grateful I am."

A flicker of understanding, a light shrug, a squeeze of her hand.

"I'd better get a wriggle on or you'll be late."

Heading out on the drive, Harriet felt acutely aware of Tom's proximity. She liked it. She liked his smile, the way he smelt, the way he flicked his floppy fringe back off his face. Mostly she liked his quiet, gentle strength. Tom accidentally brushed against her leg, changing gear. He apologized, but she caught the sparkle in his eyes and thought about going Dutch, praying she would have enough money to go halves.

****

Tom felt relieved he'd managed to ask the question. To be friends would be good enough for him. He loved the comfort he found in her intelligent words. He loved her kind and beautiful face, her wit and unerring generosity of mind. He thought about them going out together for the meal. He could—he must—keep their relationship platonic. She was far too young for him. He would keep an eye on her without her ever being aware. Yes, they would make great friends. He felt glad he'd taken the courage to ask.

Harriet waved her thanks, standing outside of Luigi's, holding onto the flutter of excitement. She was looking forward to her developing friendship with Tom, and her heart's tight knot of grief unraveled just a little bit.

Chapter 14

Luigi's restaurant was closed to customers. In a quiet corner, at the back, Sofia entered receipts into the accounts ledger while Harriet finished clearing tables and collected the variety of newspapers arranged for the lunchtime trade. The headlines caught her eye and her imagination: *The launch of the Soviet satellite Sputnik*— it sounded rather grand, that their generation would be thought of as the space age.

"There's a bit of a bonus for you." Sofia pushed a curtain of silky hair behind her ear, smiling, handing over her pay packet.

"Papa and I agree, you're doing a wonderful job. The customers like you, not to mention the handsome Mr. Rutherford, who seems smitten since you arrived. But above all, you're a natural, and you've really taken the pressure off me."

Harriet blushed, her heart racing. By the end of her first month, not only was she astonished that her tips almost doubled her pay, but now Sofia was giving her a bonus? Things like this just didn't happen. Not in her world. Well, at least not in the world of Miss Macy's unmentionables!

She heard Luigi singing out the back. This was another world. A kinder one than the one she'd left behind at Dingham's.

"Thank you." Harriet slipped the pay packet into her

apron pocket, too embarrassed to open it.

Sofia smiled, amused at Harriet's obvious confusion.

Harriet left Luigi's with her wages safely stowed in her handbag, trying hard not to skip along Stanhope Street. Life had taken her on a path she could never have imagined. Life without Nana was slowly but surprisingly becoming more bearable.

Entering the haberdashery, Harriet was impressed by the layout and the volume of stock in such a small space. Little wooden boxes made for purpose, filled with skeins and balls of wool in all colors. Knitting needles of every length and thickness were dotted in between. Patterns were held within books on little stands. Lengths of materials were folded neatly in tidy pillars on shelves, some draped for display. The place was wonderful. A haven, and Harriet knew for sure, somewhere, a woman's monthly needs would be discreetly stored, probably under the counter.

"What a wonderful place," she exclaimed, unable to contain her admiration, "and what a lovely suit you're wearing." The frosty-faced woman behind the counter, melting at the praise, immediately asked how she could help.

"I would like some lemon baby wool. I'm not sure how much I would need for a layette. I have two newborns in mind, but don't know how much I can afford."

"I have just the thing." Miss Two-Piece smiled. "And I believe we could come to an arrangement of weekly payments?" She reached across to one of the stands of patterns. "Here."

Harriet did a quick calculation in her head, including

the pattern. It would be all too easy to get into trouble on the Never, Never; she had seen it before—one missed payment, one dip of cash, and interest rates doubled.

"I'll just take enough wool to make bonnets and booties today, thank you."

"You are not interested in a repayment plan?"

"No. But thank you for the kind offer, all the same."

"Very well." The shopkeeper eyed her curiously. Harriet blushed. She would have loved to spend more but needed to be frugal. With her purchases safely stowed, she walked home thinking about tomorrow. It would be Sunday. After her chores she would attend mass, and then once her gifts were complete, she would visit her friends and neighbors in Ham Street. It had been far too long.

****

Later that afternoon, after washing her smalls and hanging them out to dry, Harriet borrowed a kitchen chair and sat outside in the back yard knitting. The sun hung three-quarters in the sky, and though the shadows of the day began to chill the air, she preferred it to retreating to her tiny room.

Mrs. Gaffney brought out a tray of tea, and they sat chatting amiably over the noise of children playing in their own back yards.

"We always wanted children," said Mrs. Gaffney suddenly. "Had four pregnancies. Lost them all. Sleeping, every one of them."

Though she effortlessly tapped a long column of ash into a saucer from her cigarette holder, her face said it all.

"How awful. I'm so sorry, Mrs. Gaffney."

Her landlady barely shrugged, as children's shrieks

of laughter clipped the air. The cries and sheer joy of youthfulness stirred old emotions in Harriet, with the pang of days lost forever. Nana's back garden, the memory of mothers and children who visited. Harriet stopped knitting and reworked a skein of wool into a ball.

"How would it be if I invited some of the mothers and their children around for a pot of tea?" She rushed on, seeing the expression of doubt.

"I'll pay for the milk and tea. I might even be able to rustle up some cakes, hm?"

Mrs. Gaffney held the cigarette holder to her lips. Another moment of sadness crossed her face.

"I don't know, Harriet. Since my old friends in the street moved on, we never kept in touch. Then the young mums moved in…" She crossed a leg over the other. "I worry they'd think me too old and stuffy."

"Age doesn't matter, Mrs. G, and I promise you're not old or stuffy. I'll organize it, if you like."

"Very well. But I'll provide the tea, if you could arrange cake?"

"Of course."

Harriet resolutely rearranged her glasses. No matter what, she must visit Ham Street. She didn't want to lose her friends, not like her landlady.

Chapter 15

October, late afternoon, Harriet was prepping for the evening trade when Fabio whipped her glasses off her nose and popped them on his own face. Pretending to be Buddy Holly, singing the new number one hit, "That'll Be the Day" and catching her hand, he expertly twirled her around in the tight space of the kitchen. Harriet giggled nonstop, feeling light as air, joy in her heart.

Luigi came off the telephone and burst into the kitchen.

"Sofia!"

The dancing stopped.

Luigi, breathless, flustered, red with excitement, announced, "My darling Sofia, she having the baby. Baby Carlo Luigi, he weighing seven pounds six and quarter ounces."

Fabio, looking goofy in Harriet's glasses, went cross-eyed in response. Harriet laughed.

"I going to see my bambinos!"

Thrilled, Harriet asked if she could go with him.

"Come, come! Hurry, hurry!" Luigi sang with delight. Fabio flicked his apron at Harriet before solemnly handing back her specs.

"I see again. Oh, you pretty girl."

"Fabio!" Harriet laughed, putting her glasses back on and collecting her coat.

****

Luigi sang *Figaro* at the top of his lungs throughout the whole drive. Harriet smiled contentedly, sitting next to the proud grandfather, her gift on her lap. The late afternoon held a happy, sunny glow, a tribute to the child.

Family were already trooping into the house when they arrived, and Luigi's wife, Elena, welcomed Harriet with a warm embrace, instantly making her feel a part of the family.

"Congratulations, Sofia," whispered Harriet, when at last she got to see her and the baby. "What a darling little angel, but I didn't realize there would be so many visitors."

Sofia smiled and sighed as Harriet placed her gift beside her, a pair of homemade knitted booties and Dr. Seuss' new book. "I know baby Carlo is too young. I expect you think I am quite mad, but everyone's talking about it. Maybe when he's older."

"Oh, Carlo." Sofia raised her eyes to her husband. "Meet my best friend Harriet."

"Ah, Harriet, welcome."

Carlo had been hanging around by the door, appearing bemused with the ever-growing queue and newly bestowed fatherhood. Now he charmingly kissed Harriet, cheek upon cheek.

"Harriet thinks I should have some rest. Carlo?" Sofia looked plaintively at her husband. "Baby needs a feed."

It was all he needed to hear. He began herding the well-wishers from the room.

"Come, come, I have cake and drinks for you all," said Elena, stepping in, appeasing disgruntled family, by offering Sunday lunch to celebrate.

"And you, Harriet. I am thinking you bring a friend also? It is possible you will be lost amongst us, never to be found again."

Harriet laughed, thrilled at the suggestion, and thanked her for the kind invitation, with her first thoughts instantly drawn to Tom.

****

Saturday evening, Harriet and Tom walked to Pete's café. They liked the brightly lit place with sparkling clean melamine tables, and chose their favored spot, next to the window. They enjoyed the limited menu consisting of meat pie, mutton pie, sausage, and black pudding. Everything came with mash, mushy peas, and gravy. The food was homey, filling, and the entertainment, provided by the owners, Pete and Mel, could not be ignored. First time customers might think murder was on the cards as Mel and Pete shouted, yelled, and bashed pots and pans around in the kitchen.

Harriet and Tom waited for their order of pie and mash, trying to ignore the commotion, and smiled at one another. Another five minutes and the shenanigans should be over. Sure enough, Mel came through the swing door, beaming with an order.

"Sorry about that," Mel said to the couple on the right, placing their food on the table. "Pete's had a bit of a meltdown. Thinks I should cook tonight. I ask you! *He's* the chef!"

Whilst peace reigned, the customers went about eating and chatting, and Harriet spoke about the invitation to Luigi's. Tom happily accepted and decided he would bake an angel cake by way of a small gift. Harriet was delighted.

"Do you know, I've just had an idea."

Mel arrived with their meal.

"There we go, you lovebirds. Two pie and mash. Enjoy."

Harriet polished her glasses, embarrassed. Tom gave her a lopsided smile, waiting for her to continue, and by the time she finished with her ideas, Tom's eyes were twinkling.

"Do you really think Luigi might be interested in outsourcing?"

"If you don't ask, you don't get. Maybe you could batch-make the dough, and they could bake it?" Tom looked surprised.

"That's not such a bad idea, especially as we don't have enough ovens right now, though plans are to expand."

They heard Mel shouting, "Have you completely lost your marbles, Pete? I said one sausage and one black pudding." Harriet and Tom glanced at one another in mock amusement.

"I really don't know why we come to this place," said Tom. "It's so noisy. Perhaps we should find somewhere else?"

"Never," said Harriet firmly. "The food's good, and the entertainment's a bonus."

****

Sunday lunchtime, Luigi waited at the front door, welcoming his guests whilst his wife ensured the paternal grandparents were given pride of place at the top of the table. Once the blessings were made, Luigi began singing, and Harriet was simply spellbound.

"It is beautiful, isn't it?" said Tom, quietly in her ear.

"I've never heard anything quite like it. It's stunning."

" '*Nessun Dorma*' is one of Puccini's most famous arias. You can easily understand why, but the translation makes no sense whatsoever!"

In Harriet's heart, the aria sounded wonderful. She wished she could be held in the moment with Tom forever.

Chapter 16

Mrs. Smith was the first to arrive at Mrs. Gaffney's. With baby Elizabeth fast asleep in her pram, the landlady suggested she come in the back way so as not to wake the sleeping child.

"As it's such a lovely day, we're having tea in the garden. I'll walk with you and open the gate," offered Harriet.

"Don't be long, Harriet," said Mrs. Gaffney, looking pensive.

"We won't, Mrs. G."

"I'm so glad you could make it, Mrs. Smith." They were making their way along the back lane with its mishmash of wobbling back walls and weeds nudging between mortar.

"It was such a kind invitation I could hardly refuse." Mrs. Smith expertly traversed the pram past nettles and under an overhanging purple laburnum. They arrived at the back gate just in time to hear the doorbell.

"Mrs. Smith, please make yourself comfortable."

And Mrs. Smith thanked Harriet, parked the pram in a shaded spot, and found a seat.

Harriet found Mrs. Gaffney talking to a woman on the doorstep.

"Good afternoon, Mrs. Harris."

"Call me Dotty, luv." She smiled, exposing two crossed front teeth. "Don't suppose you want us to stand

on ceremony. Especially if we are gonna be friends."
Dotty glanced through to the hallway and adjusted the
apron covering her robust figure.

"I'm glad you could make it, Dotty," said Mrs.
Gaffney affably. "Harriet will show you through. Mrs.
Smith is already here."

"Nice gaff, Mrs. Gaffney," Dotty called back the
moment she reached the kitchen, having opened every
door on the way, including the under-stair cupboard.
"Now, you behave yourself, Charlie. No pickin' your
nose or touching things. I can't afford no breakages!"

Harriet caught Mrs. Gaffney's wry smile. Charlie, at
three years old, was certainly growing to be like his
mother, eyes and hands everywhere. If Dotty didn't keep
a close watch, something would surely be broken, and it
just might put the kibosh on the whole thing. As Dotty
disappeared into the garden with Charlie, a heavily
pregnant Mrs. O'Connell arrived carrying her youngest,
Mikey, angled carefully on her hip. Her other three
children stood obediently by her side, all very well
turned out, the boy with his hair slicked down, and the
girls' bunches tied in pink ribbons.

"Welcome! Shall I take the weight off?" Mrs.
Gaffney offered to carry Mikey, her eyes innocently
traveling to Mrs. O'Connell's underdeveloped legs
supported by calipers.

"Thank you," said Mrs. O'Connell, surprised at the
offer.

Polio, thought Harriet. She had seen so much of it in
children as she grew up but puzzled why the woman
would wear a roll-neck jumper on such a hot day.

"Such pretty girls, Mrs. O'Connell, and your boy, so
handsome," said Mrs. Gaffney. Declan looked quite

embarrassed, but the girls wriggled in pleasure at the compliment.

"As it's sunny, we are having tea in the garden. Children, go with Harriet. There are crayons and paper. I expect you like to draw." Mrs. Gaffney seemed to have lost her concerned edge, and in its place softness crept in.

"Hello, Florrie, 'ow's business?" Dotty Harris wandered out from the kitchen. "Lovely tea set, Mrs. Gaffney." She turned to Florrie. "You want to see this place. Done up real good, and the garden's a treat." She held out a strong hand.

"Come on, girls, my Charlie's out the back, and you'll never believe who else is!"

A light sigh escaped Mrs. O'Connell as Dotty herded the children along. Harriet smiled and quickly introduced Mrs. Smith as they entered the warmth of the garden, but Mrs. O'Connell instantly pinked.

"It won't come off, you know," said Dotty. "I thought it would come off. Look!" She showed the palm of her hand to the women.

Harriet and Mrs. Gaffney's eyes flashed in dismay. Harriet was about to interject, but Dotty was on a roll.

"Sorry, luv, but we all thinks it, don't we?" She continued full pelt. "Your skin, Mrs. Smith, it's just like chocolate. I always thought it would come off." She shrugged. "'eard that from ignorant folks 'round 'ere. Not you haven't got great skin, by the way. All smooth and seam-free. What do you use on it? Some super new cold cream or what? Whatever it is, I need some! My face and legs have gone just like a crusty old loaf."

Mrs. Smith began laughing, rich and warm as the summer breeze.

"What?"

"My, my, and here I was thinking your skin so pasty white must be like icing sugar and sprinkling dust everywhere," said Mrs. Smith wryly, "but I guess your skin won't taste any more like icing than mine does chocolate."

The rest of the women's eyes were wide, waiting for Dotty to fly off the handle, but all she did was laugh her head off.

"You're a funny one, Mrs. Smith. Never thought me skin to be like icing sugar. But thinkin' about it, you got a point. That makes us both kinda sweet, don't it?" She grinned. "I think we're gonna get on like a house on fire, Mrs. Smith."

"I do hope so. Why don't you call me Patience?"

"Right-e-oh, Patience." Dotty smiled back.

Harriet saw the relief in Mrs. Gaffney's face.

"My name's Florrie." Mrs. O'Connell's calipers clicked as she sat down, drawing a breath and looking more flushed in the heat. "I reckon we could *all* become good friends, don't you?"

"That would be lovely," said Patience as Dotty smiled a crossed-tooth grin.

"She's all right, ain't she, girls?" And the women allowed themselves a nod and a smile, and with it the awkward moment passed.

"Dotty's right, though," said Florrie, looking closely at Patience. "Your skin is beautiful. What is it you use, exactly?"

Mrs. Gaffney was just bringing a tray of tea and buns cut into quarters when Dotty yelled.

"Charlie, you little bugger! What did I tell you?"

Charlie, holding a china ash tray in his pudgy

fingers, immediately dropped it. The ashtray smashed on the ground and into a thousand tiny pieces. Dotty flicked him around the head with the back of her hand.

"What did I say?"

Mrs. Gaffney stood stock still, holding the tea tray, gazing at Charlie's face puckering into a cry, and then calmly took control.

"Tea is served, ladies." Casting an eye over the area dotted with broken china, she added, "A gift from my mother-in-law. I didn't care for her, and I hated that. Now, children, who would like a piece of sticky bun?"

Chapter 17

Harriet knew she'd lost weight, having adjusted the only two work skirts she owned with elastic. But when she put on her Sunday best, she found her light blue wool coat gapped at the front, having previously moved the buttons to allow for girth. Harriet groaned. She had no time for alterations. Pushing her shoes on, shone to their shiniest best, another discovery. The hole in the sole had grown to the size of a crown. No wonder it felt like she was walking on a bullet.

Harriet flew her grandmother's pretty powder compact up and down, attempting to gauge the overall effect. It was impossible. She shrugged. What was more important, the way she looked, or her friends? Popping on her beret and stringing her grandmother's handbag across her arm with gifts carefully stowed inside, she headed off to church.

Ten thirty mass was full, and as she squeezed into a pew, acknowledging a sea of unfamiliar faces, she was welcomed with a congenial ripple of handshakes. As the service began, Harriet studied the congregation. Mouths opening, closing, singing, praying, standing, sitting, kneeling. Incense wafting, candles burning.

Church had once given her peace, a time to reflect. Now instead, raw emotions exposed themselves. Harriet felt like a phony, an interloper, a doubting Thomas. Undoubtedly others felt it in times of grief, but it only served to confirm once again the biblical arguments didn't hold water. If there was a God, why did he take the good, and save the bad? She once had dared to challenge Father O'Leary, but he immediately batted her away as if she were an irritating fly.

Harriet glanced at her watch. The flicker of candlelight took her mind off the priest and his droning sermon. Her decision to come to the church was ill judged. Most likely she would never go to mass again but didn't feel brave enough to leave mid-service. She would escape by timing her exit to coincide with the priest's retreat to the vestry.

Standing at the corner of Ham Street, Harriet realized how quickly it had become a stranger. The houses somehow seemed smaller and the potholes bigger. Wind cartwheeled debris along the pavement, sending a shiver down her spine. She stopped outside her old home. It looked different. The new tenants had put their mark on it. Nets hung in the window. Nana hated nets, preferring a clear view to wave to passers-by. Harriet sighed. The Donaldson's would be her first port of call. Hopefully, she would feel better after seeing them.

The moment she knocked on the door, a dog began barking. Mr. and Mrs. Donaldson never owned a dog? Stupid! Of course. They planned to move. Someone else must live there now. Why had she left it so long? She knew. Deliberately avoiding the moment, using her new life as a poor excuse. Coming back felt like picking at a weeping wound. An older man in a string vest, a towel wrapped around his neck, opened the door before she could leave. Quickly apologizing, she explained herself hurriedly, embarrassed, and he sniffed, nodded, and muttered something she could not hear before closing the door, the dog still barking from somewhere.

Harriet turned and looked across the road. Rosa, Mr. and Mrs. Singh, Mrs. Dart, Ron Oatley, Winston, surely there was someone left? Walking up the short path to Rosa's, the smell of food eased out of the house warm and inviting. Even before she put her knuckles to the door she heard the shout.

"Coming!"

The door flew open, and children met her with screams of delight. Harriet put her hands to her ears in mock defense.

"They saw you first, Harriet, through the front window." Rosa tutted. "Trying to use my curtains to play hide and seek. I'm surprised they're still hanging!" Throwing her arms around her friend, bringing her into a tight welcoming embrace, she whispered how lovely it was to see her and stood back casting a thoughtful eye over her.

"You've lost weight. It suits you."

The children, still pushing and shoving, almost wrestled Harriet to the ground.

"Behave! Harriet's dressed in her Sunday best, for goodness' sake. Away now!" Rosa laughed, ushering Harriet straight into the kitchen, with the children running ahead, giggling and shrieking.

"How is Alan, and your mother-in-law?"

"Old Mrs. Flowers still keeps my Alan on his toes, and mine, I might add." She looked glum. "I visit twice a day. Alan does Sundays. I'd have her here in an instant, but she can't get upstairs. Besides, these places are so small there's no room downstairs for a bed."

Rosa looked bothered. They were in the kitchen.

Pots were boiling, steam filled the tiny room, and the smell of garlic pressed in as warm as a blanket.

"You'll stay and eat." Rosa stirred a pan with a wooden spoon and raised a brow. "No argument." She turned to the children, shooing them outside into the back yard.

"Anyway, with Alan visiting," she winked, "it gives us a chance to talk."

Once the children disappeared, Harriet took out tiny cone paper bags, each filled with two ounces of mixed sweets.

"Is this all right?"

"How kind of you, Harriet. They'll be delighted. Perhaps you can give them out after we've eaten?" Rosa gave the pot one last stir, and, switching the heat off, covered it with a lid. Harriet settled on a stool, and Rosa began updating her with the comings and goings. It was strange, thought Harriet, how rare it was anyone left Ham Street when she lived there. Now, since Nana's passing, most of their old friends had gone. Mr. Singh, who had long been looking for business premises, found a suitable property just outside of London. His notion of selling spices, and making his own brand of bottled curry sauce, had begun to take off.

Ron Oatley had a couple of lodgers. Rosa suspected the landlord had no idea, but they hadn't caused any trouble up to now, and if it meant they had somewhere to live, what did it matter?

Mr. and Mrs. Donaldson had moved just two weeks ago. They said they would write to Harriet with their forwarding address, but Rosa scribbled it down on the back of an old envelope anyway.

"You'll never guess who's pregnant."

"Not Mrs. Dart, surely not, so soon after little Ethel!"

"Yup!" Rosa's eyes rolled to the heavens.

Harriet laughed at Rosa's hip-thrusting actions and nudged her in the ribs.

"So is there a man on the scene, Harriet?"

"No." But as her mouth opened, out fell Tom's name.

"Well, what's this Tom like?"

"Oh, he's just a friend. He's the baker at Daisy's." She wished she hadn't mentioned him.

Rosa smiled. "Ah, yes, the tenor? Nice-looking, in a plain sort of way. Bit old for you, though, isn't he?"

Rosa's eyes drifted across toward the back window where the children were shrieking in the yard. The daylight was changing to a sickly mustard tinge. She called them in.

"He's not interested," confessed Harriet, with a feeling of disappointment. "But we're really good friends."

Rosa's eyebrows shot up.

"Really. Just friends, eh?" The front door rattled, and a draught wandered in. "That'll be Alan. He has impeccable timing. Dinner's just about ready."

"Reckon it's going to be a pea souper tonight, love!" Alan called out from the hallway, wheezing and panting. He stopped in his tracks the moment he clapped eyes on their visitor.

"Well, bless my soul if the wanderer hasn't returned!"

"Daddy!" cried the children, pushing each other aside to get in first for one of his mammoth hugs.

Alan was huge, like a giant teddy bear. He folded

his arms around his children, kissing each of their heads one by one, grinning. Then, giving his wife a sloppy kiss, finally turned to Harriet and gave her a bear hug. She smiled contentedly. How she missed his cheeky ways.

"You've lost weight, my girl," he tutted.

"Just what I said, Alan. Go on and take the load off while the children lay the table."

"I hope you're staying, Harriet?"

"Of course she is!" admonished Rosa. "Got to feed her up somehow."

The children did as they were told and washed their hands before squeezing themselves around the table, fighting for position. Happy chatter filled the air, and the family ate with passion. Harriet absorbed their sense of wellbeing, laughter, and generosity, but by the end of the meal, the sky had turned to gloopy gray. Alan's surprising prediction of a pea-souper seemed on the cards, and they understood Harriet's reasons for going home sooner than planned. Making her promise faithfully to visit again, Harriet gave her knitted baby gifts for Mrs. Dart to Rosa and gave the little two-ounce cones of sweets to the children. After squeals of delight, more cuddles, hugs, and exchanged thanks, Harriet headed home far happier than at the day's start.

London's smog could be dangerous, a killer. Harriet shivered, carefully crossing the road. Her view was distorted, like looking through a dirty net curtain. She knew the sodium streetlights could easily disappear in the thick oppressive air if it got worse. Peering down the road looking for the bus stop, a sliver of ghostly headlights emerged through the mist. She strained to see the number...yes, it was the twenty-three. Perfect timing! It would be a luxury, but one she would afford today.

Stepping aboard, Harriet settled into a spare seat and rubbed the window but remained unable to see out. Bus drivers knew their routes well. In this weather, caution was a must. The ticket collector hung tightly onto the silver pole at the doorway, briefly poking his head out every now and again, adjusting his peaked cap, and pinging the bell twice in advance of the stops ahead.

Harriet, exploring her feelings for Tom, could not deny when she thought about him her heart would skip a beat. She *loved* being with Tom. Their first "friends" meal out. Going to Pete's café had become a real treat at the end of every second week. She loved their conversations, and their easy relaxed companionship. She loved Tom's gentle manner, and how he checked she was okay without prying too deeply. She loved their shared laughter at the most stupid of things. Just thinking about him Harriet felt a rush of excitement. She hoped it would be enough, just to have Tom as a friend— wouldn't it?

Chapter 18

News of the success of Lord and Lady Carmichael's garden party quickly spread. With specialist orders growing week on week, Daisy offered to extend Harriet's shift, but she politely declined. Sofia was right. The tips at Luigi's more than doubled her wage, but more, she enjoyed the diversity of work and its customers. With Luigi's restaurant providing a confidential atmosphere, it drew a high-class patronage. From academics to Harley Street consultants, politicians to barristers, with a belly full of good food and wine they often allowed their stiff professional guards to peel away.

Harriet swiftly learned odd but not yet published facts about the political world and law, and particularly enjoyed waiting on those who engaged her in their lively banter, making her audience laugh with delight. It earned her the title of the Witty Waitress and an even better tip.

One week, a small group of barristers, who often enjoyed a late lunch, remained long after closing. They had the privacy of the segregated table, the trellis work acting as a partial barrier to the rest of the restaurant. One raised a hand for more wine.

"Harriet, you still okay with table seven?" Luigi asked. Harriet glanced over at them. "Any nonsense, you letting me know." Luigi nodded.

Harriet shivered. She'd come across one of them

before, arrogant, drinking too much, privately dubbing him the Toad. Her blood curdled as she arrived. They were earnestly discussing the widely reported case of a man accused of beating his wife to death.

"It's a shamble," said one.

"I agree," said Toad. "By all accounts, she was asking for it." He leaned back in his chair pontificating, puffing his neck, and linking fingers across his swollen belly. Toad caught Harriet's expression of revulsion.

"Ah, our Witty Waitress appears to have an opinion on the matter." Grinning lecherously, he seized the opportunity to play with her. "Another bottle of your fine Rioja and your company, if you please." A fly in his trap.

Toad glanced around at his companions, laughing at his own importance whilst attempting to pinch her bottom. Harriet swiftly moved out of reach and collected the wine.

"I'm sorry, Luigi, table seven?"

He nodded thoughtfully. "Customer no right?"

"No."

"You taking the wine, I come."

"So," said the disgruntled Toad upon Harriet's return, trying unsuccessfully to grope her again. "What are your thoughts on the matter?"

"What matter, sir?" Harriet said politely through gritted teeth, steadfastly remaining two paces from his grasp. "The weather or the state of politics?"

"You see, our Witty Titty has an opinion on everything!" He smirked. The other men shifted in their seats, thumping the table in unified agreement. Harriet glanced over her shoulder for Luigi.

"What I want to know is what you think about this!" He pushed a newspaper toward her. Harriet's eyes narrowed, angry at his rudeness and the men's lack of mettle, but read the headline aloud:

"*Twenty-three people are killed in the Munich air disaster, including eight Manchester United football players.*" She frowned. "It's simply dreadful, so terribly sad."

"No, silly gal. This!"

Her lips tightened as she scanned the article, already suspecting what Toad alluded to. She'd been following the story with morbid curiosity each day. Mr. Reginald Thwaite was standing trial for battering his wife, Mrs. Dorothy Thwaite, to death. The defense appeared to be leading the argument Mr. Thwaite's wife pushed him to *the boundaries of reason which no common man could be expected to endure. Mr. Thwaite, in one moment of terrible madness, accidentally killed her.*

The provoking title in the paper suggested, "*One moment of madness.*" Having previously read Mrs. Thwaite's skull had been smashed with an iron, more than once, she thought otherwise. One thing for sure, Harriet knew Toad already held his own skewed view. Women were worthy victims.

"Would you really like to hear my view, sir?" Hiding her contempt was difficult. "Or would you prefer I agree with you, sir?"

The men laughed. One tapped his empty glass, making it ring.

Toad smacked his hand down on the table. "Give me your view, Witty Titty." He smirked. "I believe it's good to *allow* the uneducated to air their perspective every now and again."

Harriet sucked air through her nose, while her mantra *the customer's always right* sat uncomfortably in the pit of her stomach.

"Very well, sir, but you may not like what you hear." All eyes were on her. "I believe you suggested Mrs. Thwaite was *asking for it*?"

Toad nodded.

"I don't believe any woman ever asks to be bullied or battered to death." She locked eyes with Toad. "Everyone should be treated with kindness, dignity, and respect!"

Toad touched each of his waistcoat buttons as if he were counting them, the silly smirk still on his face.

"However, it appears that if men in elevated positions, such as your own, who have no moral compass, can empower men to brutalize women without retribution, surely then, sir, justice would never be served."

Red blotches appeared on Toad's neck. "Why, you!" Unsteadily getting out of his chair, he raised a hand to her.

Harriet nimbly took another step back.

Toad scowled, steadying himself. "You think you know better than the law?"

"It appears so, sir," Harriet bit back, indicating to his raised hand. "Even when asked to give an opinion, unnecessary brutality can occur."

The men murmured, reluctantly acknowledging her assertion. Toad sat back in his seat, in a defeated but furious heap. Luigi tapped Harriet on the elbow, giving her permission to leave.

"Gentlemen, I hope everything was to your satisfaction?"

Toad, unable to contain himself, stood unsteadily, throwing his napkin and money onto the table.

"Just tell Titty…" He stopped, appearing unable to gather his thoughts, and mumbled, "Forget it. I'll tell her myself another time," and weaved his way out of the restaurant, rudely pushing past another customer.

Luigi returned to the kitchen, his usual easy smile gone. Harriet's head hung, heavy with shame. How stupid to get drawn into Toad's vile web. How vain to think she could put one over on him.

"Luigi, I'm so sorry for letting you down." She could barely bring herself to lift her coat off the peg. "I understand. You don't have to tell me to go. I just wanted to apologize first."

"No, Bella," said Luigi gently. "I sorry. If he try touching you again, he no longer welcome. You going to home, an' I seeing you tomorrow."

"Really?" Harriet hugged Luigi, gratefully, tearfully, thanking him and promising she wouldn't let him down again.

Harriet pulled on her coat, her mind working overtime, her stomach lurching between anger, shame, and gratitude. She walked directly to the library, mulling things over. Not all men had an endemic view of women like Toad. Luigi for one, and Tom another. She was sure of it. How dare Toad suggest the poor woman deserved her fate. The quicker Harriet's mind worked, the faster she walked. Toad's view was clearly not in isolation. She suddenly stopped. A man who had been keeping pace behind almost collided into her.

"Excuse me." They both apologized. Harriet could not look up. The man stepped past murmuring something she could not quite catch. But as he disappeared amongst the crowd she noted a pleasant and somehow familiar fragrance. Harriet's steps became slower, pondering life.

She had been a victim at school; did she deserve it? Her eyes flickered. Did she *allow* it?

Chapter 19

Miss Farleigh, the librarian, used to Harriet's regular visits, acknowledged her with a gentle nod of the head. The vaulted ceilings and tiled flooring would encourage echoes if it were not for the soundproofing of vast shelves filled to the ceiling with hefty tomes. Even so, Harriet always found herself staring at the giant-sized *QUIET* sign and would virtually tiptoe across the floor. The librarian gestured her usual spot had been reserved and produced the requested books, placing them on the counter.

"I've got a little treat for you." Miss Farleigh excitedly raised her whisper just an octave. "You have permission to use our microfiche room. Microfiche is a much quicker way to research. I hope you don't mind. I've booked you a slot."

"Really? How kind. Thank you."

Harriet carried her books to the area of anthropology, usually the perfect place to study undisturbed, and followed Miss Farleigh, who, for someone of a certain age, was surprisingly sprightly, and with small swift steps she led Harriet to a glass-and-wood-paneled side room. With the door closed behind them, Harriet listened to instructions on using the equipment and was amazed at the information she could scroll through in an instant.

"I'm trusting you will treat this with the utmost

respect," advised Miss Farleigh.

Harriet, thrilled, thanked her profusely and, finding the equipment easy to use, soon began scribbling notes. One hour later she came across a headline that stopped her in her tracks:

Freddie "the Fish" Craddock stands trial for
"Fish Market Murder"

The crisp black-and-white photograph set under the headline left no room for doubt. Frederick Craddock's small dark eyes, devoid of empathy, stared back. Tall and lean, his sour face enhanced an aquiline nose. He was the male mirror image of Dorian Craddock. The school bully. Her nemesis.

Harriet swallowed hard. Rumor at school had it Dorian's father was a gangster, a member of the seedy underworld during the war, one of those loathsome, creatures who dealt blows if rents were not made on time or debts not repaid. Harriet, trembling, had a flashback. A day at school she would never forget. She could still see Dorian curled into a ball in the back schoolyard, battered and bloodied, a shoe discarded, oddly alone, midway between the schoolyard and the woods beyond. Finding Dorian changed both their lives forever. Harriet, wide-eyed, read on:

The man accused of the "Fish Market Murders" has entered a plea of "not guilty" at the start of his trial.

Frederick Craddock, also known as "Freddie the Fish," denied murdering and dismembering the body of George "Silver Smith" Blaney, a rival gang member.

Mr. Blaney's companion, Miss Dorothea Wall, shot and left for dead, survived and picked out Mr. Craddock at an identity parade from her hospital bed, where she lay paralyzed from the waist down.

Mr. Craddock has not been charged with the attack on Miss Wall, who is expected to give evidence from a wheelchair during the trial.

In his opening statement, Prosecution barrister Lord Felix Sutcliffe, QC, said Mr. Craddock may have murdered Mr. Blaney "for no better reason than to rid himself of a rival."

The trial is expected to last up to three weeks, during which time approximately seventy-five witnesses will be called.

Harriet left the microfiche room reeling. Had Dorian's prophecy come true? Had it been her father's way of dealing with "*the situation*" as she so coldly, so bleakly, put it that day?

Chapter 20

Sitting in her usual spot, Harriet watched a young woman, wearing kitten heels, noisily clattering across the library floor. Mr. Baldwin, chief librarian, gesticulated wildly, unable to silence her, pointing at the massive *QUIET* sign hanging in full view.

The young woman, wearing high-waisted trousers cinched in at the waist, with braces over a beautiful white puffed-sleeve blouse, appeared oblivious. Harriet remained fascinated, studying her style. Her hair stood on end in short, tiny black tufts, made more bizarre by being tipped in bright pink. It suited her. Her fingers ran along a column of books, and she pulled them out one by one, gathering them into her arms, four in all. They fell to the floor with a thud.

"Whoopsie! Need to be quiet, me thinks." She caught Harriet's eye and put her fingers to her lips, and with a smile began picking them up. But the books seemingly took on a life of their own and slid from her grasp. Harriet quickly helped. She could have sworn there was a whiff of alcohol on the girl's breath.

"Thanks, I might get booted out of here if I'm not careful." She grinned, shoving the books under one arm and holding out a free hand. "Kate Westfield."

The first thing Harriet noticed was her accent—a rich, warm burr she'd never come across before.

"Harriet Laws." She took the young woman's hand

114

and, noticing Mr. Baldwin making his way across, she wiggled her brows as a warning.

After a curt but quiet word, Kate found a chair close to Harriet and pulled out a sketch book from her bag. Then, swinging her chair backward onto two legs, tilted her face toward the ceiling. Harriet, convinced the chair would tip over, couldn't help but watch.

"Great arches," Kate said, turning toward Harriet. She pointed to the ceiling. "Though your arches aren't so bad."

Harriet tried desperately to control the urge to laugh.

"I'm thinking about transferring some of those shapes into my designs." Her voice carried around the library. An angry shush vibrated, clearer than St. Paul's whispering gallery.

Harriet bit down on her bottom lip trying to stop the quiver, hoping her eyes did the talking, jerked her head in Mr. Baldwin's direction. Kate, taking the hint, smiled innocently, mouthing widely "S-O-RR-EEE." Mr. Baldwin, huffing, returned to the counter.

Harriet was intrigued by Kate Westfield. Her clothes, her hair, the way she carried herself. She dared to ignore convention. It appeared liberating. Harriet considered her own clothes with embarrassment. Boring, old, and desperately unfashionable. About an hour later, with Harriet settled well into her studies, Kate began shoveling all her belongings back into a cloth satchel and strung it across her shoulder. Clattering over to Harriet, she handed her a business card and, waving goodbye, clip-clopped back out of the library calling with a beatific smile, "Nice meeting you, Harriet Laws. Call me. Take it easy, Mr. B. Hope to see you soon. Bye, everyone!"

Mr. Baldwin looked like he would die of apoplexy, whilst library users looked on in hushing disgust.

Harriet, fit to burst, gathered her belongings and quickly exited the building, hoping to catch up with Kate. Once outside, she looked about. There was no sign of her. She studied the business card. Beautifully crafted, with swirls of ocean and shells—and Kate's name with a telephone number embossed in pink and purple lettering. Miss Kate Westfield, Fashion Designer, London SW1. Harriet felt something more than disappointment for not catching up with her. Whatever it was, she felt a strange kind of connection. She really would have loved an opportunity to talk to her. Harriet took one more look at the business card and placed it securely in her handbag. Maybe, she just might be brave enough to call.

Chapter 21

Tom's invitation to take Harriet to the performance of *Le Nozze di Figaro* came as such a wonderful surprise she instantly said yes. But even before Harriet got home, she realized her mistake, and as her landlady poured her a thimble of sherry "for medicinal purposes," she listened carefully to her young lodger working through her dilemma.

"I've been stupid, Mrs. G. I don't possess a decent day dress, let alone a gown. How can I tell Tom without upsetting him?" Mrs. Gaffney put her glass down.

"Come with me, young lady."

Puzzled, Harriet followed Mrs. Gaffney to her bedroom. An opulent 1930's cherrywood wardrobe stood weightily against the side wall, and a matching dressing table with mirror filled the front window, with a double bed directly opposite.

"My husband and I used to go out all the time, before the war." Mrs. G sighed, moving toward a woven golden ottoman at the bottom of her bed. "We especially loved the opera. Even if you can't speak Italian, you can't fail to understand the story." For a moment she looked lost in her own thoughts. "But of course, I can't afford to go these days." She raised the lid of the ottoman; a waft of mothballs drifted out. Taking out a large parcel wrapped in butter muslin, she placed it on the bed.

"I had to sell the rest, but I couldn't bring myself to

get rid of this one." She paused briefly before unwrapping it. "It holds so many happy memories." She removed one layer after another until eventually she revealed a beautiful sea-green gown. Harriet gasped.

"It's absolutely stunning, Mrs. G!"

"I have to say I felt like a film star when I wore it." She smiled, lovingly fingering the material. "Even my husband couldn't take his eyes off me." She looked at Harriet. "I think it just might fit you, with a little bit of creativity here and there. What do you think?"

"No. Really?"

"I can't think of anything better than to see it being worn again. Even if it isn't me." She sighed wistfully, holding the dress up against herself, and in a girlish moment twirled around, allowing the fishtail to spin outward. "How about trying it on, right now?"

Harriet trembled with excitement and possibility—if the dress fitted, and hopefully the smell of mothballs was eliminated…

****

Harriet discreetly glanced at her watch, thinking her shift would never end. Most customers had left over an hour ago, including the handsome Mr. Rutherford Sofia mentioned every time he visited. However, today the Toad and his colleagues seemed as if they would be there forever.

They had been in a good spirit from the start. Even Toad's behavior superseded his usual arrogance, being politeness itself. Privately she hoped it was due to a combination of her speech and Luigi's intervention. One of the men threw his napkin down, signaling he wanted the bill. As he rose, to Harriet's relief the rest immediately followed suit, and to her delight, she received an even bigger tip than usual. With everything cleared away, Harriet spoke to Luigi, her excitement rising. It was Saturday, and not just any Saturday.

"Is there anything else you need me to do, Luigi?"

Fabio, the Commi's chef, flicked her with a tea towel.

"Give me a kiss an' I do the rest for you!" Harriet laughed at his teasing, whipped off her pinny. Fabio, being a huge flirt and perfectly harmless, she flicked him back.

"Hey, watch it!"

"Off you going and getting yourself to be the ready!" cut in Luigi, picking up a ladle, brandishing it in their direction.

Harriet grinned back. Everyone knew where she was going. They could not fail to, having not stopped talking about it for days. Tonight, she was going to the opera. Harriet gave Luigi a peck on the cheek and waved Fabio goodbye before slipping on her coat and walking out into the sunshine. She felt light as the air around her, and happiness danced in her heart as she thought about Tom and the night to come.

Mrs. Gaffney opened the door before Harriet could get her key out of her purse.

"At last, young lady. I've put the boiler on so you can have a bath, and I found these." She held up elbow-length gloves matching the gown. Harriet, delighted, hugged her, thanking her for spoiling her.

As Harriet slipped into the bath, soaking off the day's sweat, she could not help but reflect how her life had turned around. Could it really be eighteen months since Nana died and Tom saved her from her darkest hour? Now the man who gave her back her life, the man whom she knew she cared for deeply, would be taking her to the opera. Harriet slid right under the water, and as she surfaced she squealed with joy. "Nana, I'm so lucky!"

****

Whilst Sofia fussed around sorting Harriet's hair, Mrs. G double-checked the gown, laying it out ready to be worn. And though Harriet didn't usually wear cosmetics, they both agreed a little rouge and lipstick were a must.

Stepping into the dress, Harriet felt her heart pound, and she prayed she would make Tom proud. Sofia clapped her hands in delight as Mrs. G admired their handiwork. Nodding with approval, she pushed Harriet toward the full-length mirror.

"You look gorgeous, young lady. The color brings out the blue in your eyes."

Harriet looked at herself in the mirror. Her strawberry-blonde hair had been whipped into cut-glass clips, and gentle curls framed her face. She was thrilled—the gown was a masterpiece.

"Thank you so much!" A tremor of a tear caught in her throat.

The doorbell rang, and her eyes widened with eagerness to see Tom.

"Don't rush. Don't show him you're keen."

"Oh, Mrs. G, stop it. Tom's made it perfectly clear we are only to ever be friends."

"Ha! Friends, my eye," said Sofia. "I've seen the way he looks at you. If he were aware the times Mr. Rutherford comes to our restaurant just to look at you, why, I believe he would snatch you up in an instant!"

"Don't be silly!" said Harriet hotly.

"Who is this Mr. Rutherford?" asked a miffed Mrs. G.

"Sofia's making a mountain out of a molehill, trust me."

"I'm most definitely not!" The doorbell rang again. "Mr. Rutherford is a very handsome, wealthy antiques dealer. Since Harriet started with us, he has become one of our most regular lunchtime customers. You should see how he watches Harriet's every move. Trust me, he even asks about her when she's not there."

Harriet scowled. "Well, perhaps if he's so wonderful, *you* should consider marrying him, Sofia!"

The doorbell rang a third time.

"Shall we get the door now and put the poor man out of his misery?" said Mrs. G, elegantly lifting her cigarette holder and placing a cigarette in the end.

"Now, young lady, when you get back, I want to hear everything, and an explanation as to why I've never heard about this mystery man Rutherford before."

Harriet took a deep breath as Tom was invited in. He just stood there, tall, lean, and, yes, she could call him handsome in an unusual sort of way. His dark hair had been slicked back, and he looked extremely smart in a dinner suit and dickie bow. Holding a small white rose in his hand, he appeared dumbstruck.

"Well, will I do?" said Harriet, wishing he would fall at her feet and profess undying love.

"You look, um…"

"She looks fantastic!" said Mrs. G, stepping out from behind a door, unable to hide there any longer. "What's the matter with you, man, cat got your tongue?"

Harriet burst out laughing.

Sofia, smiling broadly, and with baby Carlo

straddled on her hip, looked at the flower Tom held. "Would you like a hand?"

Tom suddenly came to his senses. "Yes. Thank you. It's good to see you both looking so well."

"For God's sake, man, forget about us. What about Harriet?" demanded Mrs. G, plucking Carlo from Sofia's arms.

Harriet whispered her thanks to Sofia as she pinned the corsage to her gown.

"Now, don't stay up too late, Mrs. Gaffney." Tom winked. "We don't want you to miss your beauty sleep."

"Well!"

Harriet took Tom's arm, laughing, as he led her toward the taxi. Some of the neighbors were already outside, their husbands dragged out to watch. Some let out low wolf whistles. Harriet tried to hide a grin. Tom leaned close to her ear. She felt a frisson of excitement.

"You look absolutely beautiful, Harriet. I feel the luckiest man on earth."

As they drove away, Harriet looked over her shoulder, waving, and felt sure she caught Mrs. G dabbing her eyes.

Chapter 22

Harriet absorbed everything as they stepped through the doors of the theatre—the architecture, the opulence, the dazzling, beautiful audience, the gentle murmur of conversation whilst the orchestra tuned up. Tom ushered her to their row and sat proudly beside her, watching her every expression.

"I'm sorry we're so far back, Harriet. Hopefully this will help a little." Tom slotted a penny into the binocular holder and tried to control his nerves as he thought about his plan. Once he crossed the threshold, would they ever be able to return to normal?

"I could never have imagined anything quite like this, Tom. It's so beautiful. The seats and the night are absolutely perfect." She beamed at him. He smiled in return and tried to relax, her words giving him a little courage.

During the second scene, Harriet closed her eyes, and Tom, who had tried all night not to keep staring at her, whispered, "Are you all right?" Worrying she was tired, or worse still, bored.

"Oh, my goodness, Tom, it's so beautiful! All this time I never knew what I've been missing. Mrs. G was right. It's unbelievable. You are so kind to bring me here."

Tom smiled, awkwardly patting her hand. Harriet smiled back, squeezing his hand in return, and somehow their hands were allowed to rest together.

"I've taken the liberty of ordering champagne. Just a glass. It seems fitting for the occasion," said Tom during the interval.

"Champagne? I've never tasted wine, let alone champagne," said Harriet, wide-eyed. "It must have cost a small fortune."

Tom put his finger to his lips. "Enough! I just hope it's all it's cracked up to be."

****

From across the room, Harriet was being studied. Mr. Rutherford knew she would be here somewhere, and when his eyes fell upon her, he felt vindicated. His instincts were right all along. The waitress from Luigi's most certainly could carry herself appropriately, and when dressed in the right attire, she looked stunning. A smile crossed his lips. Luigi's daughter had given far more away than she realized when he pressed her for information. Leaning into one of his party, he discreetly pointed toward Harriet.

"Do you know her?" His friend shook his head. "I wouldn't mind, though. She's gorgeous." It was all he needed, if George didn't recognize her, none of his acquaintances would.

"CJ?" one of the women in his party pouted.

"Margaux, don't simper," he replied, irritated. She really was grating on him lately. "I'm not in the mood for one of your sulks. Go fuss around Bartie. He fancies you something rotten."

Margaux, looking hurt, began to speak, but he took her hand and squeezed it, just enough so she didn't cry out.

"Like I said, talk to Bartie!" And he moved swiftly

toward Harriet. She was alone, and he wanted to capitalize on it.

"Well, what a happy coincidence!" His comment took Harriet by surprise. "How wonderful seeing you here. Are you enjoying the performance?" Harriet blinked, puzzled.

"Don't tell me you don't recognize me? I'm most hurt. Let me introduce myself properly. Charles James Rutherford at your service." He smiled at her confusion.

"Luigi's?"

"Of course."

Harriet blushed. "I'm so sorry." His cologne had reminded her.

"Tell me you have been foolishly abandoned so I can rescue you."

Just at that moment Tom was making his way through the crowded bar. When a pathway opened, he could see Harriet talking to a man he didn't recognize. Tom stopped and stared. They looked like they knew each other. He felt sick. Somehow, they looked so right together. Harriet laughed at something, animated in her response. A surge of jealousy was quickly followed by a feeling of stupidity. What was he thinking? Harriet would never agree to marry him. The man looked much more in her league.

"Tom!" said Harriet, clearly elated at his return, but her eyes immediately returned to the man standing beside her.

"I would like to introduce you to Mr. Rutherford."

"Gosh, Harriet. Mr. Rutherford? How formal, especially when we know each other so very well. Call me CJ, old boy," and Rutherford held out his hand.

"Harriet?" Tom proffered the glass toward her just

as the auditorium bell rang.

"Five minutes, ladies and gentlemen, please make way to your seat."

What followed next Tom could not be sure but had his suspicions as Mr. Rutherford stumbled into him.

"Oh, dear old boy." Rutherford looked at Tom's trousers, the champagne splashing unfortunately onto Tom's groin area. "Gosh, some people are really clumsy." CJ looked about as if he were admonishing the man next to him.

"Look, allow me to help." He went to hand Tom a clean crisp pocket handkerchief, but swiftly withdrew the offer.

"Actually, I don't think it will help after all. You must feel an absolute fool. Look, why don't I escort Harriet to my box whilst you arrange yourself. We've a couple of spare seats. Join us?"

On the face of it, he sounded genuine enough. Tom knew there was no option but to try and resolve the situation, and noticed Harriet desperately trying not to look at the growing patch of wet.

"It's all right, Tom. Let's go and collect our coats," said Harriet. Tom felt instant gratitude, but Rutherford interrupted.

"Harriet, Thomas would not want to spoil your evening. Would you, old boy?"

"Really, Tom, I don't mind," she said. "Come on, let's go." Tom hesitated. It would be unfair to ruin her evening.

"No, Mr. Rutherford's right. Why spoil your evening because of a silly accident? If you don't mind, I'll meet you later in the lobby."

"There, you see, Harriet, Thomas is being sensible."

126

Rutherford caught Harriet's hand in an overly familiar way and leaned toward Tom, quietly speaking so only he could hear. "A man should know when he's beaten, old chap."

Tom felt a surge of anger, powerless against the fait accompli.

"Please come back, join us?" Harriet called, already being guided away with purpose.

"I'll wait, Harriet." Tom watched Rutherford closing in on Harriet, making the action like a lover's, and he felt sick.

"Harriet, would you do me a huge favor and keep my friends guessing as to how we know each other? Make it our little secret?"

Harriet assumed Mr. Rutherford might be embarrassed if he were to introduce her as the waitress from Luigi's. Even though she was not ashamed, for some inexplicable reason she agreed to go along with it.

CJ smiled at her. "And just one more thing. I trust you are no longer being bothered by one of your rather unpleasant, overstuffed customers?"

Harriet looked at him in surprise. "I beg your pardon?"

"I couldn't help but notice the disrespectful way you were being treated a while ago. Those bloody Silks. Think they own the place. It really is unacceptable."

Puzzled, Harriet contemplated his words. Did he mean the Toad? Had he been there the day Toad had been particularly revolting? Harriet tried desperately to recall. It was a curious fact Toad appeared more subdued recently.

****

Harriet soon came to realize just how charming and

127

attentive Mr. Rutherford could be. He insisted she call him CJ. And he was right, his friends could not help but pry. CJ winked at Harriet, drawing her further into his lie, swiftly dancing around the subject, alluding to Luigi's only once in the greater sense. But Harriet could not help but notice how Lady Sutcliffe watched his every move. As the curtains rose, Harriet felt guilty. Tom brought her, paid for her. This simply would not do. Five minutes into the second act, Harriet whispered to CJ, "I'm sorry, I have to go."

"Tell me there isn't anything I've done, said?" he faltered.

"Of course not. You have been most gracious."

CJ swiftly gathered his composure and together they quietly left the booth. With the door closed behind them, CJ looked at the blushing Harriet.

"I'm really sorry, you have been so kind. It's just, well, Tom brought me. I don't feel…" CJ was staring at her intently, and she realized just how attractive he really was. Embarrassed she may have given her thoughts away, she glanced to the floor.

"May I?" Catching hold of her hand, he placed it on his forearm. "I confess you're breaking my heart, Harriet. But let's go find the lucky blighter. I hope he appreciates what he has!"

"Tom's a friend, CJ. Nothing more," she replied without hesitation, but as the words left her lips, she wanted to kick herself. She loved Tom. What was she thinking? Why did she say that? But Tom had not come back to find her, and hadn't he made it clear from the moment they met they were only ever to be friends? Her heart sank. She was a fool to think otherwise.

"It's such a shame." CJ guided Harriet slowly down

the staircase. "I hoped you would have done me the honor of joining me at the after-show party." He paused. "Thomas is invited, of course."

"Thank you, CJ, but I think not." They were at the entrance. Tom was waiting with her wrap, wearing his coat, presumably to cover the stain.

"Ah, Thomas. Thank you, old chap, for allowing me to take care of Harriet." CJ smiled generously. "I've invited Harriet to the after-show party, but"—he laid his hand protectively over hers—"you would be welcome as well, of course."

"Thank you, CJ," cut in Harriet, guilt rising in her chest. "I am very grateful for your offer, but I'm ready to go home."

"Are you sure, Harriet?" Tom asked searchingly. "I've already spoilt your evening."

"It's been wonderful, Tom, but if you wouldn't mind, I would like you to take me home."

"Thank you for taking care of Miss Laws for me, Mr. Rutherford," said Tom, proffering his arm toward Harriet, knowing the words sounded hollow, matching the emptiness he felt inside.

Harriet thanked CJ before leaving. He watched, but she didn't once look back as they walked away.

During the taxi ride home, Harriet thanked Tom for the evening, admonishing him for leaving her with CJ. Yes, his companions were friendly, and yes, of course the performance continued to be magnificent. But she made it clear she would have enjoyed it much more in his company.

Tom listened halfheartedly, his mind working overtime. Thinking about the tiny box with its precious cargo, wondering how Harriet knew the man who had seemingly managed to manipulate the situation in one fell swoop. Frustrated, annoyed, Rutherford, much younger than himself, appeared so self-assured. Tom never felt so inferior in his life. Something had changed. Harriet seemed to have changed. She never even offered an explanation as to how she knew the man, and he felt he had no right to ask.

Tom rolled the small box over in his pocket. The question he'd worked himself up to ask now seemed foolish. Instead, he hid the box deep in the bottom of his pocket and the sadness deeper in his heart. He could never ask her. Not now, not after seeing Harriet with Rutherford.

****

Mrs. Gaffney did not bother with her beauty sleep as Tom had so cheekily suggested. She suspected there was more to the evening than a night at the opera, especially when she saw the way Tom looked at Harriet. How she loved a romance! She sighed, deciding to put out the sherry ready for their return, and re-polished the already sparkling glasses.

Mrs. Gaffney heard the front door open, then muffled voices. Mr. Noble was already in, and Jim was on nights, so it had to be Harriet arriving home. Puzzled, she gently inched her door open, and she heard Tom's voice.

"…I'm so sorry for spoiling the evening."

"You really haven't, Tom."

Mrs. Gaffney held her breath. The floorboard creaked, and she retreated into her room, worried about being caught eavesdropping.

"Harriet, I'm such an idiot. I don't believe I could have spoiled tonight more if I tried."

"Tom, you haven't spoilt anything. You have been nothing but kind and generous."

Tom looked at the crack in the step. Kind and generous? Is that how she saw him? If only he had a way with words. If only he could be the person Harriet deserved. He rallied his thoughts into sensible actions.

Harriet searched Tom's face, waiting, wondering, hoping. Tom leaned forward. Harriet's body tingled in anticipation of his lips upon hers. Instead, Tom kissed her cheek, lingering only momentarily.

"Harriet." Tom's voice was deep, croaky. "You need someone who can provide for you. Someone who is more in your league, and someone who is nearer your age. I just hope we will be able to remain friends?"

"I don't understand, Tom, what are trying to say?" Harriet stood there surprised. He took hold of her gloved hands and shyly kissed them one by one. "It would be wrong for me to expect more." He turned to go. For a moment Harriet remained still.

"What do you mean?"

"Goodbye, Harriet. I am really sorry."

"Goodbye... How... What?" But her words fell on deaf ears as Tom was already hailing a passing taxi. Mrs. Gaffney, trying to hear the exchange, heard Harriet crying, albeit softly. This would never do! She could not contain herself anymore—she just had to find out what had been going on.

"Oh, Mrs. G…" Harriet's voice trailed off dismally when she saw her in the hallway.

"What's happened, young lady? Come on." Mrs. Gaffney led her to her parlor, where the sherry stood waiting for celebration. Instead, it would be used for listening, support, and for medicinal purposes. Mrs.

Gaffney sat Harriet down and poured the sherry. "Here, I think you may need this." Harriet burst into tears.

"I just don't understand. The evening started out so wonderfully, and now Tom seems so distant."

Mrs. Gaffney's lips drew to pencil-line seriousness. If that Tom was a bounder, he would have her to answer to.

"Tell me everything. From the beginning." Harriet told Mrs. Gaffney everything, from the moment they sat down, the music, holding hands, the glasses of champagne, and finally the accident. She talked about CJ being the perfect gentleman, offering to look after her whilst Tom sorted himself out. Harriet said she felt awful when Tom virtually insisted she remained with CJ.

"Don't be silly. He's probably just embarrassed," said Mrs. Gaffney, giving her a little nudge.

"Well, yes, at first I thought the same. But he was so quiet on the way back—he just sat there like a lemon, and not like him at all."

Mrs. Gaffney pondered.

"None of it makes sense, Harriet. Men are such strange creatures. In fact, I thought he was going to…" She stopped abruptly, picked up her cigarette holder, and fiddled with the cigarette in its end.

"What were you thinking Mrs. G?"

"Oh? Nothing."

"Go on, tell me." Mrs. Gaffney looked flustered for a moment.

"I was just thinking poor Tom seems to have crash landed, a bit like the Luna thingy on the moon, in the paper the other day." She finished her sherry and poured herself another. "Tom will come to his senses in the cold light of day, my girl. He's obviously embarrassed by the circumstances. At least he didn't try anything. You know." She coughed self-consciously. "Now, finish your glass. I want to know all there is to know about this Mr. CJ Rutherford."

Harriet went to bed that night bewildered. What Mrs. Gaffney had said kind of made sense, but Tom seemed so distant. As she slept, she dreamed about Tom and about CJ, then woke with Tom's words of his friendship ringing in her ears. How could she have been so foolish as to think anything else. He never indicated there would be more to their relationship. She had to be content, but in her heart, just being friends would be the most dreadful agreement to have to stick to.

Chapter 23

Monday came and went. Disappointingly, there was no sign of Tom. Harriet wanted to clear the air with him. She wanted to make sure their regular meetings remained the same, just like before, in that funny, shiny, brightly lit little café on a Saturday night. Harriet wanted normality back, but she doubted that would ever happen.

Two days later, Tom left a message with Daisy. Harriet tore open the envelope and unfolded a sheet of paper:

Dear Harriet,

I am sorry if my abysmal behavior ruined your evening and hope you can find room in your heart to forgive me? If you would care to join me at Pete's café, six thirty, on Saturday as usual, I will look forward to seeing you. If you decide not to come, then I will completely understand.

Yours most sincerely,
Tom

She re-read the short note. "Yours sincerely," thought Harriet, "sincerely," she mused again. Daisy studied Harriet's expression as she read the note.

"Well, my girl, I don't know what has got into Tom lately, but he is walking around like a sack of spuds. Didn't you enjoy the opera?"

Harriet's eyes glistened. "I loved it, Daisy. It was the most wonderful thing ever, and Tom..." She trailed off. "Did Tom say anything to you?"

"No?" Daisy looked at her hopefully, but Harriet had a faraway look in her eyes. "He didn't say a word. But I know something's up with you two. Tom's been working so hard to make the business grow, and he seemed so happy that night, but now... Did you have a row, dear?"

"If only we had," responded Harriet.

Just then Mrs. Turpin bumbled into the back room to collect a bread basket. She could be tactless at times, but in fairness called a spade a spade and stood there with her hands on her hips, speaking plainly. "You and Tom should sort things out."

"And what do you know that I don't?" demanded Daisy.

"It's obvious, ain't it? Harriet's going around like chickin' lickin' with the end of the world about to fall in, and Tom, well, enough said."

"You're right, I need to sort this out," said Harriet, a smile flashing across her face as she remembered their last visit to Pete's Café. She and Tom were in the middle of a serious debate about the CND Peace Campaign for Nuclear Disarmament when a wooden spoon flew out through the open kitchen doorway. It could have hit anyone, but it bounced off his wife's head. The whole café fell silent waiting for Mel to go ballistic. But before she had the chance, and to their amazement, Pete came out of the kitchen and dropped to one knee, begging his wife's forgiveness. The customers roared with laughter as Mel clipped him around the ear and told him to stop being a clown.

But it was in that moment she had looked at Tom. Their eyes met across the table, recognizing the devotion between the couple who ran that little café. Their arguments vanishing in an instant. Pete picked his wife up and swirled her around between the tables, nearly knocking the food off. Their customers responded with a huge round of applause when he kissed her firmly on the lips. If only Tom would do the same—pick her up and swirl her around and plant a kiss firmly on her lips—then everything would be perfect. Yes, of course she would go.

****

Harriet pushed her glasses up her nose. She felt drab, her clothes were shabby, and for the first time in her life she hated feeling poor.

"Hello, Miss Harriet, you look like you've lost ten shillings and found a penny." Patience was walking toward her with the O'Connell children holding tight to the pram and looking rather glum.

"Patience! Hello, children." Harriet beamed. "How are *you*?" Harriet reached into the pram to tickle Elizabeth under the chin, only to find baby Mickey propped up at the opposite end of the pram. She quickly disguised her surprise to see him there. "My, oh, my, don't you two look a picture together? And don't you look pretty with your hair done like that, Elizabeth. Your mummy is very clever, isn't she?" Elizabeth's tight black curls were stretched into tiny pink ribbons that covered the whole of her head. She gurgled her appreciation at the attention. Declan O'Connell piped up, looking worried.

"Me pappy's sick and me mammy's hurt." Patience flashed a look at Harriet.

136

"I'm sorry to hear that, Declan. What's the matter with Mummy?"

"She broke her arm, so she did."

"Oh, dear!"

Patience flashed another look at Harriet and spoke quickly. "We thought we would go to the park while the light is in our favor. Then, if you are really good, we can go back to my home and have some jam and bread. How does that sound?" Harriet noticed how the O'Connell children brightened up at that.

"Why don't I call in on Mummy," said Harriet. "I can let her know you are having your tea, so she doesn't need to worry, and perhaps I can give her a hand."

The children looked at her with a look of bewilderment. The rumors about Sean O'Connell were a concern, and the issues discussed in private by Dotty Harris seemed to be escalating to possible truths.

"Thank you, Harriet, that would be wonderful. Mr. O'Connell doesn't favor my color and blames my husband for taking his job."

"How about I collect them from yours around sixish?" They clasped hands in solidarity.

Harriet listened to the echo as the ball of the knocker struck the door. There was no answer. She tried again. This time she heard someone calling from inside.

"Florrie, may I come in?"

Florrie eased the door open, just enough for her to peer around. "I understand you have broken your arm. Is there anything I can do?" Florrie inched the door wider, and she could see her arm, in a makeshift sling, rested upon her swelling pregnant belly.

"You ought to go to the hospital, don't you think, Florrie?"

"No, I'm fine, really. It's just sore when I move it." Her face, pinched and pale, tried for a smile but failed. "To be truthful, I've no idea how I am supposed to manage the children, though." She sounded broken. "Patience has kindly taken them for the afternoon, so she has, and said something about giving them tea."

"Yes," said Harriet. "I bumped into her. She's taking them to the park first, and if it's all right with you, I can collect them at six?"

Florrie looked doubtful. She held her arm. The pain from her movements was clearly expressed on her face.

"I could help put the children to bed. How does that sound?"

Florrie paused. "If my Sean comes home, you might want to give him a wide berth. He's a bit…" She paused as if thinking what to say, then magnificently rounded up a reason. "His mammy's ill, so she is, and what with him not affording to go to Ireland, he's got upset." Her mouth twisted. "What with him being out of work and dependin' on me getting on with the laundry, so he is."

Harriet held her tongue. The man could help with his children and help with the laundry rather than get drunk and do whatever else he spent her hard-earned money on.

"It's women's work, so it is," Florrie said as if she read Harriet's mind.

"Well, let's get you better first. If I ask some of the mothers in the meantime, I'm sure we can all pitch in and give you a hand."

"You think?" Florrie looked hopeful.

"Of course. In fact, if you have laundry to do now, why don't I make a start?" A tear started in the corner of Florrie's eye. "Come on, you can tell me what to do,"

Harriet smiled, brushing aside her worries, and followed Florrie's loping gait through to the back and into the kitchen.

Next to the copper used for the boil wash were two huge piles of laundry tumbling out of baskets and split into colors and whites. The dolly tub was outside, along with the mangle. Harriet had always thought the children were turned out well. Clearly Florrie took care of her children and took pride in her work.

"It's the shirts that need tending first. Businessmen need their shirts. Perhaps I could do the collars while you do the whites, Harriet?" There was a pile of unclipped collars in a heap on the side.

"Hmm," mumbled Harriet doubtfully. "You're supposed to be resting."

"Don't be daft. To be sure, I can't sit here like a lump of lard and watch you work. Look, I'll put the irons either side, and I can scrub them with my good arm."

Harriet looked at her. Given the size of her, she could never be called a lump of lard, and her legs were so thin, so wasted. Harriet exhaled, partially defeated.

"All right, but if I see you in any pain, I will be taking it straight from you."

Harriet heated up the copper and carried the water through to the dolly, and with laundry soap she put the cleanest items in first and used the posser, agitating it this way and that. An hour later, up to her arms in lather and sweat, she began rinsing the items out, using the dolly in the same way. The whole day had become so strange, she thought, checking her watch she'd laid out on the kitchen table. Five thirty. Half an hour to finish one load and perhaps get it through the mangle.

"You're doing a great job, Harriet. So kind, so you

are," Florrie said appreciatively. "This will keep us heads above water for a day or two."

Harriet put the clothes, as many as would fit, on huge clothes airers strung from the ceiling, with the rest around the house wherever possible. No wonder the house always felt so damp, she thought. So much laundry to dry and often without the sun or wind to help. Harriet checked her watch again. It was six o'clock. She was shattered.

"I'll go and get the children. Then we can get them ready for bed. Or would you like to collect them?"

Florrie hesitated. "I feel a bit of a fool with this arm. Would you mind doing the fetchin'?"

"Of course." Harriet dried herself off and promised to return as quickly as possible.

The children were waiting, clean and tidy and not a hair out of place. They looked warily at Harriet as she instructed them to put on their shoes.

"They have been such good children, and all have had a wash and played so nicely with Elizabeth. You took such good care of her, didn't you?" Patience smiled kindly at the children. "I don't have any spare toothbrushes, so we used our fingers, didn't we? And I wonder, would you mind telling Florrie I would be pleased to have them again. I could take the older ones to school."

Declan looked on anxiously. "Is me pappy home?" Patience and Harriet exchanged brief glances. "Your father is out at the moment, Declan," said Harriet. "It'll be good if I get you straight to bed. And I think as your mother is tired, I might put her to bed as well." The children giggled.

"Silly Harriet. Me mammy won't be put to bed.

She's big and stays up later than us."

"Perhaps we can catch up tomorrow and come up with a plan, Harriet?" Patience whispered, looking bothered and coddling Elizabeth in her arms.

"Of course. Tomorrow," said Harriet.

Chapter 24

Friday afternoon, almost one week after the opera, Harriet collected her coat and umbrella at the end of her shift at Luigi s. Calling goodbye, she looked out through the window. Rain continued to fall heavily—dark clouds and a dark day, even at three p.m. She had planned to hang out Florrie's washing and her own. Now it would have to hang around on clothes airers, waiting for the weather to change. Harriet pumped at her umbrella, which got stuck halfway, and then with success at last, she headed home, batting off the rain.

Harriet did not see the man who crossed the road and followed her along the pavement as she hurried along. Eventually, after several turns, she stopped and checked the road was clear before crossing. He stopped at a discreet distance, using the cover of his umbrella as a shield. Harriet, unaware, ran up the two steps with a key in her hand, pumped her brolly, turned the lock, and closed the door behind her. The man turned on his heels and went back the way he came.

Harriet dashed upstairs and undressed. She felt cold and shivery. Rubbing herself dry with a towel, she snuggled up, warming herself under her sheets for a while, studying the painting with the geese in it, imagining one day she would find such a spot and maybe even get a chance to draw it herself. Realizing the time, she picked up Tom's note, though she knew the words

142

by heart. She read it again. She liked to see his penmanship, but she wished it sounded more favorable. She looked carefully through her small collection of clothes, wanting to look her best for him. Checking her watch again, she knew she would have to hurry to make sure she was on time.

****

Tom sheltered under the bus stop near Pete's café. He guessed in this weather Harriet would most likely use the bus instead of walking. The bottoms of his trousers were already wet, and others in the bus queue muttered amongst themselves as the damned rain turned from vertical to horizontal.

He checked his watch. Harriet was never late. Then he read the number of the next bus heading his way. He backed out of the queue and, from under his umbrella, watched, waited, hoped. Harriet stepped off the bus, and his heart soared, then dipped. He could understand why Mr. Rutherford would be enamored with Harriet as was he. But did Rutherford realize she was not only beautiful but also intelligent, kind, and thoughtful? Tom imagined her in ten years, twenty years from now, and knew that even when Harriet grew old she would always be beautiful, gentle, and generous of heart. How he would love to share his love and life with her.

Harriet saw him and waved. She looked a little apprehensive, he thought. Most probably all down to him. He would have to try and put things right.

Harriet settled herself at their usual table, just by the window, while Tom placed their brollies in the stand. The wind whipped up and beat the rain against the pane. She looked at him as he sat opposite, his dark fringe flopping down over his forehead. He pushed it back. She loved that about him. He smiled his awkward, quirky, lopsided smile. She loved that about him.

"How are you, Harriet?" Tom sounded stilted, and she worried why.

"I'm fine, thank you, Tom, and how about you?"

"I'm well, thank you."

Tom felt stupid. This was stupid. They were dancing around one another. This wasn't them. They were always honest and open with each other. He reflected they were never like this before the evening at the opera. Damn the opera. Why did they ever go! What was it that happened that night that changed their relationship so much? Surely it couldn't be the accidental spill on his trousers? Or Rutherford's intervention?

"I understand business is taking off." She sounded hopeful.

"Yes." For a moment, Tom relaxed, his old self returned, and with it an air of excitement in his voice. "We're hoping to extend the bakery, and the plans are in, along with a new home for Daisy, purpose-built in the back yard and all on the flat. It should make it easier for her to get about, being on the level, I mean."

"Wonderful!" She sounded excited.

"I've made an appointment to see Luigi. You remember you suggested making specialist breads?"

"You've spoken to Luigi? He didn't say. I'm pleased for you." Her face was wreathed in smiles.

"I need to be on top of my game. You know how I like to get things right. There's no point going armed with samples if they don't suit the customer."

Harriet pushed her glasses back up her nose, looking thoughtful. "I wonder if you could work with his staff. They're really helpful, you know. You could look at their methods and ingredients beforehand. I suspect you know just how different they are to ours?"

"Do you think Luigi would be up for that?"

"I can't see why not." Tom went to reach across to squeeze her hand—the gesture was innocent, grateful—but instead he caught a glass, and it went flying. The glass smashed and splintered right across the room. Pete's wife was just coming out of the kitchen with an order. She shrieked melodramatically, and Pete came out to see what was going on. Tom immediately started picking up some of the shards, and Harriet helped and asked for a sweeping brush, but Pete and his wife insisted on doing the clearing up whilst their guests returned to their seats.

"Seems I'm becoming a little accident prone of late," said Tom, embarrassed.

"Seems like you've cut yourself." Harriet pointed to a trickle of blood running down his index finger. "Here, let me check there's no glass inside." She adjusted herself to get a better view and held his hand to the light. "I can't see for sure, but"—she squeezed his finger gently—"can you feel a prickling sensation?"

"No. I don't think so." Tom watched her every move as she studied his wound, gently twisting his finger this way and that, and he wished she could stay with him forever. When he looked up and caught the look, he felt himself flush.

"I think you'll live. Here, let me wrap my handkerchief around that. It's clean, no germs lurking, and it should help stop the bleeding." She smiled as he allowed her to make a bandage.

"It's a bit big for a little cut," said Tom waggling a fat, white-covered finger at her after she finished. "I don't think I will be kneading dough with this on."

"Maybe not. Look, it's soaking through already. You need a proper bandage, Tom." Tom was astonished to see a crimson stain growing through the handkerchief.

"Perhaps I should go. I'm sorry, Harriet. I really am. You stay, my treat, if you don't mind eating alone?"

"Don't be daft." She sighed. "Come on, I don't want to argue. Let's just go."

Mel arrived to take their order just as they were about to leave.

"Here, I'm sorry for the mess, I'll pay for the damages," he said, offering some money. Mel rested her pencil over the top of her ear and shrugged.

"Don't want your money—put it away. Accidents happen all the time, especially here. You should know that by now." She looked at the handkerchief. "But I agree that needs looking at. See you lovely people next time eh?"

They stepped back out into the rain. It wasn't about to let up. There was nothing for it but for Harriet to get back on the next bus and Tom to return home to fix his finger. Tom insisted he wait at the bus stop with her until the bus arrived, but he had to wrap his own handkerchief around the outside of hers to stem the flow.

Once Harriet was safely installed on the bus, he waved goodbye. How could a simple piece of glass spoil an evening? How could he have been so clumsy? If only, he thought, if only he had age on his side, or at the very least money in his pocket, he might feel able to be more honest about his feelings for her, and she might even look at him in a way he could only dream. He was a fool. She would never think of him that way. He must be deluded. Annoyed with himself, he decided to walk back home, punishing himself by allowing the rain to burn his face with its needle-like fingers.

Chapter 25

By Monday, the weather had broken, the skies were kinder, and though a few clouds lurked, nothing came of it. Harriet checked that Mrs. G had managed to hang Florrie's washing out, and clutching a small parcel, she smiled to herself, having bought wool to knit a pair of booties for Mrs. Dart's latest baby. Not fifteen minutes from home, Harriet was stopped in her tracks as a man blocked her path. She smelt a familiar fragrance.

"I'm so sorry!" she exclaimed, trying to sidestep, but managing to stand on his shoe.

"Harriet?" She looked up, surprised. "What a happy coincidence, even if you did stand on my foot." She blushed hotly, instantly recognizing CJ.

"I'm so sorry."

"No need to apologize." He laughed but couldn't resist polishing his soiled shoe with a handkerchief.

Harriet returned his gaze and smiled faintly. CJ was immaculately dressed in a dark gray suit complementing the color of his eyes. She reached to her hair and felt a mess. For some reason she didn't want him to notice how shabby her clothes were.

"What perfect luck, seeing you like this."

"It is?" Tugging at her coat, she wished she could afford a new one.

"I wonder…" She listened to his silken voice. "I don't suppose you would care to join me for a cup of tea.

It would be a wonderful welcome break to have your company before I see a client."

"I don't know," Harriet began, flustered.

"Am I being presumptuous? Are you worried about...what's his name, Thomas?"

"No. I've just finished work. I'm not really smart enough."

"Nonsense. Besides, I would like to talk to you, Harriet, not your clothes. Go on, what do you say?"

A smile played across her lips at the comment.

"Very well, a cup of tea would be lovely, thank you." CJ quickly proffered an arm, putting her at ease.

Two streets down, they arrived at a smart little tea shop and entered. Lady Sutcliffe was sitting at a table on her own. Her face soured the moment she set eyes on Harriet.

"Ah, Margaux, so glad you're already here. You remember Miss Laws?"

Margaux's eyebrow raised with light disdain but smiled politely. Harriet acknowledged Lady Sutcliffe graciously, unconsciously tugging at her hair, her coat, her bag.

"Margaux's my partner in crime," said CJ, ensuring Harriet sat comfortably next to him before raising his hand to the waitress. Margaux watched CJ's every move, and as he placed the order she spoke quietly to Harriet.

"I'm surprised CJ would bring you here."

CJ must have overheard.

"Business is business, Margaux." His eyes narrowed, but his voice remained silky. "Where better than to conduct it in a small establishment highly unlikely to entertain our competitors?"

"I'm sorry, CJ, I understood this was to be a short

break before your meeting. I'll go." Harriet began to rise.

"Don't go." It was almost a command. Then added more softly, "I should have explained. It was just such a lovely surprise seeing you. Anyway, we're meeting a new client later. Margaux speaks five languages, including Russian. I need her by my side."

Margaux looked triumphant. Harriet automatically became mother, offering to pour tea to give herself thinking time. If Margaux wanted CJ, it was no skin off her nose.

"Do you speak languages, Harriet?" she asked.

"I can get by in French. Latin was compulsory."

"Latin? Which school did you attend?" There it was. Mocking sarcasm. Harriet had felt sorry for her.

"Lansborough."

"Lansborough High? I believe it has an excellent reputation. I'm surprised." She trailed off, glancing at CJ, who was watching, listening, looking relaxed in the chair. A trickle of pleasured anticipation crossed his lips. He raised a brow at Margaux.

"Harriet, I know it's extremely short notice, but I wonder if you would consider helping me out?" He flashed an enigmatic smile. Though Harriet didn't look at Margaux, she sensed her every move.

"I confess my request is wholly selfish. You will be doing me a huge favor." Harriet looked confused.

"What I'm trying to say, and very badly, is I need someone to be my plus one at a dinner party next Saturday. I wonder... Well, in truth, I'm hoping you will say yes." He looked deep into her eyes with such intensity Harriet felt heat rising in her chest.

"Margaux usually entertains my clients' wives whilst I discuss business." CJ paused, shaking his head.

"But she's unavailable... Oh, dear, I can see I shouldn't have asked. Forget I said anything."

A moment's silence descended.

"I'm not sure I would fit in." Harriet inadvertently glanced down at herself. Her clothes *were* an embarrassment. Her face flushed.

"Nonsense. I wouldn't have asked if I seriously thought it for one minute. I promise the business side of things shouldn't take long, so it won't be boring." CJ slipped his hand to her elbow, touching it lightly.

"It would be so helpful if you said yes. You'd be doing Margaux and me a good turn." He paused for the briefest of moments. Margaux stepped in.

"All you'll need is a cocktail dress, Harriet. You must have one tucked away."

Harriet caught Margaux's smirk from behind her raised teacup and thought about Tom. There had been no mention of meeting up again. Plus, she knew her budget hardly stretched to a new coat for winter, let alone a cocktail dress.

"I'm sorry. Thank you for the invitation, CJ, but I don't think I can make it."

She clenched her fists under the table. How she wished things were different and wondered if Mrs. G would have something else hidden away. A night out sounded exciting, even if it was for business.

CJ glanced at his watch. "Now, please don't be offended. Look on this more as a business transaction." He handed her a card. "Margaux goes there all the time. In fact, why don't you gals go together?" It was as if they were completing a pincer movement between them as Margaux instantly brightened.

"Do you mean Madam Raines, CJ? Yes, why don't

we go together, Harriet. It would be such fun, getting to know one another. Madam Raines has an excellent reputation. You have to have an appointment just to get through the door!"

There was the rub. Margaux obviously knew the prices would be way out of her league.

But CJ leaned into her, whispering, "A beautiful outfit for a beautiful girl. Trust me, it won't cost you a thing. I need you by my side. Choose anything you like." CJ leaned back in his chair. "It's settled. I'll book the appointment. Friday at four p.m. And I'll collect you at seven thirty sharp on Saturday." He handed her a pen and his card for her address.

"Sorry to leave you like this. Make sure the gal gets the tip, and thank you, Harriet, for being such a sport."

Harriet stared at the ten shillings, then at CJ.

"Four p.m., Harriet." Lady Sutcliffe was already on her feet. "Just think, we can have a jolly good catch-up." Margaux placed her hand protectively on CJ's arm with a sly smile on her lips.

"Thank you again for agreeing to be my plus one, Harriet. So kind." And they left with no time for her to refuse.

The waitress immediately came to the table. She must have been in her twenties. Thick black eyeliner matched her black uniform. She wiped her hands on her little white apron.

"Is everything all right, madam?" She tried for professional but fell short of convincing.

"Yes, thank you." Worrying. "Um, could I have the bill, please?"

"It's been taken care of, madam. Can I get you anything else?"

"No, thank you." Harriet stared at the tip. Did CJ really mean for the waitress to have this? It was probably more than the woman would earn in a week, but she followed his instruction.

"I believe this is meant for you."

"Why, thank you, madam." Her mouth flapped in disbelief, and she virtually curtseyed before vanishing with the tip and the tea tray.

Outside, Harriet twisted the business card over in her hand, reading the address. Should she really accept CJ's invitation and the offer of a new dress? She mulled over the proposition.

CJ had made clear the dinner party was purely business, and she would need to look the part. The atelier was plainly upmarket. Harriet shrugged. If CJ didn't mind having a waitress on his arm, then why not? Tom obviously didn't feel about her the way she felt about him. Otherwise, he would have left word. Perhaps she was dolly-daydreaming. Their relationship would only ever be platonic.

Harriet felt a surge of defiance. Why shouldn't she live a little? To hell with it. Mrs. G might be right. Perhaps if Tom found out she was stepping out with someone, it might make him pull up his socks.

Chapter 26

That night the commotion coming from the O'Connells' could be heard through the walls. Doors slammed, furniture crashed, and the volume of a ferocious argument grew. Then came screams, so high and fearful the whole street must have heard. The screams grew louder.

Harriet, dizzy from sleep deprivation, dragged herself from her bed and slipped on her dressing gown. There was no sign of Mr. Noble or Mrs. G, and she knew Jim was on nights so would not be back home yet. Harriet stepped out the front door. The screaming didn't stop.

From opposite, lit hallways cast long shadows on the street. Harriet, blinking, still in a sleep-filled stupor, watched Dotty's husband cross the road to the O'Connells'. Another man followed. Harriet heard a crash.

"Christ! Get an ambulance, quick," a voice shouted with rage. More men arrived. A shattering of glass followed by a shout.

"He's over there, boys!"

A short, stocky figure ran out of the side alley in awkward staggers. The shadows moved after him. Harriet shivered in fear, watching the scene unfold. Sean O'Connell tripped over the curb, sprawling to the ground, heavy as a lorry load. He grunted, staggered back up, and hobbled away. The shadows were gaining.

Shrill cries from children woke Harriet from her trance. Moving swiftly in the cold night air straight to the O'Connells', she peered inside the open door. Florrie, crumpled like paper, lay at the bottom of the stairs. Harriet gasped and rushed to her side. Glancing upward, she saw three small children standing at the top of the stairs, fear pouring out in torrents, terror caught in the whites of their eyes. Harriet heard Florrie groan. Thank God! Harriet crouched beside her.

"The baby…I…" She drifted into unconsciousness as an acrid smell reached Harriet's nose. A pool of pale blood eased from between Florrie's iron-braced legs.

Harriet pulled off her dressing gown and covered the frail body, calling up to the children, trying to calm them, "Everything is going to be all right. Mummy's just sleeping." It was evident in their faces, even in their fragile, early years, they knew it to be a lie. Torn between the worry of Florrie and the children, Harriet put her finger to her lips to silence them.

"I'll be right back. I'm going to get help." Harriet was surprised her voice sounded so calm and in control. The children sobbed. Declan, the eldest, nodded. Harriet, grim-faced, ran outside and saw the outlined figure of a lone woman in the middle of the street.

"Dotty? Please, we need an ambulance, right away!"

Dotty called back, as if pulled out of her own daze, "Oh, god! Yes."

Harriet, shaking from head to foot, hurried back to the O'Connells' and checked Florrie was still breathing. Yes, thank God. She ran swiftly to the little ones and scooped the children into her as best she could, folding her arms around them, cooing over their shock.

"Now, my little kittens, who has lost their mittens?"

Declan, short and stocky, stopped crying the moment Harriet came through the door. He looked at her straight in the eye, a six-year-old wall of silent acceptance.

"Me mammy's dead, isn't she?"

"No, sweet pea," she said, her heart breaking. His sisters were wide eyed, terrified, by his side. "Mummy's going to be all right. I just need you to be a big boy. Can you put some warm clothes on and help your sisters get dressed?" Declan nodded solemnly, catching hold of her tightly, his little fist tugging at her nightwear.

"Me mammy's not going to die? Promise?" Harriet laid a comforting hand on his shoulder.

"Promise. Now, where's Mickey?"

Declan pointed to a bedroom door. It had been battered. Harriet rushed inside the bedroom, petrified at what she might find.

The bedroom was cramped, filled with a double bed and a cot. It was evident the children slept top to toe. Little Mickey, a fat bundle of tantrum, had his tiny hands fisted around the bars, his face, hot and wet from silent, worn-out screams. She took the child carefully out of the cot, cooing softly. Mickey's fiery hot body rigidly resisted being placated. Taking a blanket, she wrapped it around him.

"There, there, Mickey, everything is going to be fine," she cooed gently, and felt his body slowly relax in her arms. As she turned, ready to move, Declan and his sisters were standing right behind her, the girls crying. Forcing a smile, she sat on the bed, placing the solid figure of Mickey on her lap. Holding him with one arm, she reached out with the other, until they were all safely gathered in.

Harriet silently prayed her promise to Declan would not be broken, and one by one their cries turned to gentle hushes, like tiny waves caressing shingles upon the shore.

"Declan, can you wait in here? I'll be back as quickly as I can."

He nodded solemnly. "Promise you will come back?"

"Promise. By the time you've helped your sisters to dress." She tousled his hair. "But I need you to stay in here. Don't leave this room. Okay?" The girls started weeping again, but Declan put his arms about them.

"Mammy is poorly. Aunty Harriet will help."

With little Mickey carefully locked in her arms, deliberately burying his face into her shoulder, Harriet moved quickly, and stepping over Florrie's unconscious figure, she hurried home.

"The ambulance is on its way," said Mrs. G. in short rasping gasps, stopping her on the path. She looked at Harriet's charge snuggled into her shoulder.

"Here, give him to me and bring the rest of the children." She held out her arms, and the small child was transported without a sound into her soft, warm, comforting folds of love.

Harriet turned to go back just as a milk-cheese moon painted the road, bearing witness to a dark vicious cloud of thuggery. Sean O'Connell had become the victim. She couldn't stop herself rushing over.

"For God's sake, stop!"

"Come away, child." Jim's voice was thick, unsteady, and even his face, partly hidden in shadow, could not mask his anger.

157

In the distance the disjointed peal of bells announced the ambulance pulling into the road. The pack quickly dispersed into thin ribbons of black velvet and vanished into the night.

"The children!" Harriet cried, and her feet carried her toward them with a speed she didn't know she possessed.

Chapter 27

Harriet stayed at the hospital with Declan who, with all his miniature but powerful might, refused to leave until he knew his mammy was safe.

The nurse frowned, turning to Harriet. "Can you explain this?" she asked, with Declan trying to wriggle free of the tortuous stinging of antiseptic as she bathed the welt on his face.

"I can't explain any of it." How could she? It was beyond her.

When Mrs. O'Connell came out of theatre, the nurse relented, allowing a distressed Declan to see his mother alive. Harriet gasped at Florrie's white-ash face, pinched and gaunt against the plump brilliance of a white starched pillow. Her eyes were closed, her hands crossed over a white, crisply folded hospital sheet. She looked more dead than alive.

It was too much for Declan. He tried biting back tears, his small hand trembling in Harriet's. She knelt to hold him. Instead of rigidity, Declan fell softly into her, tears wetting her shoulder. A tragic, wretched little boy who only needed to know his mammy would live. Try as Harriet might to console him, Declan could not stop crying. He wanted to be close to his mammy. Nothing would change his mind.

Two hard seats served as their bed, sitting in the sterile hospital corridor outside his mother's room. They guarded entry as Harriet cradled Declan, and antiseptic invaded their senses. Far away down the hall, Harriet saw a nurse move swiftly toward them. Her broad hips, ample bosom, and posture held confidence oozing years of experience. She arrived with a tray with a glass of warm milk for Declan and a welcome cup of sweet tea for Harriet, and a blanket. There would be no more questions tonight. Harriet, amazed at her kindness, mouthed her grateful thanks.

Declan sat upright, glad of the offer, and as he drank thirstily, a white moustache painted his top lip. At some point, Declan fell into a guarded sleep, his warm head on Harriet's lap, his legs curled under, her arm wrapped around his body holding him tight. Harriet found it impossible to sleep. Once or twice Declan woke with a frightened whimper. Harriet stroked his hair, telling him everything was all right.

Nearing five in the morning, Harriet rubbed her neck, stiff from her head lolling forward and jerking awake. She looked down at the little man-boy, his chubby round face, pinked cheeks, tiny, upturned nose, brown hair in wild, knotted disarray. He looked perfect. How could anyone harm a child? The stab of reality seared her thoughts. What would become of the O'Connells?

The quiet of the hospital suddenly crashed alive, rudely waking patients with early morning routines. Bright lights flicked on, the changeover from night to day staff imminent. Voices murmuring, tea trolleys clattering, medicine chests rattling, and the smell of disinfectant re-infused their world. Next, uniformed nurses hurried about at matron's orders, moving swiftly, lightly, through gleaming corridors, opening, closing doors, working hard. More antiseptic, more cleaning, sweeping, stripping beds, laundry carts wheeling, porters transporting patients—until silence fell once staff were inside their designated wards.

Later, a white-coated, silver-haired doctor cast a dispassionate glance their way before entering Mrs. O'Connell's room. Other white-coated figures scurried behind him, clipboards at the ready, pens in top pockets, stethoscopes around necks. The door closed tight. Harriet prayed.

Declan woke, rubbing sandman eyes. Harriet smiled.

"Mummy is fine," she soothed instantly, before he had the chance to ask. "Let's get you looking a bit smarter, ready to see her, shall we?" Harriet said, keen to vanish before the consultant reappeared.

Declan obediently slid off the seat and slipped his hand into hers, and they walked to the toilets. Harriet helped him smooth his hair from standing to flat and persuaded him to wash his face. Declan looked about, embarrassed.

"I shouldn't be here. It's for girls."

"It doesn't matter. No one will come. It's too early."

Surprised at the child's resilience, Harriet washed her face, tidied her hair, and straightened her clothes. All the while she watched sideways as Declan scrubbed himself clean, pushing his shirt back into his shorts, pulling down his jumper, and pulling up gray socks.

"Well done, Declan. You look very smart. Mummy will be proud of you."

"I want to see her." The quiver in his voice betrayed his bravado.

"We will see what we can do." As they exited the

ladies', the same nurse who had brought the milk and blanket passed by.

"Excuse me, Nurse?"

She stopped, looked between them, and put her finger to her lips.

Declan moved swiftly to her side. As far as he was concerned, he had a co-conspirator and capitalized. He grabbed her hand and gave her a sweet smile.

"Please, will you take me to see me mammy? She's been very poorly."

"Why, you dear little thing. You know you're not really allowed." But the nurse was smitten. "Come quickly before your mother is moved to the main ward. I'm surprised Matron didn't insist you go home last night."

Harriet thought the same and smiled. Declan must have cast the same spell on her. The nurse stood on guard outside the room as they went in. They found Florrie propped up in bed. A tiny baby lay in the crook of her unbroken arm, trying to suckle her breast. As soon as she saw Declan she cried with delight. He ran and jumped onto the bed and knelt across the baby, hugging her with such power Harriet choked back a sob.

"Mammy!" As cool as you like, he stared at the infant. "Are you sure he's ours, Mammy? He looks older than old Grandpaps Malone!" Trying to disguise her pain, Florrie laughed.

"Yes, he's ours, Declan. Meet your new little baby brother. And, as you are the first in the family to see him, you can name him."

"Easy." Declan, grinning from ear to ear, announced, "I'd like him to be called Harriet."

Harriet shook her head, smiling widely, but Declan

looked at his mother, his smile so endearing, she laughed with tears.

"Well, Harriet is a lovely name, Declan, but do you think your little brother should have a girl's name? I know, how about shortening it to Harry?"

"Harry." Declan beamed. "Yes, hello, little Harry." His small child's voice choked with emotion. The infant, as if he understood every word, linked his tiny fist around Declan's finger as if it were a sign of approval. It was clear Declan would be the best of friends and closest of brothers.

All eyes on the scene changed as the door opened. The nurse guarding the door told Declan off for being on the bed. Gently removing his little brother's finger, Declan slid off the bed and rushed over to Harriet, reaching as far around her middle as he could, giving her the biggest cuddle.

"Mammy is all right, Aunty Harriet. Me mammy's all right."

Florrie nodded toward the nurse, who quietly coaxed Declan to leave them for a moment with the promise of some warm milk and a biscuit.

"Harriet, I know this may sound stupid, but I believe Sean has a good heart. It's just the drink gets him all fired up." Her eyes traveled to her baby. Her words came out in a tumble. "But I need to get away, right away. I tried before, but he always finds us, and then the troubles get worse. I can't allow it no more. Please?" Florrie was crying softly. "You know things, you know people."

With the tears, she continued, "His family live in Ireland, so they do. They don't understand. Harriet, please. I can't risk the little ones. Not anymore." Harriet touched her shoulder gently.

"Florrie, trust me, I will do everything in my power to help."

****

On the bus home, Harriet kept a firm eye on the road, bewildered, worrying, trying to stay awake. Eventually they got off at the closest stop. Wide eyed, Declan grasped Harriet's hand tightly.

"What's the matter, Declan?"

"Me pa. Will he be there?" The fear in his voice said it all.

"No." Her heart beat unevenly. "Don't worry." She felt awful. What could she say or possibly do to protect them? She wished with all her heart she could make all the horror vanish. No one should have to deal with such things, and she began praying someone might have an idea.

Chapter 28

Harriet found Mrs. Gaffney in the kitchen smoking, her eyes half closed and puffy, her usually smartly waved hair disheveled. She shook herself awake.

"Mummy and baby are fine," Harriet said, pleased to give a small hope of normality but desperate to talk in private about her promise to Florrie.

"I bet you're starving, young man." Mrs. Gaffney stubbed out her cigarette. Declan inched closer to Harriet.

"We've got a new baby brother. His name is Harry."

"Well, well. How lovely." Mrs. Gaffney half smiled. "Sit down. You both look like I feel. How about some toast?" She began cutting a loaf of bread, but before she cut the second slice, Declan had crossed his arms and rested his head on the table.

"Off to bed, young man," said Harriet.

"They're in my bedroom," Mrs. G whispered.

Harriet took Declan to the room where his brother and sisters were still fast asleep, arms and legs sprawled east to west. Somehow baby Mickey remained cocooned between them. She watched Declan snuggle under a blanket, his siblings still out for the count. Quietly closing the door, she tiptoed back to the kitchen.

"Poor little mites." Mrs. Gaffney was lighting another cigarette. "Now tell me, how is Florrie, really?"

The smoke made Harriet's eyes water. She rubbed

them and, pushing back a tangle of hair, spoke about her promise.

"What on earth am I going to do? I can't let them down."

Mrs. Gaffney tapped ash into the saucer with a thoughtful expression. She poured stewed black tea and heaped three spoons of sugar into Harriet's cup.

"Well, my girl"—she pushed the cup across— "Dotty Harris has a finger in every pie. Best not waste time."

Dotty gathered their little clan together within the hour, relaying information.

"Me brother works at the 'orspital as a porter. Seems that bugger Sean's gonna live but they reckon he's likely out of action for at least a month." Dotty sighed. "If Florrie had been thinking straight, he could have 'ad a permanent place at 'er Majesty's."

Harriet raised a doubting brow.

"The way I see it, if we all work together, we can share the load, so no one feels put upon."

Within half an hour the group of friends had a semblance of a plan in action. Harriet would do the laundry, Patience agreed to do the school run, Mrs. Gaffney would look after little Mickey, and Dotty would do tea for the children.

"They can sleep in my room, whilst Florrie's in hospital. I don't think it would be good for them to go back home, not just yet," said Mrs. Gaffney. Harriet smiled. Her landlady was a real softy. The only bed she would have would be the sofa. When the women were gone, she would offer up her own.

"We'll wash up, Mrs. G, while you keep an eye on my little monster?" said Dotty. Charlie was pulling a little wooden train along the hallway, bashing it into the skirting board, while Dotty drew Harriet into the back yard.

"You asked me to find out some business. What I have to say stays with us, promise?"

"Of course!"

Dotty rubbed her chin. "I know what others think of me, a nosey old bat, can't keep a secret, finger in every pie. But those pies sometimes have a way of helping others out, and I can most definitely keep a secret."

"You've found somewhere?"

"It weren't easy, but yes, most likely. But like I says, if anyone—especially her bloody monster of an 'usband or even one of his drunken mates—gets a whiff, we can say goodbye to it. One word, and it puts a whole heap of others at risk."

Harriet listened to Dotty in surprise and complete admiration as she passed a telephone number over.

"I don't want to know anything, Harriet. It's up to you now."

Harriet quickly dried the washed cups and saucers, bemused, relieved, hopeful. Perhaps her promise to Florrie could be kept, and she and the children would have somewhere safe to go.

****

The *London Times* lay on the kitchen table, and the radio was on. Mrs. Gaffney took a sip of tea listening to the news reader: "*...in the first protest march for the Campaign for Nuclear Disarmament. The march begins in Hyde Park and finishes in Aldermaston, Berkshire.*" Mrs. Gaffney shook her head.

"I don't know what the world's coming to."

Harriet smiled halfheartedly, her mind elsewhere.

There was so much to think about, so much to do, it gave her a headache. Harriet made the call not fifteen minutes after speaking with Dotty. A woman answered, asked a series of questions, and wanted assurances. As she listened, she felt like a spy. The instructions were clear, explicit, and in no way could be changed. Everything depended on the instructions being followed to the letter. No one else, other than Florrie, must know.

That same afternoon, Harriet visited Florrie in hospital, outlining the plan. Once put into action, no more contact could be made by her to her family or anyone. It sounded so final. So unreal. Harriet knew there would be challenges, but Florrie remained resolute.

"Thank you, Harriet," she whispered, holding her closely. "I will forever be in everyone's debt."

Harriet had two weeks before Florrie would be well enough for discharge. Two weeks to prepare. Without Florrie's knowledge, Harriet put all her own hard-earned savings into a sealed envelope at the bottom of one of the suitcases, wishing her luck for the future, praying they would be safe.

****

Sofia popped into Luigi's to see Harriet for a quick catch-up. They sat at the back of the restaurant, chatting. Harriet's concern for Mrs. O'Connell far outweighed everything, but the promised secret would remain just that. She would only share one incidental piece of worry with Sofia, the business arrangement with CJ.

"I said Mr. Rutherford had eyes for you, now, didn't I?" said Sofia, beaming, with one eye on little wobble-legged Carlo Luigi, who tried standing, using a chair for support. Sofia dropped a napkin and rushed over before he fell.

"Look! Carlo is desperate to take his first steps." The boy held tightly onto her index fingers, raising one chunky leg after another, taking her along with him.

"I think you are also taking your first steps. They may be a little unsteady at first, but you will find your feet."

Harriet, folding napkins, smiled at the analogy.

"And as to the clothes." Sofia shrugged. "Why not? It's business, after all, isn't it? How about I ask my Carlo to collect you at the end of the evening, if you're feeling unsure of Mr. Rutherford's intentions?"

"No, really, thank you." She squeezed her friend's hand. "I'm sure I'll be fine."

Chapter 29

It seemed stupid to think visiting an atelier could cause her such angst, but it did. Knowing she would look out of place whatever she wore, in the end Harriet decided on the only dress she possessed, with her newest knitted cardigan. Fear, panic, and a kind of calm took over as she neared Madam Raines' establishment. Arriving early, she checked her hair, added a smidge of lipstick, and waited for Lady Sutcliffe.

At seven minutes past four, Harriet began pacing the street. She hated being late. Five more minutes ticked by, and with no sign of Lady Sutcliffe, she took the plunge and pressed the doorbell. Moments later, a young woman arrived.

"Miss Laws?"

"Yes."

"Welcome. We have been expecting you. My name is Sarah." She held the door open.

"Has Lady Sutcliffe arrived?"

"No, madam." Sarah sounded faintly surprised. "Please, come this way." Harriet followed Sarah into a side room. There were two comfortable chairs, a large floor-to-ceiling mirror, and hanging space.

"I see you are a size ten. Mr. Rutherford explained you will need something appropriate to wear for a dinner party. Something understated but elegant?"

"Yes." Harriet couldn't control the shakes. No way

on earth could she go on with the charade. What a fool to even consider the possibility.

"I think I've made a mistake."

"Mr. Rutherford has the account covered," Sarah added quietly. "Choose whatever you like, and if I may, I would like to introduce you to our newest designer, Kate Westfield." Harriet puzzled over the name for a second, and there was a polite cough from behind the door.

"Hattie!"

"Kate?" Harriet instantly recognized her. "What a lovely surprise!"

"You know one another?"

"No, not really," said Kate. "We met quite by chance, and now fate has stepped in again. Why didn't you phone? Anyway, not to worry, you're here now. First, madam, we must fulfill your wishes."

Working in unison, Kate and Sarah displayed a range of cocktail dresses, assisting Harriet when required. The choice took no time at all, as she selected an elegant slash-necked black dress.

"Good choice," said Sarah. "It's one of Kate's designs, and with just a small adjustment around the bustline we shall ensure your comfort."

Whilst Sarah made tea, Kate started working her magic, somehow managing to speak even though holding pins in her mouth and taking measurements. Up close, Harriet noticed the freckles across Kate's nose, and how it wrinkled when she smiled. And as they chatted, it was as if they'd known one another all their lives.

"There. Would you be kind enough to slip this on? We will have tea, and you can tell me how you know the most sought-after bachelor in London, and I'm given to understand he's great in bed."

Harriet, shocked, flushed deep salmon pink and remained tight-lipped.

"Seriously? Give over. You're no more a saint than I am. CJ is gorgeous. Not my type. But given half the chance, who knows?" Kate giggled as Sarah brought in the tray of tea, grinning.

"Kate! You're scaring our customer half to death. Don't take any notice. All Kate thinks about is sex."

Harriet's mouth dropped open.

"Sex gives me a creative edge, releases pent-up tensions, and clears my mind." Kate shrugged. "How else does one survive? Take drugs and smoke like a chimney?"

"Just as well Madam Raines isn't here," said Sarah.

Kate's eyes glittered with mischief. "Whilst the cat's away."

Chapter 30

Mrs. Gaffney winked at Harriet, already waiting nervously in the front room reserved for guests only.

"Mr. Noble will be rewarded with a Chelsea bun if he does a good job." She smiled, hearing a rap at the door.

"Ah, at last," said Mr. Rutherford when Mr. Noble answered. "I believe Miss Laws is waiting for me?"

Mrs. Gaffney poised herself elegantly on the sofa, her hands folded across her lap. Mr. Noble brought Mr. Rutherford through to the lounge.

"I'd like to introduce you to Mother," said Harriet awkwardly. Never having a mother, it sounded odd to her.

"Mrs. Laws," CJ said without skipping a beat. "How wonderful to meet you, but surely you are far too young to have a daughter Harriet's age?" Flattered half to death, Mrs. Gaffney appeared to forget her new persona.

"Mrs. Laws, is everything all right?"

Harriet stared, horrified, but Mrs. G recouped the lost moment admirably.

"Ah, yes, Mr. Rutherford. I trust you will be bringing my daughter home at a reasonable hour?"

Harriet's eyes widened.

"Of course, Mrs. Laws." CJ smiled to himself, hiding his thoughts as easily as breathing air.

"I plan to have your *daughter* back by midnight. I

trust this won't be a problem?" CJ raised the back of Mrs. Gaffney's hand to his lips and looked into her eyes with such intensity Harriet felt sure her landlady would faint.

"No, no, of course not, Mr. Rutherford. May I offer you a sherry?" CJ glanced at his watch.

"I'm sorry, would you be offended? Time is of the essence. We are expected at seven forty-five sharp."

"But allow me." CJ, taking charge, poured her a glass. "You don't have to miss out, do you?"

"Thank you, Mr. Rutherford. Perhaps we could do this another time?"

"How kind." CJ proffered his arm to Harriet.

Mr. Noble remained by the front door, opening it as if he were the butler.

"Have a good evening, sir, madam."

Harriet wanted to scream with laughter.

CJ held the passenger door of a shiny red MG, allowing Harriet to slip in before sliding in beside her.

"Is everything to your liking, madam?"

"To be honest, I've never been in a car before, let alone something quite so fabulous. Why, it even has a leather interior!" CJ made an adjustment to his rearview mirror, bringing her attention back to Mr. Noble, still standing at the front door.

"Who is that, exactly?" He pulled the choke out and turned the key in the ignition, and the engine surged with power.

"Oh dear, I'm sorry. I can't keep up the pretense. Mrs. Gaffney wanted to make sure you weren't a villain or something. I don't actually have family. Not anyone."

"To be honest, I guessed so—you look nothing like her."

"Oh." Downcast, she said, "I'm sorry for the lie."

CJ reached across, lightly touching her hand.

"I understand. I don't have family either." He looked genuinely sad. "But I don't like to talk about it." He turned to look out the side window and pulled out into the road, taking charge. She didn't see him hiding a smile.

"Now to business. You'll need to know exactly what to do. I'll teach you before we get there, okay?"

"Of course." She tried to hide her concern.

"I like your outfit, by the way. You really look the part." Harriet half smiled.

"Shall I get the dress cleaned and take it back next week?"

CJ pressed his foot on the accelerator, and they shot forward toward an amber light.

"You will do no such thing. The dress is yours." They flew through the lights at the crossroads as amber turned red and sped on.

Harriet felt exhilarated at CJ's recklessness. She had seen London before, of course, walking, once from a van, and then from the upper deck of a bus, but not like this, driven in a fantastic car with a handsome man. Lights poured from shops, cabbies weaved themselves expertly between heavy traffic, and pedestrians overflowed paths. CJ adjusted his speed, raising the thrilled flush in her cheeks before making a show of checking his watch.

"Will we be late?"

"You will learn, Harriet, I hate being late, and I believe we are right on time." He was slowing down, almost grinding to a halt, allowing a car to pull out from a side street. They were right outside Pete's café. CJ glanced across. A light smile played across his lips. Tom was in the window, sitting opposite a female. They appeared deeply engrossed with one another.

"I say, what a coincidence, isn't that your friend, what's-his-name?"

Harriet's instinct, her natural curiosity to look, had already seen them. CJ caught her frown and the faint quiver of her bottom lip.

"Is everything all right, Harriet?"

"Yes, thank you." There was a crack in her voice. "Are we nearly there?"

CJ smiled, changing gears, and pulled away. "Not long."

Chapter 31

CJ was so attentive, so very composed, so very, to use Kate's word, *sexy*. Harriet blushed at the mere thought of it. Kate had been right. Up until now her feelings and desire had been for Tom. But the champagne seemed to give her an edge, a confidence she had never known until now, and when they stepped out into the cool night air, she felt relaxed and surer of herself than she ever had before. The evening had been a complete success.

"I've had the most wonderful time, CJ. Thank you."

"No, thank you, Harriet." He turned her gently toward him. "Is this all right?" Before she could respond, he placed a slow, lingering kiss on her lips. Harriet shuddered. The sensation, warm, thrilling, divine—her first real kiss. He pulled her gently, tantalizingly, out of the embrace.

"Your carriage awaits, Miss Laws. I don't want to get on the wrong side of *Mother*."

Harriet laughed. She was happy. Happy she had a kiss from an extremely attractive man. Happy there were no secrets between them, and as CJ drove her home, he made her promise to meet him again, suggesting they go to a club, one he knew in Soho. This time it would be a date, not a business proposition. Their first real date. Her first real kiss. She remembered Kate had given her a business card. She lived somewhere in Soho. She would pay Kate a visit. It would be good to see her again. Kate said she had a new range of clothes she wanted to show her before they went "live," whatever that meant.

The curtains twitched. Mrs. G was in the front room. The moment the door closed, she appeared.

"Good evening, Cinderella."

"Oh, Mrs. G, he was a prince. And he knows I don't have family—he guessed. Can you believe it?"

"Oh, my goodness! Come in here, child. I think a glass of sherry's in order." They went into the parlor, where she poured two glasses. "Now sit and tell me all about it."

There was so much to tell. The people, the food, the wine, but most of all, the kiss. That bit she would keep to herself.

****

Harriet lay on her bed, dreamily, as she thought about the night. Her gaze wandered toward the painting. It looked incongruous in her miniscule bedroom, but it was a beautiful reminder of her grandmother and their life together. Tonight, of all nights, she would have loved to be able to talk to Nana about Tom and CJ.

"I think you would like CJ, Nana. He's rather handsome, a little younger than Tom." Her voice trailed off. Tom had moved on. All thoughts of him had vanished during the evening, but she realized he popped into her head now without her even trying. She shook herself. She valued Tom's friendship above all else and would make a special effort to see him on those terms only. But even now, having seen Tom with another woman, and in Pete's café, and at their table, a little pang of hurt crept into her heart. It felt a teeny bit like a betrayal. Harriet shook herself.

"*You're being silly*," she said out loud. "Didn't you just go out with CJ? And isn't he taking you out again, and didn't he kiss you?"

Harriet hung up her new dress on the dado rail, switched off the light, and snuggled under the covers. As her eyes adjusted to the dark, she could just make out a few stars through the tiny roof light. She imagined her Nana being there, one of them, and whispered, "Good night, Nana, I love you."

Chapter 32

Kate arranged to meet Harriet in a coffee shop in Soho. It was Thursday, early evening. The place was buzzing. Music she didn't recognize drifted from somewhere out the back.

Kate arrived much later than the agreed time, but Harriet, having found a seat, enjoyed soaking up the atmosphere.

"Hattie!" Kate pushed through the throng of people.

"Hattie!" the crowd echoed back, and Harriet waved a hand in embarrassed acknowledgment. Kate pulled up a spare stool from another table and leaned in to give her a hug, with a kiss on the cheek.

"How is the eligible CJ, and how was the sex?"

Harriet pulled a face, amazed she could be so loudly frivolous in public about such a private thing.

"Would you like a coffee? I'll treat you," replied Harriet, trying to contain Kate's exuberance.

"No, thanks, don't touch the stuff."

"But then why here?"

"You'll see." Kate laughed. "Come on, we'll go to my place. It's not far, but not easy to find. I want you to be my model." Harriet's eyebrow rose with uncertainty as she downed the very last dregs of her coffee, not wanting to leave one expensive drop.

Grabbing Harriet by the hand, Kate pulled her through the crowd and out into the street swarming with young people. Teddy boys, wearing drainpipe trousers and velvet-collared jackets, were hanging around on corners, cigarettes in one hand, watching platinum blondes and brunettes sashay by. A couple of the men keenly eyed Kate and Harriet up and down and gave long, low, wolf whistles.

"Put your eyes back in their sockets, boys," Kate huffed. "And your brains back inside your pants."

"Kate!" Harriet hushed her, hiding a giggle.

"Well, how would they feel if we stared at them and did the same to them?"

Harriet sighed resolutely. Kate was right, but on the other hand, it was nice to have a little attention.

The two girls came to a stop outside a casino.

"We're above." Kate was right. It would have been difficult to find. She darted into an alley and opened a side door. Harriet followed. As they climbed the stairs, muffled music beat a rhythm, but by the time they reached Kate's apartment, the sound had completely disappeared.

"We're over the casino," explained Kate. "It has to be quiet for them, most likely soundproofed, so a perfect spot for us."

"Us?"

"Sarah and I live together. It's cheaper."

Kate led her into the front room, beautifully laid out with an arrangement of flowers on the coffee table set between two facing Chesterfields.

"My goodness, that's fabulous, Kate." Harriet admired a mural of a large hand cupping the galaxy made up of the heavens and stars.

"Isn't it wonderful? It's by Davey Craddock. Poor thing had a blow to his head, rendered him crippled, but clearly still has an enviable talent."

Harriet's mind worked over the surname. Surely not?

"Is Davey related to Dorian Craddock, by any chance?"

"He most certainly is. Do you know her? She's one of my clients. That's how I found out about Davey."

Harriet wanted to tell Kate about her once-nemesis but decided against it.

"Take a look around." Kate flicked her slender hand between the room where she slept, Sarah's room, and the third bedroom, where she worked. "It's hard not having a really big space to operate in, but anything I create at Madam Raines' atelier becomes hers by default."

"Really?"

"Yes, I'll tell you about it another time. But now to business. Come on, strip off!"

"What?"

"Bloody hell, Hattie! How can you try anything on if you don't take your clothes off?" Kate was serious. "No one else has seen these, other than Sarah," she whispered, putting her finger to her lips. "Have to be careful about industrial espionage."

"You what?"

"Oh, stop asking questions." Kate began closely watching Harriet's face as she studied the garments on the rail.

"Where did you get the material?"

"Oh, here and there. Markets, you name it. This one started out white, so I dyed it."

"Really? How clever. Can I touch?"

"Of course. How else will you put it on, levitation?" Kate giggled naughtily.

One dress looked like a shimmering waterfall, with swirls of shells and stars flowing down from the top. The shoulders crossed over at the front, allowing a cleavage to be disguised or shown off, whichever the wearer chose. The length was unusual as well, with a long train at the back but just below knee height at the front.

"There's a bazaar in Markham Square and Kings Road, Chelsea," Kate chuntered on. "Do you know it? The girl there is a designer. Her name's Mary Quant. She's just bought another shop. I know she's going to make it big." Kate sighed. "I want to make it big. I will, just you mark my words." She looked worried. "I guess you're not impressed with my designs. Go on, tell me. Be honest."

Kate on the surface seemed so in control, and yet within a few short seconds Harriet discovered just how vulnerable she really was.

"You Dopey Norah! I think they're gorgeous. And you know it. And I'd love to try the waterfall on first."

"Waterfall?"

"Yes, this one." Harriet lifted the dress off the rail. Kate laughed, sounding relieved.

"Of course. Waterfall, eh? I'm going to call this my Waterfall Collection. And if you ever need something to wear, like when you go out with the super sexy CJ, for example, Kate's the name, fashion's the game."

Harriet giggled shyly, slipping off her clothes.

"So, was sex with the sexy Mr. Rutherford all it's cracked up to be?" Harriet was stood in front of a long mirror. The dress was enchanting, exotic, sensual. Kate sat on the floor, just outside the room. "I thought with your coloring—and fabulous figure—it would be perfect. I was right."

Harriet flushed. Fabulous figure indeed. She was far more used to chants of Fatty Hattie. Harriet twisted to the side and gulped.

"It's truly magnificent. Like a piece of fine art."

"Thank you, Hattie." Kate's eyes looked suspiciously misty. Harriet wondered. To cover whatever her emotion, Kate went to the fridge and pulled out a bottle of white wine. "When you're finished, we can have a tipple."

Wine and a fridge? Harriet never knew anyone who owned a fridge in Ham Street, let alone had bottles of wine. Larders and cold buckets of water with bottled milk were far more familiar.

Whilst Harriet dressed, Kate kept prying. CJ. Harriet flushed. How could she admit to Kate she was still a virgin? She prided herself in the fact. But when Kate discussed sex, it was as if it was a rite of passage.

"Well, was it good or what?"

"What?"

"S-E-X!" Kate spelt out.

"I think you've been drinking too much. I've told you already, we haven't!"

"Seriously? That's not CJ's style." Kate shook her head. "He must have it bad. I bet he's asked you out again."

Chapter 33

Dorian Craddock owned one of the most exclusive memberships in London. Club 59 was hidden behind an anonymous sort of door in an eighteenth-century Mayfair townhouse. Spread over five floors, it offered sanctuary, relaxation, and entertainment for the social elite. Dorian prided herself on her achievement, checking each room daily to ensure the highest standards were maintained.

Dorian was speaking quietly to Edis, who replied, "Yes, madam, he is in the steam room."

"Excellent." Dorian occasionally mused what it might be like to have Edis. Handsome, muscled, and well educated, for a Turk. Edis bowed as she left to continue her inspection. The imported marble and the Turkish designer made every penny spent well worth the luxury it gave her clients.

A massive Turk stood near the marble table, arms folded, the tiniest tea towel wrapped around his middle, barely covering him for modesty's sake. He nodded his head toward the steam room.

"I hope he's enjoyed the experience?"

A slight twitch of muscle in the corner of the Turk's mouth indicated he may have also enjoyed the experience.

Dorian continued her tour. Having to rid herself of one of the attendants recently aggravated her. How the girl came to be pregnant was not her concern. The confidentiality clause in the contract was clear. Any sign of weakness could never be allowed. If a hint of further indiscretion reached her ears, the girl would be dealt with. Permanently.

Dorian stepped into the elevator. Room thirty-seven. Reserved for the super-rich. Jules, one of the croupiers, had been with her since the day they opened. She liked Jules. She was always the consummate professional, and great in bed. They had an understanding. Dorian looked toward Fabio. She'd liked him immensely from the moment of interview. He did anything she asked of him. Anything. His skills were more than managing the casino. He managed the back room where the most private of meetings took place. Vetted all the guests, arranged memberships, took care of the occasional messy side of business, keeping detailed accounts of immoral conduct for future reference. Fabio leaned into her, speaking quietly. Her very special guest was obviously enjoying himself.

"She's not being forced to do anything she doesn't want to?" Dorian tried not to flinch at Fabio's response.

"You have the evidence?"

"Yes, madam."

"Well, for God's sake, man," she hissed. "What the hell are you waiting for? I don't care who he is. Sort it. Now! And double the agreed fee."

Dorian angrily watched Fabio's retreating figure. It was most unlike him not to take the initiative, but he'd been mixing with CJ more and more lately. She wondered about that and had her suspicions. She would look into it personally, but her special guest would become a useful pawn now, nonetheless. With her check complete, she took the back stairs. She would be hosting the party tonight and needed to be ready.

Chapter 34

The call from CJ came as a surprise. Not because he asked permission to bring a guest, that was a given, but the name of his lady friend made her sit upright. Could it really be her? It had to be, but what a strange coincidence. Or was it? Dorian swiveled in her chair, checking her nails, admiring the pink opal polish, pondering.

Dorian re-read the prison visiting order, rolling her thumbs one over the other. Another interesting development. Maybe her father was toying with her one last time. After all, who in their right mind would have given the plods evidence to put him away for good? But he deserved it. She took a deep breath, thinking about Davey, and shuddered. Her father always played mind games. Perhaps he was planning to escape? The gallows were looming. She shivered, even though her office was warm.

She would never forget her thirteenth birthday, when the turf war between her father's gang and rival George "Silver" Smith escalated. If Harriet had not arrived in the schoolyard when she did... Dorian's face contorted, having spent hundreds of pounds on therapy trying to rid herself of the nightmares. It took three years just to get five simple words out: "*It was not my fault,*" pinging an elastic band on her wrist, like her therapist told her to. But nothing could stop *that* day from unfolding in her mind's eye. The same bubble of horror welled in her throat just thinking about it.

****

Her father's thin smile, his lip curling over small top teeth, slow and mean. His instruction, *"Remain silent."* Pushing her into the priest hole behind the bookcase. "I'll show you how *I* deal with the likes of him."

Two hours, in pain, misery. Unable to stop shaking. Terrified, sure she would vomit. Two hours her father just sat at his desk, calm and composed, as if he were waiting for a tray of afternoon tea.

Then two of George "Silver" Smith's henchmen had burst through the door. Two seconds, and they were dead. Sent on a fool's errand. A distraction. Everyone knew Craddock was a marksman. The first man flew backward, hitting the wood paneling, sliding to a sitting position, childlike, legs straight out in front. The second dropped to his knees as if he were praying, falling forward, a sprawling hulk across the floor.

George "Silver" Smith was next, his cane flying. He should have run for his life. The horrors filled every single sense. She remembered when the priest hole slid open and her father found her rocking. He dragged her out as she fought to keep her ears and eyes closed.

Dorian grabbed her office wastepaper basket from just under her desk, and vomited.

****

"Good evening, Dorian." CJ smiled as her bodyguard allowed them entry to her private office. "May I introduce you to my friend, Miss Laws."

Dorian eyed Harriet in the way she once used to at school.

"Dorian?" Harriet stared. She had no idea. CJ had

said he would introduce her to the proprietor of Club 59. He'd never once mentioned the owner's name, or indeed, that the owner was female. To be fair, she hadn't asked.

Dorian extended a thin hand.

Harriet's gaze traveled swiftly, noticing how her clothes shaped her well. Dorian even appeared to have developed a bust.

"You know each other?" CJ appeared backfooted. "How? You never said…"

"Harriet and I attended the same school, CJ. Harriet was clever enough to win a scholarship."

Harriet's nose flared. Dorian gestured for CJ to leave.

"I was going to show Harriet around." There was an odd, simpering inflection in CJ's tone.

Harriet breathed in deeply, unable to get the facts out of her head. Dorian Craddock, her once-nemesis, the school bully who made everyone's life hell, a murderer's daughter, owned Club 59 and knew CJ.

"Why don't you have a flutter. On the house?"

Harriet caught CJ checking his watch, noting how easily he was swayed.

"Will you bring Harriet to me?"

"CJ." Dorian's curt response was enough to silence him. She beckoned to her bodyguard, mouthing something in his ear, and he chaperoned CJ out. Dorian indicated for Harriet to sit.

Harriet, steeling herself, looked at an ornate chair delicately embroidered in gold and with a small red rose.

"Louis Fifteenth?"

"You know about antiques?" Dorian sounded interested.

"I'm beginning to."

"You always were a fast learner." Dorian flicked an imaginary piece of lint off her sleeve. "CJ's been helping me to develop my understanding of such things." She looked at Harriet's hands and rolled her thumbs one over the other. "I haven't forgotten."

Her words were loaded. Harriet flinched. How could either of them ever forget the day that changed everything? Finding Dorian in the schoolyard. A silver flash of cane, the man ready to strike. And afterward, capitalizing on Dorian's vulnerability. Harriet felt guilt, but it was worth swallowing down; it kept all the girls safe from Dorian's tyranny.

"How about a drink for old times' sake?"

Harriet's mouth twitched uncertainly. She would need to keep her wits about her. Dorian pushed a button and placed her order.

"I guess life's treating you well?"

"I can't complain. You've clearly done well for yourself, Dorian."

"Hmm." Dorian picked at imaginary lint again. "Did you know you taught me two things *that* day?" The waiter arrived with a bottle of champagne in an ice bucket.

"Just open the champagne. I'll do the rest." The waiter quickly completed the task, and she waited for the door to close.

"I'll deny ever saying this," Dorian said, studying her hands and linking her fingers together. "I learned integrity and the true meaning of respect from you.

"Until then, I always thought instilling fear meant it gained respect. You taught me all fear does is create dread. Don't get me wrong. People still fear me. Fear protects me, and my businesses. But respect? Well."

Dorian collected two cocktail glasses from a cabinet. She poured a shot of sloe gin into each glass, topped it with champagne, then looked Harriet straight in the eye.

"You earned my respect the moment you offered your help without hesitation. You had absolutely no reason to." She gave a wry laugh. "Quite the opposite. You even had the guts to insist safety for all the other girls. For that alone you earned my respect." She handed her the cocktail.

"The offer still stands, should you ever need my help."

Dorian lifted her glass and took a sip. "How about I show you around?"

Dorian charmingly introduced Harriet to politicians, industrialists, actors, and, at one point, Harriet saw the chief of police being shown into a *meeting room*, with a pretty girl on his arm. Harriet blanched at her thoughts. She caught Dorian watching her. Back at the office, and with the door closed firmly behind them, Dorian purred, catlike.

"You haven't changed a bit, still questioning everything, still intuitive. So much so, I would like to offer you a job."

Harriet, stunned at the offer, stood up and found herself making a pretense of studying a small painting on the wall.

"I'll be candid, Dorian. I had no idea what to expect when I came here, and I most certainly had no idea you were the proprietor. I'm impressed with what you have created."

Dorian waited patiently.

"But I'm sure you won't be offended when I say I

am already fully committed. Therefore, I cannot accept your kind offer."

Dorian seemed unfazed.

"Such a shame, and you didn't even ask how much I would pay. Though I'm sure it would be much more than the bakery or Luigi's."

Stunned, Harriet drew herself to her full height.

"Don't be upset, Harriet. It isn't my intention to undermine you. I have everyone vetted. I can't afford to make myself or my clients vulnerable." She languidly picked up the bottle of gin liqueur, poured a shot into fresh glasses, and pulled the champagne out of the ice bucket. Icy water slid down the bottle's side, dripping into the silver ice bucket before she wiped it with the napkin.

"Well, as you are not interested in my proposition, we will become friends. When you change your mind, we can have this discussion again. In the meantime, I will arrange full membership. You can use all my club has to offer, whenever you like."

Harriet accepted the glass in complete amazement. "Thank you, Dorian." She sipped the cocktail, which was, again to her amazement, very pleasant.

Chapter 35

During the next five months, when Harriet was not working CJ transported Harriet from her world and into his. No two dates were the same. They drove for miles into the countryside and drank in small taverns along the way. They went to the theatre, and to fashionable dance clubs, and ate out in exclusive restaurants, and no expense was spared.

When CJ introduced Harriet to his friends at the Lawn Tennis Club, she was immediately befriended by Norah Shann-Kydd. Norah, tall, elegant, would have been quite pretty if her nose weren't quite so big. CJ once told Harriet that Lucan, Norah's husband, was one of his best customers. Lucan apparently introduced him to an extensive network of wealthy businessmen who had little to no idea about art or antiquities, and they made a killing.

Today, they were watching CJ play singles with Lucan—or, as Norah called him, Lucky. It was obvious CJ was by far the better tennis player, but he kept Lucan sweet by strategically losing the occasional match.

"I guess you've met Margaux?" Norah began limbering up, ready for a game.

"Yes, she tells me she speaks five languages. Very impressive." Harriet curled in on herself for sounding so bitchy.

"Hangs on CJ's every word." Norah laughed.

"I believe she helps CJ with his business?" Harriet could never get the measure of their relationship.

"She's madly in love with him."

Harriet, shocked, gathered up a tennis ball, and repeatedly struck it to the floor with her racquet. CJ never expressed any romantic interests.

"Have they been together for long?"

Norah shrugged. "I wouldn't quite call them being *together* in the courting sense. Margaux's been his right arm in business for some time, managing his shop..." She counted back. "Around three years. Lucky says CJ *uses* poor Margaux not only for business but anything else he fancies." Norah stopped abruptly. "I'm so sorry, Harriet. That was tactless."

Harriet kept bouncing the ball, hiding her feelings. CJ had never once demanded anything of her other than a kiss. Norah was blunt. No two sides. They got on well, and she felt sure it wasn't malicious, as Norah looked embarrassed.

"Before you came along, CJ had a history of drawing women into his web and tossing them aside, like discarded fish paper. I think Margaux will be one of them, poor thing." Norah was swishing her racquet in ever-increasing circles.

"It's clear, from what I've seen, CJ is simply besotted with you." Norah smiled widely, then quickly turned the conversation around.

"Margaux!"

Harriet's neck prickled at the name.

"Norah, I just had drinks in the clubhouse." Margaux ignored Harriet and gave her friend a peck on the cheek. "I guess you heard the latest on Felicity Jones-Shaw?"

"Is she better? More importantly, is she out?"

"No. By all accounts, she's likely to be in the loony bin a while longer," Margaux continued, happily regaling the story. "Seems her husband's mistress won't have her back home." While Harriet remained excluded from their conversation, she wanted to scream how terribly unjust it all sounded.

"How awful. What's it been, nearly a year? How does he get away with it?"

"It seems all you need is a little financial persuasion, and the right doctor."

Harriet watched Margaux's eyes fixate on CJ. The conversation stopped abruptly as Lucky reached set point.

"Is CJ *actually* going to lose? I think *I* may get lucky tonight." Norah shivered with a sensual stretch. "Can't wait." She cast a coy glance at Harriet. "Lucky is so much more attentive in bed when he wins."

Harriet allowed a smile to cross her lips, but Norah and Margaux provoked questions she wanted answered. There would be no way she would continue stepping out with CJ if Norah was right about Margaux, and what about this poor Felicity Jones-Shaw?

****

Once back at Calvert Street, Harriet stripped off and threw her clothes crossly onto the bed. It was true Margaux got under her skin, and in more ways than one. She considered the difficult conversation between herself and CJ. He'd sounded annoyed when she asked about his relationship with Margaux. Theirs was a professional arrangement. Nothing more. When questioned, he apparently didn't know Felicity Jones-Shaw and advised her to keep well out of it. She gritted her teeth, wondering what, if anything, she could do, and planned to talk to Norah.

Harriet studied her tennis gear. CJ had bought her the whole ensemble. At first, she hired a racquet. Now she was the proud owner of a Slazenger. Another gift. She would have been just as happy with CJ's company. Nothing else. She sat on the bed, spinning the racquet in her hand.

He was so generous it made her feel awkward. When she explained, he looked hurt, making her feel guilty. She cast her mind to their first, and only, formal business meeting to date. CJ had instructed her carefully before they arrived. He used little signals each time he wanted her to be by his side. He drew her into conversations, and she bowed out gracefully when required. It was exciting, and she enjoyed every minute.

Harriet had studied CJ with a fascinated eye, seeing his capacity to woo businessmen, becoming enthralled with his game. Was he really the same with women? Had he really tossed Margaux aside for her? Norah was intuitive. Margaux *was* always in the background. CJ would casually drop the odd word about her into conversation. Margaux apparently having a fine arts degree, which he used to his benefit, it was only natural he should talk about her. It was business. But perhaps he had more feelings for her than he knew himself? A rotten thought crept into her head. Did CJ really use Margaux for more than business?

Harriet quickly buried the notion, hoping against hope she was wrong. CJ never made demands, but she dared to imagine what it might be like to share his bed. How exactly would she react if it happened?

Harriet locked the racquet in its press and stored it

in the corner of the room. Gathering all her clothes into a bedsheet, she went to the outhouse and began scrubbing. Without warning, Tom flashed into her head. It seemed Saturdays were always taken by CJ these days. She often found herself wondering what Tom was doing, who he was seeing. Once she found herself walking along the route to Pete's Café and caught herself standing outside, peering in. How absurd. But she missed him and always would.

Harriet sighed, wringing her clothes through the mangle, ready for the line. Thinking about CJ and the world he shared with her was fantastic, and he was wonderful. Maybe she had begun to fall a little in love with CJ and felt comfortable with the thought.

Chapter 36

Harriet checked her tin. The tips were a godsend. She had enough money at last to get her shoes re-soled, buy a new pair for evening wear, and purchase material to make a new skirt. Dotty had told her about a new thrift shop, so she visited it the very next day. There were two beautiful coats in the window. *"The latest creation,"* bragged the display, along with the other coat described as *"distinguished elegance."*

Harriet tried them both and bought the pale green one. It felt more stylish. When the proprietor offered her the handbag to match, she could not resist.

****

Harriet looked out the front window, checking her watch. CJ was late. He was normally fastidious with timekeeping. It didn't matter. She had asked if they could go for a stroll. He agreed. It sounded wonderful. She wanted to spend time just talking with him, desiring far more than clubs or fancy restaurants. Go for a walk? It had never been in her vocabulary when she lived with Nana. Now she loved the freedom of walking around parks away from the fumes of the city.

There was a thud at the door. She opened it. CJ stood there, casting his eye over her. He spoke no word of greeting.

"I've not seen that coat before." She felt pleased. "Looks like some old tat your landlady would wear."

Her eyes burned. "I…"

CJ cut her off. "Harriet, I fancy a flutter. I'm going to Club 59. There are a few deals I need to seal. If you want to come, you'll have to change into something more appropriate."

Club 59, where their relationship began. She never took advantage of the generous membership, knowing it was well and truly out of her league.

"I don't think I'll join you, CJ."

"Very well." CJ looked irritated. Nothing indicated an apology.

Harriet watched CJ get into his car; the engine roared; a second later it died. He got out and looked across the roof. "Another time, Harriet." He restarted the car and shot off, leaving her quietly perturbed.

CJ turned up on Harriet's doorstep unannounced the following evening. He looked rough.

"I'm sorry about last night, Harriet. I was a total cad. How do you put up with me?"

Mrs. Gaffney appeared. CJ had never been farther than the parlor, but Harriet wanted to talk to him in private. It would not do on the front doorstep, or in the garden, where they might be overheard.

"How about we go for a walk, so we can talk?"

"It's beginning to drizzle." CJ appeared odd, his voice edgy, petulant.

"I have an umbrella." Harriet felt uncomfortable with her landlady hovering close by.

"Very well, I'll wait in the car." She deliberately collected her pale green coat and matching handbag, knowing it didn't meet with CJ's approval. *If he says anything, he can go to hell.* Harriet stood there shocked at her fury, then collected an umbrella from the hall stand

and exited, head held high. CJ sat in the car, holding the steering wheel in a death grip. She tapped at the window, and he wound it down.

"Can you put up with my outfit, CJ?" She could've kicked herself but glanced at the sky. "Come on, let's walk, air the cobwebs. It's not raining."

"Really?" He sighed, irritated.

"Yes, really, CJ. Come on."

To her surprise, he got out of the car. They walked along the street, neither speaking until they turned right at the next junction. Half a mile and they would be at one of her favorite parks. No fumes, traffic, or prying ears. Harriet glanced at CJ. His jaw was set firmly, as if he was thinking about something distasteful. They entered through the park gates. A dog bounded by with a huge stick in his mouth, followed swiftly by another dog yapping at his heels. His owner whistled in the distance. The dog obediently bounded back with the little dog still chasing.

Lovers were taking a late evening stroll. The last vestiges of sun played tricks through the clouds and trees, sending a gorgeous pink glow across the heavens. Harriet relaxed.

"Isn't it beautiful?" she began. "I often come here. It helps me think and sort things out in my head."

"It does, does it?" He refused to meet her halfway. "Does it also help sort out business and put money in the bank?"

She was right; he was hurting.

"Money isn't everything, CJ."

"Really!" He sounded angry.

"Do you want to talk about it?"

"Tell me you don't like nights out at the theatre,

201

going for meals, wearing expensive clothes."

"Of course I do, but I can live without those things. I've done so all my life."

"Well, I don't want to live in the gutter."

"I've never considered myself being in the gutter, CJ," she flashed back.

He turned and looked to see the hurt in her eyes. Rage was all she could see in his.

"I'm sorry," he capitulated. "I didn't mean *you're* from the gutter. I've been dreadfully rude. What amazes me is you really wouldn't be bothered if I didn't have a bean, would you?"

"No. Why should it bother me?"

"You're lovely, Harriet. Kind, thoughtful. I don't deserve you. I came to eat humble pie." He glanced at her sideways. "All I've done is manage to ruin things again."

"Tell me what's happened, CJ."

"I like you, Harriet. You care." He shrugged. "You work hard for a pittance and don't expect anything from anyone." CJ stopped and breathed deeply. "Can you forgive me?"

"Nothing to forgive." He caught hold of her hand, placing it in the crook of his arm, a slight smile playing across his lips.

"I'm starving, but you'll need to change out of that coat first."

Chapter 37

Nine thirty. He would be here in fifteen minutes.
They both liked to keep good time; they suited one
another well. Excitement reigned as the Commonwealth
and the rest of the world were informed Queen Elizabeth
had given birth to Prince Andrew, the Duke of York.
Harriet smiled. The child was blessed. He would never
know the meaning of poverty.

She looked at herself in the mirror. CJ had the suit
delivered two days ago. It made her skin look pasty, and
the collar itched, but she wore it as requested, to please
him. Harriet wondered what he planned. CJ wouldn't
offer her a clue. Even now, after being together for seven
short months, he would try to surprise her. Harriet liked
surprises of the good kind, but in the same breath didn't.
Sometimes she worried about how to react to his obscene
generosity. It had to be natural, instinctive, a pleasing
response to make him happy and not to offend. CJ
seemed so easily offended. She wanted to make him
happy. He was generous, kind, thoughtful. Recently he
told her he loved her, complimenting her at every turn.

Harriet walked into the kitchen and poured a glass
of water. Mrs. Gaffney called from the front room, "He's
here. Can't see his flashy car, though."

"Thank you, Mrs. G." Harriet puzzled, frowning.
The doorbell rang, and she opened the door to CJ, as
always smartly dressed. His suit, deep gray, enhanced his

203

eyes. Her Nana would have called him debonair.

"You look wonderful, Harriet, and you're wearing the suit like I told you to." He lifted her hand to his lips. "Perfect."

"Thank you, CJ. Are you going to tell me where we're going?"

"I told you it's a surprise. No more questions. Promise?"

Harriet knew not to argue, and just nodded as he guided her to a waiting hackney cab. The cabbie flicked a cigarette onto the street. CJ opened the door and slid in beside her. As soon as the door shut, he placed his hand tenderly across hers.

"I want to make you happy." CJ put his finger to her lips to quiet her. They drove to the park where she'd taken him the month before. He paid the taxi driver to wait. Taking hold of Harriet's hand, he guided her toward the lake, and, as they neared a large oak tree, he quite suddenly dropped to one knee.

"Are you all right, CJ?"

"Perfectly, and you are perfectly perfect." He withdrew a small box from his jacket pocket. She stared in disbelief. "Harriet Laws, would you do me the honor of becoming my wife?"

"I…" She faltered, astounded.

He opened the box. It contained a diamond ring that caught the early morning sun and sparkled brilliantly.

"I love you, Harriet. You must say yes."

Harriet's immediate thoughts were of Nana, wishing with all her heart she could be there to share her joy. Tears sprang to her eyes—the moment so romantic, so wonderfully perfect.

"Yes. Yes!" CJ placed the ring on her finger, picked

her up, and as he swirled her around, Harriet laughed.

"I have another surprise."

Her mind reeling, confused, she looked between him and the ring. "You do?"

"No time to waste. We're getting married."

"But? What? When…"

"Stop with the questions!" He pulled her along, chuckling, sounding delighted with himself.

"I'll explain once we're in the cab."

"But CJ, don't you want to share this with our friends?"

"No. Besides, they'll understand. Please, Harriet. For me. For us. I have so much to give you. My heart, my soul, my undying love." He placed a lingering kiss on her lips, the web already spun.

"I have a special license."

Harriet, swept along in the moment, wanted to believe everything because she loved him. She would do anything for him. Anything, and CJ playfully pulled her along, as if he would never let go.

****

CJ glanced at Harriet, she with no family. She would be grateful. She worked hard to make ends meet, never expecting anything from anyone. When he plied her with gifts she declined, accepting only when he insisted. Harriet was nothing like the usual, rich, spoilt bitches he bedded. They were selfish and greedy. She was the opposite. She would be grateful for the life he would provide and devote herself entirely to him—his plan already coming to fruition. Smiling contentedly, he wanted all of it. She told him she loved him with or without his money. No one had ever said that to him before. No one had truly loved him before.

The taxi took them to the registry office, and CJ charmingly plucked two witnesses from the street. Afterward, pulling her close, he gave her a deeply passionate kiss on the top steps of County Hall. He felt her shiver in delight and watched her blush deep crimson as car horns blared, honked, and hooted.

"I have another surprise, Mrs. Harriet Rutherford." CJ felt full of an emotion he only ever felt and understood when he sealed a truly successful business deal. Elation. Trying to forget what would come next.

"I can't cope with any more surprises, CJ. Please, it's just too much." Harriet laughed with him, flushed, giddy with excitement, allowing him to guide her into the cab with the witnesses waving them off.

"Please, Mrs. Rutherford, just one more surprise. I promise you will not be disappointed."

"Very well, just one more surprise, Mr. Charles James Rutherford." She smiled at him. "Mrs. Rutherford," she mused, twiddling with her ring that felt just a little too tight. "Mrs. Charles James Rutherford."

The taxi driver nodded, and the journey began.

Chapter 38

Harriet drifted into quiet agreement not to ask questions as they drove out of central London. They held hands, and he kept kissing her. The cabbie, she felt sure, was watching. But today she felt free. If it amused the driver, it most certainly amused her. As they came to suburbia, it reminded her of Lady Carmichael's garden party, and Tom. A flash of sadness caught her heart. She composed herself. She was with CJ; she was married. She was married! And still unable to believe it, it had happened all so quickly. What would Mrs. G say? What would her friends say? She looked at her new husband. CJ looked so complete, so delighted. He was right. Their friends would understand; they would share their joy when she told them. She couldn't wait.

CJ pulled her in close and kissed her again. Her suit collar itched, but a shiver of delightful anticipation ran up her spine. A whole new life was about to unfold. The cabbie pulled into a driveway outside a large, detached house.

"Where are we?" Harriet whispered.

The place was huge. She rubbed the back of her neck where the collar made it sore.

"Wait and see, Mrs. Rutherford." CJ paid the cab and, taking her by the hand, led her toward the steps. She watched in astonishment as he produced a key. He unlocked the door and immediately swept her off her feet, smiling.

"Welcome to your new home, Mrs. Rutherford."

"No, surely not?" She giggled uncertainly.

"Don't you like it?" He looked hurt.

"No—I mean yes, silly. But this surely can't be ours, it's so grand. Can we afford it?"

"Enough!"

Harriet smiled, elated, as CJ carried her over the threshold and kissed her passionately, deeply, insisting she stop talking. Pushing the door closed with his heel, he climbed the stairs with her still in his arms.

Chapter 39

Harriet could not believe they had been married two whole months. Her excitement bubbled over when CJ suggested they celebrate their union with friends, and she began looking forward to Friday. He would not say who would be coming, only to prepare a meal for ten. Harriet, desperate for social stimulation, accepted the order without argument. Being married, living in a beautiful house with a wonderful husband should be everything, she told herself after weeks of housework and pulling weeds. She shouldn't be so self-absorbed, so selfish, but other than general housework and at times being allowed to explore beautiful parks, she missed her friends, and the structure of work.

The only person she'd spoken to since their wedding, other than CJ, was the gardener. She needed to laugh, to share a joke or debate the latest topic. But it rarely happened. CJ was usually irritated when he got home, and she felt it difficult to start a deep, meaningful, conversation—or any conversation, for that matter. There wasn't enough money to visit her friends, either, though she did manage to write them letters, and CJ kindly offered to post them. How she missed the camaraderie and affinity with her friends, old and new. But what puzzled her most was that she hadn't one response to her letters. In fact, thinking about it, there hadn't been any mail, first or second class, since she moved in.

Harriet thrummed her fingers on the work surface, waiting for the kettle to boil. CJ had given her a recipe for a special Polish dish he particularly wanted her to make as part of the celebration. He gave clear instructions where to buy the ingredients, but she had no idea what the meal should look or taste like and hoped she could do it justice. Harriet found Stan, their gardener, in the walled garden, digging the vegetable plot. He downed tools, smiling at her arrival.

"I can't stay today, Stan." The love of gardening was still deeply rooted in her heart, reminding her of Nana. "I've got some shopping to do, and a special meal to prepare." She put a plate of homemade biscuits and a cup of tea on an upturned plant pot.

"Thank you." Stan accepted the tea and biscuits, winking. "Me missus is always tellin' me a woman's work's never done."

****

Six forty-five. CJ had said he would be home by six, latest. It was not like him to be late. His friends would be here by seven. CJ hated tardiness and insisted on perfect symmetry. She double-checked the table. It looked elegant. She'd spent time starching the tablecloth, squaring it neatly, making sure the best china was arranged just so, and polishing the glasses until they sparkled. Everything was flawless and in regimented formation. Stretching the money CJ gave her, she'd managed to buy a bottle of the red wine CJ enjoyed, and placed it on the table, ready.

Harriet stirred the pot and placed the soup tureen on the work surface next to the dessert. The lemon meringue pie would go into the oven when she took the main dish out. Harriet quickly checked the sauce for the Polish dish. To her great relief, it hadn't dried out and tasted good. She heard CJ pulling into the drive and went to open the door.

"Hello, darling, you're late." She planted a warm kiss on his lips and took his coat.

CJ sniffed the air. "Something smells good. I'm starving."

Harriet laughed. "Just as usual, then."

"I've left a bottle of bubbly in the car. Can you get it? I need to wash my hands." She took the proffered car keys.

"How lovely."

"I've so much to tell. Now, off you go." He patted her bottom. Harriet, a little puzzled, worried their friends would arrive and CJ wouldn't be ready, went out to the car. When she returned, bottle in hand, CJ was in the kitchen readjusting the stripe of the tea towels into vertical lines.

"Time is creeping on, CJ. Aren't you going to change?" He laughed, pulling her close, gently nuzzling into her.

"Put the champagne in the fridge. We can have it a little later. Now, how about that meal?"

Harriet pulled away. "But what about your friends, CJ?"

"Oh, didn't I say?" He shrugged. "They can't make it."

"What? All of them? When were you going to tell me?" Harriet felt sick. "All that food—it'll go to waste, and I was so looking forward to the company, the evening."

"Aren't I enough for you, Harriet?" CJ snapped. "I

told you they're not coming, and that's the end of it!'"

Harriet blinked in confusion. There was an edginess, an underlying fury in his voice. Deciding not to question him, she re-set the table for two and brought the soup tureen through.

"You've outdone yourself, Harriet. The table looks perfect."

A deep well of pure disappointment was brewing, but she remained calm. Taking a deep breath, she said, "How's your day been?"

"Excellent," he enthused, picking up a spoon. She watched, hoping, even though her expected guests would not taste it, the meal was up to standard. Instead, CJ continued to eat without comment, right through the second and third course, but between mouthfuls, he talked about Margaux. He outlined the build-up, and how *they* wooed *their* new wealthy client, and how *Margaux* was the *perfect* hostess, and by the time he finished singing Margaux's praises, his eyes were shining with excitement.

"She's such an asset. I don't know what I'd do without her."

Harriet pushed her food around the plate, unable to eat. Margaux! Frustrated, not wanting to cause an argument—but she'd spent so much time, plus all this good food going to waste. Without one iota of thanks. Not one single explanation uttered.

"Perhaps you should have brought Margaux home to celebrate, as no one else could make it?" Harriet smiled brightly but with a link of jealousy wrapped around her tongue.

Margaux was always there, lurking in the background, and in every conversation. CJ's eyes narrowed, ink black.

"I'd love to get involved with your business, CJ. How about it? You know I'm a quick learner."

"Harriet!" CJ's response was sharp. He dropped his napkin and poured himself the last of the wine. "I don't want you to work. You're my wife."

"But—"

"Harriet, we've talked about this." He collected the champagne and glasses, reminding her as he had several times over the past month that he was her husband, he was the provider. But it was such an outdated view. Gauging his mood, she decided she would work on him another time. He raised a glass.

"To Margaux, who helped seal a very lucrative deal." Harriet could have screamed. She refused to raise her glass. He smiled.

"And, of course, to you, Harriet, my wife."

"Perhaps, as I've never seen your business, you could show me around?" Wanting to see exactly what he and the snotty, marvelous Margaux got up to.

"Of course. We'll arrange it soon. Promise." He pressed her to drink more wine. Harriet, already lightheaded, felt unable to decline but knew this would be one of his many broken promises.

"Harriet. I've been studying the painting. You know, the one in the hallway?"

"Yes?" She felt woozy.

CJ had generously agreed she could hang her painting there, and each time she stepped over the threshold it immediately came into view. To her, it looked magnificent.

"Like I said before..." He poured her another glass of champagne and insisted she finish it. "Whilst the painting has no value, it needs to be cleaned. It might improve the look and will definitely help to prolong its life."

"How kind." Her concentration blurred, as a niggle popped into her head.

"CJ? This may sound strange." She strategically placed a piece of lemon meringue pie on his plate. "We don't seem to get any post. I expected to see something drop through the door by now."

CJ dug his fork into the crisp meringue topping and took a bite.

"Ah, there you have me. Didn't I say? The post has been redirected to my business so I can deal with any pressing issues. Why do you ask?"

"I've been hoping to have a response from at least *one* of my friends. It seems odd not one of them has bothered to get back to me."

"If anything were addressed to you, I'd bring it home." CJ patted his lips with his napkin and brushed a crumb onto his plate. "Besides, I didn't know you wrote to anyone."

"But you offered to post them, CJ."

Frowning, he cut her off, placing his hands firmly over hers, so they became trapped beneath. She breathed deeply, the desire to remove herself overwhelming.

"You don't need friends. They can go to hell. We have each other." CJ poured her another glass of champagne. "Drink." The order was explicit.

Her face fell, but having got to the point of inebriation, she found the glassful slid down easily.

"Now, how about afters?"

"But you've just finished dessert, CJ." Her words slurred. Even the cheese had been polished off.

"I don't mean that." He laughed, pulling her out of her chair, grabbing another bottle. She felt giddy, out of control, and could not remember a thing after that.

Chapter 40

Daisy's back yard had been transformed. Tom moved into Daisy's old flat above the bakery, and Daisy moved into the new extension. Everyone helped with the transition from her old home—her furniture arranged just as she asked and her home newly decorated. Daisy was thrilled with the layout. She could walk into the bakery anytime through the connecting door and without requiring help.

The business, growing fast, now employed more staff to compete with the ever-increasing orders. Tom sat in Daisy's front room, a cup of tea in one hand and a list of properties in the other.

"I reckon the bank should see our business plan as a sound investment. We have the books to prove our turnover doubled last year." He handed over the addresses of two more properties he had his eye on.

"What do you think?"

Daisy adjusted the string of pearls around her neck.

"I think you've probably more energy than all of us put together. I like both of your ideas, Tom. Very cleverly thought through." She tapped at the sheet of paper with the estate agent details.

"There are loads of families in this area who need good food at affordable prices." Daisy pointed. "As for the toffs…" Her finger slid to another location as she murmured thoughtfully. "Yes, a posh tea shop and connecting bakery right there would be perfect." She looked at him, smiling brightly. "You've done well, Tom. I knew you would."

"Yes, Harriet said much the same thing." Tom pushed his hand through his hair.

"You two are still talking, then?" Tom quickly rose from his chair.

"I haven't heard or seen her since seeing the newspaper notice of her marriage. Much like everyone else, it seems. Sorry, Daisy, I need to get on." He sounded upset as he strode out the door.

He was right. No one had seen Harriet since Mr. Rutherford handed in her notice.

"A rum affair if you ask me," Daisy said to the four walls.

Chapter 41

"Harriet!" CJ called from the kitchen. His voice rattled her with fear. He would be there, sitting at the kitchen table, insisting she stand by his side. Just like he did every Friday morning. She felt like a schoolchild on detention whilst he counted the change from the housekeeping against the receipts, and Harriet hated it. CJ never performed this ritual in his office, the always locked, forbidden room. His private domain. Harriet had never been allowed to step one foot inside. She bit down on her lip. Her head was hurting. The headaches were getting worse. Her tiredness and confusions worried her.

"CJ?"

"I've been waiting more than five minutes. What have you been doing?" He was tapping the table.

"I'm sorry, CJ, I've a bit of a headache. I wonder, could I sit? I need to ask you a question."

"Very well." He pointed to a chair and leant back, waiting, his hand encircling the large bunch of house keys, studying her.

"Well?" Harriet adjusted her specs nervously. "You know I love you, don't you, CJ? And I appreciate everything you've done. Our home is beautiful. I'm so grateful."

His eyes narrowed. Her heart raced right into her throat.

"I understand you're busy with work. I wondered,

perhaps…" She blurted it out. "I'd like to visit our friends, CJ. Please? May I? We can always go together another time. When you're free? Or maybe we could invite them here, for a cup of tea?"

He shrugged indifferently.

"You'll need to be a much better housekeeper to do that. We can't afford to throw good money after bad."

"I'm trying my best, CJ, but what with the cost of living…" She paused for a second. "Maybe…" She smiled, hoping to plant a seed. "Maybe I could do a little job. It might take the pressure off a bit. What do you think?"

"What are you saying, that I can't support you?"

"No, not at all. I just want to help. Make you happy." Harriet rushed on. "Perhaps if I came with you to work— I still haven't seen your shop. I don't mind doing anything. Maybe cleaning?" The thought of cleaning around Margaux stuck in her throat, but it would be a start. She could keep an eye. "I just think—"

CJ cut her off, his tone sharp. She caught a dark glint in his eye. "You think a lot, don't you, Harriet. We talked about this before. Always asking. Always wanting. Am I not good enough for you?" He shot her a sullen look. "Maybe you should have married the idiot baker. Maybe he would have given you the life you really deserve."

"CJ! Now you're being ridiculous." The words were out before she could stop them. He thumped the table with his fist. The chair scraped loudly behind him. Startled, she rose from her chair.

"I'm being ridiculous, am I? Trying to keep you in luxury?"

"CJ?"

But he was already gone. Out of the house.

219

Slamming the door, speeding out the drive in his MG.

Harriet wrung her hands. This *was* ridiculous. He was being unreasonable. If he didn't want to see their mutual friends, so be it. But she hadn't seen her friends since the day she married him. CJ insisted they should see them together. But time rolled on, and he always found an excuse.

Harriet, frowning, rearranged the ledger and receipts tidily beside CJ's three pens squared against the paper and ledger. CJ was always fastidious, right down to making sure the canned food labels faced outward in cupboards. She shook her head in despair. It seemed no matter how hard she tried, nothing she did made him happy. What was really going on? Gathering her coat, she went for a walk in a desperate attempt to escape her palatial chicken coop and think. Was she being unreasonable? Only once people had been invited to their home, and they declined at the last minute. It was stupid. This argument was stupid.

About an hour later Harriet returned home, no further forward or satisfied she could ever change CJ's mind. He was there, waiting, clearly agitated.

"Where have you been?"

"I just needed some air and a little time to think."

Before she had time to blink, CJ was in her face, glaring, eyes glinting.

"Why can't you just be happy! You make me feel such a terrible husband. Am I not good enough?" He raised her chin with the tip of his fingers. She flinched.

"But then, maybe if you didn't drink so much!"

Harriet frowned, puzzled.

"You've got to get a grip, Harriet. Look what it's doing to you. To us. To me! Why do you think I need to keep a tight rein on our finances, and *you* from our friends? Why do you think you have headaches and are always so sleepy and forgetful?"

Harriet dared not speak. He was wrong on so many levels. CJ suddenly calmed down. His face kinder, more thoughtful.

"Come. Sit here."

Harriet, afraid, did as she was told, and he led her to a chair.

"We have one another, don't we? I'm enough for you, aren't I?" He knelt before her and, putting his head in her lap, begged forgiveness. He promised he was sorry for being cross and promised he would never hurt her.

CJ became more attentive over the coming days. Every morning he rose early and brought her tea in bed. Often it was too strong, too sweet, but she drank it, to please him. On a good day she could get out of bed and manage the general chores or go shopping, and deal with life. On a bad day, she felt too ill, confused, and mostly too weak to get up. It bothered her, but CJ loved her; he told her so. He took care of her, but there was always something she did wrong.

Money became an enormous factor in their lives. Harriet quietly worried, trying to balance the books. Every time she went shopping, she struggled with the little housekeeping money provided and having to prove every penny spent. Even sourcing the cheapest cuts and bartering with the stall holders, the money was never quite enough. Often, she went without food so CJ could eat, saying she'd eaten earlier. All she knew was she needed to be a better wife and better at housekeeping.

Chapter 42

Today, Harriet felt particularly pleased with herself. She'd managed to save enough from the housekeeping to buy CJ a small gift for his birthday. She stood by his side whilst he sat at the kitchen table, holding one of the receipts in the air.

"What's this for?" His tone was dark. Stupid, stupid, stupid. Her mind raced, having quite forgotten to exchange one scavenged receipt for the one he held.

"It was meant to be a surprise." She hesitated. "For your birthday. It's a little early. Shall I get it?"

CJ grunted, but she flew off upstairs, hoping the gift would make him happy. Harriet returned in an instant. CJ looked at the tie. Harriet saw his face contort but didn't read the signs.

"You really expect me to wear this market tat?"

CJ was on his feet before she could blink, yelling in her face. "What a complete waste of money!" He threw the ledger across the room, the receipts floating on the air. A momentary distraction. Then there was complete blackness.

When Harriet came around, she found herself on the floor. Cold. Night was drawing in. She curled in a ball, trembling. After a while, she tried to stand. Her legs wobbled, the world spun, and she passed out. Harriet woke sometime later, somehow wedged between the chair and the kitchen table. She had no idea how long she'd been there. She hurt all over. The room was pitch black. She could hear the ominous tick of the kitchen clock. Reaching out, just able to stand, holding onto a chair, something caught her foot and she shoved it aside. She found the light switch. Five to midnight. Bewildered, she looked about.

There was a half glass of wine on the table and an empty bottle. Harriet could smell alcohol all over her. None of it made sense.

Unsure what to do next, terrified CJ would return at any moment, she gathered her thoughts. There would be no telling what he might do. Unable to move quickly, Harriet found the rolling pin and put it on the table. She needed to be prepared. Shivering. This was awful. Why was she thinking like this? This was not her. Nonetheless, she kept the rolling pin within reach.

CJ returned home long after two in the morning. He woke her from dozing upright. She grasped the rolling pin.

"Good God, Harriet, what the hell happened?" CJ stepped toward her, sounding full of concern. Harriet, thrown by the question, stared, blinking. Her head throbbed; she felt muddled. Had he really forgotten, or was he just toying with her?

"Don't touch me."

He took a step back.

"What's going on, Harriet? What happened? Did you fall? You're always drinking yourself silly and falling over. Now you're about to attack me?" He looked at the rolling pin in her hand. "Harriet, for goodness' sake, what have I done to deserve such treatment?"

Harriet held the pin tight. Her head pounded.

"Come on. Let me help you. Did you bang your

head?"

CJ sounded so reasonable, so honest, so sweet. She wanted to believe him. She wobbled, feeling more bewildered than ever. He took the pin from her.

"Harriet?"

"I don't drink." She stared fearfully at CJ, waiting.

"Harriet, you're obviously muddled. Alcohol affects your memory. It does that." He shook his head sadly. "This is terrible. Why, you can't even remember this same conversation we had last week, can you?" He caught her arm. She winced. "Can you? Come see." He insisted she look in the mirror. There were bags under her eyes, her hair was a mess, and a bruise on her cheek blushed deep purple.

"Heaven knows we can't afford it, but perhaps I should get you to a sanitorium."

"No!" Harriet's mind instantly focused on Felicity Jones-Shaw. She never had managed to speak to Norah about her. She looked at her image again. She didn't drink, did she? She passed out.

When Harriet woke, she found herself in bed. CJ promised her the doctor had visited, saying she should rest. He raised the idea of the asylum again. Harriet wept, promising to be good. She didn't want to go. CJ agreed he would give her one more chance. But he would sleep in the guest room for now, until she got better.

****

Two nights later, a car horn blared, lights blinded. Rain bounced off the road. A car swerved. Harriet looked about, her head in a fog, her clothing saturated, her mind confused. She could just make out she was standing in the middle of the road, the white line leading toward oblivion. How she got there was a mystery. Everything went black.

Harriet's head swam. Her foot hurt. She looked down to see she was wearing one slipper. A man was by her side, mouthing something. A flash of light. A loud pop. Her hearing came back.

"Harriet! Thank God!"

CJ was there, wrapping warm arms about her.

"Where did you find her?" CJ was stripping off his raincoat, talking to someone, a man.

"She was in the road, sir. Seems like she might have fainted. She was lucky not to have been killed. She managed to give me her address." Harriet tried focusing.

"What, where am I?"

CJ placed his coat over her shoulders.

"You've been missing, Harriet. I've been searching for hours." CJ pulled her tightly into his chest, holding her close. The rain continued. CJ was dripping wet. She was soaked, freezing, shivering.

"I was so worried. Thank God you're safe."

"I don't understand…"

CJ's attention diverted to the man. "I can never thank you enough. My wife has been… Here, let me give you something for your trouble." CJ went to his breast pocket. The man coughed, embarrassed.

"No, thank you, sir, I'm just glad to have been of some assistance."

CJ took Harriet home. He helped her get dry and put on fresh nightwear. He encouraged her into bed and got her a hot water bottle and more blankets. The next thing she knew, there were murmurings from downstairs in the hallway. Harriet shivered, listening, horrified.

"Mr. Rutherford, sadly, some women can become a little difficult at times in their lives. A short stay in a sanatorium would be appropriate."

Harriet heard her husband reply, but his words failed to reach her ears. The doctor arrived at her bedside. Grave-faced, he took her pulse without speaking. He turned to CJ, talking over her.

"Her pulse seems to be weak. Luckily, no harm done. But you say you found her in the middle of the road, in this weather, wearing only her nightwear?" CJ nodded, glancing at Harriet. "My recommendation still stands, Mr. Rutherford."

Harriet wanted to crawl under the blankets and die.

"Please. I won't go out again. I promise."

The men traded glances. CJ ushered the doctor from the room. There were quiet exchanges outside. Harriet found herself sobbing. What if she ended up like Felicity Jones-Shaw? Sometime after the doctor left, CJ sat on the side of the bed.

"Please don't send me away, please!" she begged.

CJ shook his head thoughtfully. "I won't consider the sanatorium yet, Harriet." He opened the bedside drawer. There were two small empty bottles of whisky. "The evidence is here for all to see. The alcohol is making you quite mad. I can't keep this up. You have to start thinking about what you're doing."

"I don't understand." Harriet sobbed. "I wake up feeling so tired all the time, but I never remember having a drink."

"Never?" CJ challenged. "You always like to have a drink with me. I think you forget. I was going to suggest we visit our friends tomorrow, but we can't have them see you like this. In fact, you won't be seeing anyone for a while. Understood?"

"Yes."

"Good. Now you need to sleep. The doctor has given you some sleeping powders. I'll sort it out now."

"Yes, CJ."

The following night CJ didn't come home at all.

Chapter 43

There were times when Harriet was sure someone was in the house. A door would click shut. A murmur from somewhere. A cough. A draft of fresh air even when windows were closed. Harriet checked everything, even trying the locked door of the forbidden room. Confused. There was never anyone there.

Standing in front of the mirror, she watched the hot tears trickle down her face. How did it come to this? Their first few months of married life were blissful. They were, weren't they? Yet she knew in her heart it wasn't true. She heard the front door open.

"Harriet?"

"Yes?" She dabbed her eyes. CJ was home early. "Tea's not ready," she called worriedly from the bathroom. "I'll get it now." Terrified, quickly splashing cold water on her face, she rushed to greet him in the hallway and helped him take his coat off.

"No need. We're going out. We have been invited to Club 59."

"We have?"

"Yes. I need you to wear the red dress." There was an air of excitement in his voice.

"The *red* dress?"

"Harriet." He caught her by the shoulders. "Don't question me." Unwittingly she recoiled at his touch. His tone suddenly softened.

"Now, hurry up, get ready. I'll tell you on the way what to do." CJ gave her a playful slap on her bottom. "Just like old times, eh? Farquhar is a lecherous old goat." He raised his brow. "I want you to use your womanly charms."

Harriet walked slowly up the sweep of stairs to the gallery. Her heart plummeted as she considered what CJ was suggesting. She turned to see him unlock the study door. She always wondered what could be so private, so important in there she wasn't allowed to see. What she did know was not to ask.

Harriet picked out the dress from her wardrobe. CJ had brought it home one day. He used to ask her to wear it before they made love. Once upon a time, she didn't mind—it suited her figure and was for CJ's eyes only.

Unsure, hating the thought, Harriet pulled it on. It exposed her cleavage, the length too short. She slipped on the matching red shoes. They were high and gave her legs even more length. The ensemble made her look and feel tarty. Angry and upset at CJ, she vowed no way would she come on to this man Farquhar. Kitten heels would do. She sorted her hair and descended the stairs as CJ locked the study door. He slipped the key into his suit pocket and looked up.

"Are you really sure I should wear this, CJ? Isn't it a little…"

"Sexy?" he finished. "I want you to wear the stilettos, Harriet." He was walking toward her, his tone husky, aroused. "Put them on." Harriet turned to go, but he wrapped his arms about her. "Little wifey." His nose nuzzled into her neck. "You smell good."

Harriet felt confused. He was different.

"Go on, put them on. We have time." Desperately

trying not to show her disgust, she let him guide her toward the bedroom. Finding the stilettos, he slipped them on her one by one. She dared not look or speak. CJ gently pushed her onto the bed. He began kissing her over and over, tenderly kissing her, until she began to relax and eventually gave in to him. They had not made love for such a long time. This was the CJ she once knew. This was the man and husband she wanted, the man she once loved, gentle and kind. Afterward, CJ lay on the bed beside her with a look of quiet satisfaction.

"When are you going to give me babies?"

Harriet stared at the ceiling, shocked, horrified at the thought. To have children, with him? No, never.

"I don't know." The room felt eerily silent. "Would you like me to see the doctor, CJ?" She was planning to see the doctor anyway, to ask for a different kind of help.

"Yes. For once, a good idea." CJ walked to the bathroom. "Come on, you've a job to do." He popped his head back around the door. "Make yourself sexy." He grinned.

Harriet's mind raced. Somehow, she would need to avert any unwanted attention without either of the men being aware. It was all she could focus on.

****

Dorian Craddock always mixed with her guests. Tonight was no exception. She knew CJ would be bringing Harriet. After all, it was her suggestion. Rolling her thumbs one over the other, she contemplated the issue. She had no beef with Harriet, but CJ was becoming a nuisance. He could not resist the charms of the casino, or her "special" girls, but his debts were mounting. CJ bragged he had a piece of fine art she would love that would easily cover the debt. There had been no sign of it thus far. Dorian instructed the doorman to notify her the moment the couple arrived. She would speak to CJ in private.

To Harriet's relief, Farquhar had brought his wife, Anthea, beautifully coiffed, heavily pregnant. Anthea giggled and played coy with her husband, and he looked dotingly on. Farquhar appeared besotted. Harriet, managing a "girlie chat" with Anthea in the powder room, discovered they hoped for a little girl and talked about her husband with such devotion it made Harriet's heart hurt. Anthea truly loved her husband. It was not a show, or about money, as CJ implied. If only her own marriage were the same. Harriet blinked back a tear. How her life had changed. CJ had managed somehow to reduce her to a quivering wreck. Her independence and integrity had been completely compromised. She felt weak, a fraud.

"Are you all right, Harriet?" Anthea stared at her in the mirror, washing her hands.

"Silly me, head in the clouds. Mother Nature's just started."

"Oh, dear, I'm sorry. Never mind. Better luck next time, eh? Let me know, and we can go baby shopping together." Anthea ran her hand across her bump affectionately.

Harriet forced a smile and reapplied lipstick.

"Shall I wait?"

"No, thank you, Anthea. I won't be long." Inside she was screaming. She stared at her pale skin, a stark contrast to the bright red of her dress. Her bottom lip wobbled. She couldn't go on like this.

Harriet followed CJ's instructions to the letter as he worked his magic throughout the night. At the end of the evening, Harriet, eternally grateful for Anthea's presence, felt nothing else except relief. There had been absolutely no need to make a fuss or sell herself to anyone. The evening was a great success, but as they drove away CJ appeared preoccupied. Harriet kept quiet, fearing what might happen once they were home.

As they pulled into the driveway, the car headlights caught the front door. It was partly open. CJ swore under his breath.

"We locked the door, didn't we, CJ?"

"Stay here," CJ told her, hushed, switching the car lights off. Harriet protectively put her hand on his sleeve.

"We should call the police. There's been a spate of burglaries in the area..."

"Don't worry, I can handle myself." CJ disappeared into the gloom.

Harriet shivered. This was stupid, dangerous. Taking her shoes off, holding the heels outward like weapons, she got out of the car and crept toward the house. There was a flashlight in an upstairs window.

"CJ!" she shouted, running barefoot and armed. Suddenly the house lights went on. CJ stepped back outside.

"I told you to stay in the car."

"Are you all right? I saw a flashlight upstairs."

"Did you see anyone?" He looked bothered.

"No, but..."

His shoulders relaxed. "Look, I've checked. There's no one." His voice trailed off. "Seems you were right. We've been burgled. They've even taken that painting in the hallway."

"What?" Harriet dropped her shoes where she stood. "No, not that, please, no!"

"I'll call the police and check around." Ever so gently, he pulled her to him. "Poor, sweet Harriet, looking out for me. It's my job to take care of you." And as he held her in his arms, for the first time in ages she felt safe. Perhaps he could change. Perhaps she could change him. Perhaps she could be a better wife.

Chapter 44

Since the burglary, Harriet felt even more on edge. CJ seemed more relaxed in one way, but his moods remained unpredictable, and she tried hard to monitor his ever-changing behaviors. There were other pressing issues. Whole days could vanish in a forgotten haze, and sometimes she was unable to get out of bed. On those days CJ became the kindest, but Harriet had begun keeping a record detailing dates, times, what she ate, drank, and when she was unwell. Her aim initially was to present her findings to the doctor.

As she read through her notes, a disturbing pattern began to emerge, and increased paranoia crept in. Surely, she must be wrong? After she decided to give it one more week, her records presented the same pattern.

CJ had been bringing her tea in bed. Feeling stupid, idiotic, wondering if the tea held something undesirable, she potted a tiny lavender, taken from the garden. It kept her company on her nightstand, to calm her nerves, she told CJ, so he allowed her to keep it. The pot held two containers, like a magician's prop. Her health improved somewhat since her pot plant genius.

Harriet considered all the facts. She couldn't go on like this. She would leave him but needed to save a little money to do so. She continued acting the way she thought CJ may have expected. Confused, weak, stupid, compliant. She would have won an award if she were on film, but over the weeks, Harriet increased her scavenging. More receipts meant more money in her purse. Every penny would go into her tiny fund.

Harriet, steeling herself, began the daily chores, looking down CJ's newly compiled list.

"Check suits." Harriet loved CJ's walk-in wardrobe, with its feel of shop floor smartness. Fifteen Savile Row suits hung in neat, color-coordinated order. Ties hung in an orderly queue. Soft Italian leather shoes sat soldier-like on racks, and crisp, neatly folded white shirts were in drawers.

Taking each suit to the window, using the daylight, she inspected for the slightest speck of dirt or crease. As a matter of course, Harriet dipped into his pockets, ensuring there was nothing the dry cleaner would find. Her fingers brushed against something. She pulled out a small packet and stared. CJ never used protection. Not with her.

"You pig!" Tears flooded her eyes. "You rotten, stinking PIG!" She flung it across the room. Deep down, though hurt, she had long suspected his infidelity. This just offered proof.

Harriet left the room unable to complete the task. She needed time to calm down, to rationalize her thoughts, before doing something stupid. Moments later, dabbing her eyes, she knew she wouldn't dare confront CJ. Hating herself, her cowardice, she returned the condom to his suit pocket.

To her surprise, in the same pocket, Harriet found a key. She rolled the cold metal over in the palm of her hand, knowing instantly it must belong to the study. The forbidden room. Tears welled. She couldn't carry on like this. So what if she didn't have enough money to survive.

It was time. If Florrie could do it, so could she.

****

Harriet stayed in bed until CJ left, feigning a headache, but he'd hung around much longer than she had hoped for. It was as if he knew. Her heart had become a physical pain in her chest whilst she waited.

Now he was gone. CJ had said he would be home by five. Her watch read three ten.

Harriet had already packed her bag, waiting for the right moment, but she decided on one act of rebellion before she left for good.

Harriet put her hold-all by the back door. Should CJ return home unexpectedly, she could hide it in the glory hole, where the polish, brushes, and mops were housed. He rarely looked in there; he didn't like the smell. She would need only ten minutes to walk to the nearest telephone box. She would supply a different name and address to the operator, should CJ try tracking her down.

Knowing just how fastidious CJ was, she removed all traces of perfume, in case it left a hint. She wore white cotton gloves and socks, lest prints were noted, and wound her hair into a tight bun to prevent the fall of a stray hair.

She would allow herself fifteen minutes, max.

The key turned softly in its cylinder like a well-oiled machine. Her mouth dried as she twisted the doorknob, terrified CJ would come home and catch her in the act. Harriet went to lock the door again, but the key stuck fast. Scared, she jiggled it. At last, it freed itself. Feeling pathetic, she opened the door.

Harriet's eyes danced around the room. The pristine order and masculinity didn't surprise her, but the size of the room was smaller than she'd imagined. A huge

236

fireplace filled one wall. A carved bronze bulldog sat in the hearth. Above it hung a stunning gilt mirror. French doors led to a side path. In front of them stood a large leather-topped desk. To the left of the room were floor-to-ceiling shelves, stacked full of books. She stared, stunned. Once, just once, she had asked CJ to take her to the library, and she'd suffered the consequence. Why, she could not fathom. But all this time these magnificent works were here, right under her nose. Why would he want to prevent her reading such treasures? None of it made sense.

Harriet moved along the shelves, reverently touching the spines in blissful awe. Even first editions! The more she looked, the more she discovered. Harriet lifted slightly the volume of *Little Women*, her heart beating unevenly, her mind flashing back to happier days as a young girl sitting with her Nana, reading this very story from a treasured birthday gift. She still had the copy, hidden in the bottom of her bag.

On one of the lower shelves, Harriet came across a collection of Dickens' novels. One caught her eye, sitting incongruously between *Bleak House* and *Great Expectations*. Astonished, she saw the title of *A Tale of Two Cities* had been spelt incorrectly. Instead of *Tale*, it read *Tail*. Puzzled, she paid closer attention. Curiosity getting the better of her, she tried pulling it out. It wouldn't budge. Baffled, she tried again and felt a jolt under her fingers. Part of the bookshelf swung open, exposing a room beyond.

Harriet stared, disbelieving, into the darkness. She'd heard of priest holes. This house was certainly old enough to have one, but this surely was a modern adaptation.

Twelve minutes left.

Harriet found a light switch and flicked it on. She shuddered. "My God!" There were three of the four paintings stolen at the time of the burglary. Nana's painting was not one of them. Stunned, she turned to go but found the entrance had silently closed behind her, trapping her inside.

The light went out.

Panic-stricken, bile rising, Harriet tried to calm herself. Think! Fumbling along the wall, eyes adjusting to the dark, she noticed a thin drizzle of light seeping in from the study, filtering between shelves. Harriet peered through. To her astonishment, she found the whole of the room could be viewed from her exact position. CJ could come and go as he pleased, through the side gate, unnoticed. Maybe that was why she'd heard noises in an otherwise empty house. Maybe she wasn't paranoid after all. But why? Shuffling along the wood paneling at last, she found the light switch, hoping, praying. To her utter relief, the door slid open.

Seven minutes left.

Adrenalin took over fear. Harriet began studying the ornate desk with CJ's trademark. Three pens arranged in soldier-like order on the left-hand side of a blotting pad, and a sheaf of writing paper squared perfectly against it. The Bakelite telephone sat on the left of the desk, and on the right an art deco table lamp. Harriet began testing each of the four drawers. They were locked. Next, she ran her fingers along the bottom of the desk, searching for a key. Getting down onto all fours, she looked at the underside. Harriet saw a black revolver holstered securely under the desk and, stunned at the find, hit her head in a scramble of desire to get out from under.

Shocked, she shakily crawled out, wondering why on earth CJ needed a gun.

Now more determined than ever, she wanted to discover if there were any more secrets—and why CJ felt the need to control her.

Harriet checked quickly around the room, searching for the key to the desk. Nothing gave itself up. She returned to the desk.

There were little acorns carved into the wood running along three sides. She twisted and pressed each one. Frustratingly, nothing happened. About to give up, Harriet noticed one of the carvings looked more worn than the rest. It wobbled slightly under her touch. She pushed the carving harder, and to her absolute astonishment, a secret drawer slid open. She checked her watch.

Five minutes.

Noting its exact position, she took a notebook out of the drawer, and very carefully opened it. The pages were listed in immaculate handwriting with rows of names, some famous, others not so much. Appalled by its explicit content, she felt ashamed and sickened. How could he? Her husband, of all people? There were dates against each one, and odd little numbers against some of them that made no sense whatsoever. She puzzled for a second and started to put the book back but instead put it on the desk, then gingerly removed two envelopes from the drawer, almost expecting them to burst into flames.

Three minutes left.

Harriet cautiously slid the contents out of one envelope. Inside was a life insurance policy folded into thirds. She quickly scanned the pages. A nauseating well pushed up from her stomach and into her mouth. The policy outlined should she die before she reached twenty-one, CJ would receive a quarter of a million pounds. The signature on the bottom was hers, wasn't it? But she didn't remember signing such a document. Shakily she opened the second envelope. It held something far worse. Photographs. Horrified, disgusted, mortified, it took only a moment to realize where and why they must have been taken. In the wrong hands they could easily ruin the lives of so many. Harriet knew right then there would be no way she would leave any of it behind.

One minute.

Harriet quickly gathered everything up and was just about to leave when she noticed one of the pens slightly out of square. She heard CJ's car pull into the driveway.

No time!

Harriet raced to the door, put the key in the lock, and tried to turn it.

It stuck fast.

Panicking, wiggling, thumping, she found it resisted all efforts. She could hear the car door slamming.

Yes! She pulled the key out.

Grabbing her bag, she ran.

Chapter 45

Thank God for the secret garden. Thank God for the secret door hidden behind a wall of ivy. Thank God CJ hated nature. Thank God for Dotty's connections. Though Harriet's journey had thrown scares her way, in the main it was amazing. The people involved so far never asked questions, requested payment, or looked at her in the way she'd felt they surely would. After all, it had been her fault, hadn't it? She must have been a rotten wife.

The last ride of her journey had been in a beat-up old truck, trundling along a narrow lane.

"What on earth's that smell?" Harriet covered her nose, trying hard not to breathe in.

"What?" Albert Hannam sucked on his pipe, trying desperately to keep it alight and his truck out of potholes. "Me baccy?"

"No. Not that, the other smell. I can almost taste it." She grimaced. Albert gave up on his pipe with a smirk on his face.

"Ah, that'll be the cows, miss." Harriet wound the window up. "You'll get a lot of that around 'ere." He was laughing at her. "Best you get used to it. Besides, it's good fer yer lungs."

They arrived at a large farmhouse. It looked like it had stood there for centuries with its array of outhouses and barns falling apart.

Alice Hannam, his wife, was already at the door and greeted Harriet with the friendliest of hugs and the scent of earth and new-mown grass on her. It would be one Harriet would soon come to recognize and love.

"Back to business, then." Albert waved and climbed onto the tractor and set the engine running.

Harriet guessed Alice must be around fifty. She wore a crossover pinny, and a beret hiding any suggestion of hair.

"Come along. I want you to meet Violet." She walked her through to the kitchen. Along the hall hung countless sepia and black-and-white photographs. Alice caught Harriet's curiosity. "They were my little angels." She smiled fondly, touching one of the photos. "Evacuees brought here during the war. That one's Harry. He wet the bed something awful to start with, poor little mite. Didn't half miss his mummy." Alice had pointed to a sweet little boy before naming every child. "'Course they can't come back here, not while we have 'guests.'" Her comment caught Harriet by surprise. "And these are my land army girls." Alice pointed to the photograph of a group of five young women.

"What a laugh they were. They soon grew up, livin' 'ere, I can tell 'e. Some of them 'ad never seen a cow before, let alone worked on a farm." She had a crackly laugh that caught in her throat, making her cough. "But they were good girls, and in the end worth their salt."

They looked so young, and Harriet imagined a life here, far away from towns. Far away from smog. Like her painting, which was lost forever. This was a new beginning. She had to keep telling herself that. Praying, hoping she would be safe.

The kitchen was large, basic, functional, with huge flagstones as the floor. Under the window, a china sink was housed next to a long wooden draining board. An open door exposed a huge larder at one end, and an Aga stretched across the back wall, giving off comfortable heat, with an enormous kettle set on top and on the boil.

Harriet would soon learn that kettle was always hot, ready for a brew at any time. It reminded her of Daisy's Bakery. She swallowed, a sweet memory of a lifetime ago. A young girl looked up from rolling pastry on a huge table that seated ten. The girl smiled. She had a streak of flour across her face and quickly put her rolling pin down to brush flour from her hands onto her apron. Harriet thought she must be Alice's daughter.

"I'm Violet. I'm going to be your buddy." Harriet couldn't help but stare. She was incredibly young, and there was a hint of wild animal about her.

"I'm Bunty." Harriet smiled back, saying the name given to her on a scrap of paper along with strict instruction never to give away her true identity. The name Bunty had instantly reminded her of her childhood and the magazine for girls.

"You and Violet are our newest recruits," Alice said kindly. "I'm sure she'll help you settle in."

Harriet gaped, shocked the child was not Alice's daughter at all.

"Everyone pulls their weight on the farm. You'll be given a list of chores, and what you don't know you'll pick up soon enough."

Harriet would have done somersaults if Alice asked her to.

"We get up at four thirty and go to bed at seven, latest. Unless you can last longer." Alice laughed.

Four other women were guests at the farm. Each was introduced at the dinner table, but none of them spoke much, and Harriet felt unnerved by the lack of chatter. They shared the loft, fitted out with slatted bunks. Without electricity or the facility of a toilet close by, each woman had a potty and a candle. That night, her first night, Harriet carried a large stick she'd found in the yard and took the top bunk above Violet. No one questioned why. It lay by her side, a weapon if needed. She stared up at the ceiling, listening, trying to relax, trying to adjust herself to the very heart of the farmhouse.

The house seemed to have a life of its own. Every sound, every movement seemed to share the very air she breathed. Everything scared her. Every single creak sent a bolt of fear right through to her toes. What if CJ found her? What then? The occasional cow mooed from somewhere outside. A squawking of hens followed by the howling of dogs. There was a permanent smell. Not just cows and a sooty bonfire, but a strange whiff of cooking cabbage. It eased into the loft and hung there, submersing itself into her consciousness.

The women were already asleep. She could hear them breathing, turning over, moaning in a dream—or a nightmare perhaps. How could she ever sleep again? How could these women sleep? It was a misnomer. Surely, they should be as scared as she.

About an hour after the candles were blown out, Harriet heard another new noise. She froze, not daring to move. Her eyes had already adjusted to the dark, her ears now on high alert. The hairs on the back of her neck prickled. Was that the loft ladder creaking? Gripping her stick, she waited. Nothing. She continued to wait for what seemed an eternity, not daring to move an inch. Not wanting to give away they were there. Silently she begged no one move, turn over, or rustle a sheet. Though too frightened to get up and investigate, in her head she promised to sound the alert if necessary. Time passed. Nothing. Only the sound of the women in the room. She would remain on duty all night if need be. Eventually her lids became heavy, and though she tried to fight it, fatigue very slowly won over.

The second and third nights, Harriet tried putting order to the sleeping women. She determined the gentle snorer must be Violet, as the sound came from right beneath her. Another noise, Joy perhaps, a light raspy breath. Some of the women mumbled or cried out in their slumber, perhaps in nightmares from a memory or fear. She understood that fear. No one complained or spoke of it, but always Harriet remained on guard, terrified CJ would find her.

By the second week, Alice suggested Violet show Harriet around the village and maybe take her to the park. But even with little Violet by her side and the stick in hand, Harriet found herself jumping at the slightest sound. The distant rumble of an engine. A van door slamming, a car backfiring, a dog barking. She was on perpetual lookout. Violet made it clear she didn't like walking and would much rather be back at work in the warm kitchen. To Harriet's relief, they returned far sooner than anticipated.

It took a while for the women to accept Harriet. To her surprise, she discovered they were afraid. Afraid of her! Frightened she might be there on false pretenses, gathering information to take back to those they ran from. That night, her third week, shattered from milking cows, cleaning out the shed, sweeping the yard, and loading the milk vans, she realized just how lovely it would be to sleep. All she wanted to do was put her head on the pillow, close her eyes, and relax. But, for the first time, the women began to talk a little about themselves, sharing a morsel of their lives and their terrible experiences. It seemed to help. Talking. A gentle sigh. An understanding. Everyone listening, allowing their voices to be heard.

The following night, as they climbed into bed and each candle had been extinguished, Joy spoke in whispered hushes, sure she should return home. She'd made a mistake. Her husband wasn't so bad. He didn't mean it.

"Don't be daft," snapped Violet. "You know you're being stupid! From what you've said, if you go back, heaven knows what he'll do to you."

"I'd kill mine, given half the chance," said Doreen from across the next bunk, in a fit of pique. "I've lost my whole life because of him. I'm too terrified to even see my mum and sisters, just in case he finds out and does something awful."

"It seems no one's interested in battered women," piped up Phyllis from the bottom bunk under Doreen. Harriet heard a rustle. "Sorry, girls, can't hold it in anymore." She began to piddle. "No one knows where I am. No one cares." It was as if the thought had just occurred to her, and she began sobbing.

"Don't give him the satisfaction, Joy. Remember Ruth Ellis? Poor cow, getting hung. And for what? Him having an affair and kicking her in the stomach when she was pregnant! That was a miscarriage of justice if ever there was one."

"I would have got him drunk, and when he was out cold, I would have cut his bits off," said Violet.

"Strong words from a little 'un." Phyllis laughed. "But you're right."

The room fell silent. A sense of solidarity settled on them. Clearly, none of them had forgotten the story of Ruth Ellis, even five years on.

A month went by. Harriet felt a little surer, braver. Perhaps she could move on. Maybe try and take a step away from the farm, after chores, on her own. She would check with Alice first. With clenched fists, determined not to be afraid, or beaten, Harriet told Violet she didn't expect her company. After all, she could try the lane on her own first, see how she felt. The village was only about a mile farther. She would have the stick. The park was just a stone's throw from the village. She met no argument from Violet.

Harriet delved into her bag. Now was the time. She pulled out the hateful photographs she'd found in CJ's secret drawer and shredded them into tiny pieces and dropped them into the cesspit. It felt good, right. They would never see light of day again. CJ couldn't do anything with them now.

Harriet knew her next step must be to write fifteen letters. Dorian Craddock and Lord Sutcliffe, QC, would be amongst the recipients.

She would need to wrap and post one small parcel. The letters, once posted, would hopefully help set them free. Free from the fear of blackmail. Freedom was a gift, something she once took for granted. Now she would cherish every second.

The afternoon held a chill, but as she picked up the pace, Harriet felt warmer and lighter with every step.

The rain had fallen, leaving the smell of new mown grass, pungent, fresh, and light. As the sun warmed the earth, she could almost touch its woody scent. Harriet smiled. She even loved the smell of cows these days. No longer did she feel so in awe of their giant bodies, or frightened when they stumbled or kicked in the stalls. She had quickly learned their personalities and treated each beast with respect. Harriet could see skylarks, and a blackbird hopped between dead leaves. They were free. Perhaps, at last, she could be free.

Having finally managed the lane, she visited the post office and spent all her paltry savings on the task. It was worth every penny. Kate. To her dear friend Kate she entrusted the notebook. Kate would heed her instructions. Harriet felt a rush of energy, the sensation long forgotten. She loved walking.

A stray tear fell as she walked back to the Hannams' farm. For all her newfound freedom, she so desperately wanted to remember when things were good between her and CJ. Instead, all she could recall was loneliness and dread.

Chapter 46

Harriet arrived at the children's park. Beautiful shadows cast themselves upon lush green, rolling hills. Her vision of the countryside, and Nana's painting, had not let her down. Except for sheep dotted far away on the hillside, Harriet was completely alone. This place, this countryside, was idyllic. It both pleased and surprised her that in the last few days something had changed in her. She did not feel quite so scared nor looked over her shoulder quite so often at every unusual sound.

Harriet cast her eyes around the field as she walked the park's perimeter. Even in the half-light she enjoyed the abundance of colors, with leaves of green turning to reds, yellows, umber, and gold. Her mouth pursed. She would need to make her way back soon. Dusk was beginning to settle, but first she would sit on the park bench, just for a second or two.

Harriet briefly closed her eyes, imagining Florrie and her children. How they would have loved it here. She hoped they were safe in their journey to a new life. Time. Time perhaps would allow her freedom to breathe easy.

"Hello, Bunty." Her eyes flew open.

"Dear God, Violet, you frightened me half to death! Where did you spring from?" Violet shrugged.

Harriet still couldn't believe Violet could be any

older than fifteen. No more than a tiny scrap of humanity, her eyes constantly wide, fearful. God knew what had happened to her.

"You don't come from around these parts, do you?"

"No. Perhaps I'd better start working on my accent?"

"Nah, it's posh. I like it." Violet sat beside her, scanning the park with its two lonely swings, her eyes lingering on the witch's hat. "Don't have any fags, do you?"

"No. Besides you're too young." Violet laughed at that. She began singing. She did that, it seemed, when she was worried. "You've a good voice, Violet."

"I'm lucky. Alice lets me listen to her boy's records. This one's really catchy, isn't it?"

Harriet nodded. "What's up?" Violet wouldn't go for a walk just for the sake of it.

"It's Joy."

"Why, what's happened? Is she all right?"

"She can't be right in the head. She's left a note. Gone and run back to her bleedin' husband. Thinks he'll be lost without her."

"What! When did you find out?" Harriet pushed her glasses back up her nose.

"Not long. I've come to get you. We've been told to lie low. If we get word, we might have to move on." They looked at each other desperately, and clasped hands.

"Don't worry. Joy's not *that* stupid."

"She must be. I'd rather kill myself than let my bleedin' shit of a father get hold of me again."

"Come on, Violet." Harriet gave her hand a squeeze. "We'll be fine," she said, but a sense of unease settled in the pit of her stomach, and they began making their way back past the large houses surrounded with laurel and rhododendron, keeping them private. She wondered how their owners felt about the growing cluster of prefabs recently built not far away, then heard a dog growling close by. It never showed itself.

The lane led them directly back into the tiny high street. Wednesday was half-day closing. Everything was long closed. They were about a mile from the farm. Cottages lining the road had already pulled their curtains against the dying light. But there was the glow of a lamp in a top window, and a shadowy figure moving around.

"I had no idea it was quite so late, Violet. I'm sorry making you come for me." Violet did her usual shrug. It was then Harriet caught a movement from the corner of her eye. She glanced across and saw a woman on the other side of the road. Her throat dried. Surely not! Please, dear God! She found herself quickening her step, pulling Violet along.

"Come on, or they'll be sending out a search party." Violet's left foot stumbled over the other as Harriet gathered pace.

"Bunty?"

"They'll start worrying, like I said. Let's get a move on." Was she being paranoid?

"Harriet!" Her instinct was to flee. "Harriet Rutherford."

"Violet. Hurry home! Please. Tell them."

"Bunty?"

"Just do as you're told. Go!" Violet shook her head. "Violet. Please! Tell Alice?" Harriet squeezed her hand. "Sing one of your fast songs and run like the wind!"

Harriet turned slowly. Her heart plummeted right to her toes.

"Margaux?" How she wished she had been wrong.

"Well, well. Haven't you been a naughty girl?" Margaux's heels clicked along the pavement.

Harriet glanced over her shoulder at Violet's fast-disappearing figure. "How did you find me?" Harriet scoped out the street, looking for CJ.

"I didn't. Dorian did." Margaux pulled out a letter from her handbag. "I don't know what you've been up to, but according to CJ, you have something of his, and he's not happy."

"I don't know what you're talking about." Harriet held her nerve.

"Look. Dorian pulled out all the stops to find you before *he* does." Margaux tugged at her gloves. "Give me whatever it is, and you can go back to your simple country life and be the bumpkin I always thought you were."

Harriet glared.

"Come on, Harriet." Margaux's tone softened. "It's getting cold. You can read the letter in my car, work this out."

"I don't trust you. After all, you never stopped sleeping with my husband, did you?"

Margaux's jaw slackened. "You knew?"

"You've just confirmed it."

"He should have been mine," Margaux whined.

Harriet bit her lower lip angrily and played for time. Something didn't feel right. She shivered. Why would Dorian send Margaux, of all people? She knew they weren't on the best of terms.

"Tell CJ I don't know what he's after. Tell him I

don't have anything except the clothes I stand in."
Margaux sighed.

"Get in the car. Read the letter."

"Where is he?"

"Who?"

"CJ!" snapped Harriet.

Margaux sniffed. "Um, I'm not entirely sure."

Harriet's mind worked furiously. "All right, you
win. Give me the keys."

Surprisingly, Margaux handed them over.

Harriet turned them over in her palm. Maybe,
hopefully, Violet would be back by now. Maybe
someone would come. She shivered again.

"Hello, wifey." Her blood ran to ice as, from
behind, a nose of cold metal dug into her temple. "Not
a sound, or you're dead." She nodded.

"Move!" CJ was pushing her toward a car in a side
street.

"Margaux, you drive." CJ bundled Harriet into the
passenger side, slammed the door, and climbed into the
back seat.

"I'm so sorry. I had no choice," Margaux
whimpered, sliding into the driver's seat beside her.

"Shut up!" CJ growled, pushing the gun against
Harriet's head again. "You're going to give back what
belongs to me. Now!"

"I don't know what you mean." He closed his hand
tightly around her throat. White noise began drowning
out his words.

"CJ, she can't breathe!" Margaux tried prizing his
fingers off.

"Stop it, bitch!" CJ slammed Margaux's face with
the butt of the gun. She instantly recoiled, screaming,

her nose bloody.

Still holding the car key, Harriet jabbed it hard into the back of CJ's hand. He yelled and slapped the side of her face with the gun. Her eyes popped. The keys flew from her grasp.

"You know what I want. Don't make me ask again. Do. You. Hear?" CJ held the gun to her head again.

"Yes. I hear you." Harriet choked, her mind trying to work through the haze. She couldn't tell him what she'd done.

"I don't have it. Not here. Not on me!" Her mind began gathering momentum.

"Where, then?"

"It's with a solicitor. Should anything happen to me, he is to hand everything over to the police. He is bound by law. You will be exposed." She reasoned there wouldn't be a hope in hell with any other story. Margaux was still crying and trying to stem the flow of blood.

"Shut up. I'm trying to think!" With the weapon no longer at Harriet's temple, very slowly, she reached for the door handle. To her surprise, at that very moment Margaux lashed out at CJ. It provided Harriet with a vital distraction. She fell out of the car, stumbling, sobbing, and began running.

Running for her life.

Chapter 47

Harriet prayed dusk would be her savior. She heard a branch crack. Felt a hornet sting. A searing pain. A bloom of warm liquid ran from her shoulder. Faltering, she stumbled forward. She could hear the pounding of leather on ground. She pushed herself on, not daring to look back, praying Margaux was all right.

"You will give me what I want, or I'll kill you!" CJ panted. In the distance, an engine turned over. Moments later car lights streamed along the lane. Ghostly shadows from hedgerows loomed. A startled bird flew across her path. Harriet floundered. She could hear short rasping breaths closing in on her. The roar of an engine. Then, one perfect moment of silence before a sickening thud. She glanced over her shoulder. Something dark flew high into the air. It landed, not five feet away. Heavy. Deadweight. A body. A wheeze. A gurgle. CJ, splayed starfish, his joints at impossible angles.

The car continued to head straight at her, lights blinding, brakes squealing. It slewed left. Harriet leapt right. Hawthorn tore into sinew. The car missed her. It skidded into the ditch, backside up, headlights buried. Engine running, wheels spinning. Harriet smelt fuel. With all her strength she heaved herself upright, wrenching painfully from the grip of thorns, and hobbled toward the car. A gust of wind. A flame.

Harriet didn't hear herself screaming. She managed to lever the passenger door open. It felt, oh, so heavy. In the gloom she could just make out Margaux's silhouette straddling the steering wheel, with her head smashed against the front screen.

"Wake up! Get out!" Harriet screamed, but Margaux was out cold. Harriet reached to grab her, dragging, pulling, anything to get her out. Pain seared through her shoulder.

"For God's sake, help me!"

Margaux's coat caught on the gear stick.

"Help me, someone, anyone!" She kept tugging, pulling. A rip. Flames were growing, licking out from the engine.

Margaux groaned.

"Come on, Margaux. Please, wake up, come on! Help me. Hurry!" Dead weight. Margaux passed out with a sigh, but Harriet managed to hook her hands under Margaux's armpits and pulled hard.

She should be light, but she was oh, so heavy.

The distant sound of an engine rumbling...hefty machinery...a tractor, maybe? Margaux was now half in, half out of the car. The flames were rising higher. Then voices.

Harriet's eyes rolled.

Chapter 48

Harriet found herself in hospital. A doctor with his stethoscope and an army of white-coated medical students attentively circled her bed. Her head pounded. Questions came and went. Confusion.

The doctor spoke. Her eyes swam, and everything went black.

A nurse. Her face passive, taking Harriet's pulse, a thermometer under tongue.

"How are you feeling?" Her expression kind, professional. Harriet was bewildered, disoriented. The glass mercury stick bobbed up and down.

"Where am I?"

"Hospital. You've been in the wars. Do you remember what happened?"

Tears welled. "My husband?"

Matron glanced across at two men standing in the doorway, one in a smart gray suit and trilby, the other a uniformed policeman. "The police have been waiting." She looked on her sympathetically. "I won't let them in if you're not ready." All Harriet wanted to do was block everything out, but those last few moments kept repeating themselves, over and over. She tried sitting up in bed. A searing pain shot through her left shoulder. She felt woozy.

"Bowl!"

A nurse arrived, too late.

"I'm so sorry."

"Better?"

Harriet nodded, compliant, still heaving. "Sorry," she said, wiping her mouth between gagging.

"You've been shot. You're bound to feel uncomfortable, and most likely lightheaded from the anesthetic." She poured a glass of water and handed her some pills.

"Shot?"

"Take these. They should help." The nurse returned with a sand pail, bucket, and mop and quickly commenced cleaning. Matron observed Harriet as she swallowed the pills, marking something on a clipboard.

"Seems you were lucky. Another inch to the left and it would have severed an artery." Another wave of nausea.

"Lady Sutcliffe?"

"I understand she's in a stable condition. She's in a private room. I'm sorry." Matron looked toward the door to the waiting policemen. "I really can't answer any more questions. You will need to speak to them."

All Harriet wanted to do was block everything out.

She caught a view of a man, later known as Detective Fielding, speaking to Matron. He appeared to listen, then stepped away, acknowledging he would need to return as soon as commonly decent. He would be back tomorrow. Matron advised she would be required to identify a body. When she was ready.

The following day, Detective Fielding returned. It appeared there would be no respite. Shakily, Harriet agreed to his request. Matron organized a nurse to help her into a wheelchair. Harriet was unsure if her lack of feeling was from grief, confusion, horror, or fear.

Detective Fielding followed behind the nurse and porter as she was wheeled to the bowels of the hospital. The mortuary. Fittingly quiet. There was a side room. A viewing pane closed off with a curtain. The brakes on her wheelchair were applied, and the nurse placed a kindly hand on her good shoulder. Detective Fielding stood behind Harriet whilst the nurse murmured something as the curtain was pulled back.

Nothing could prepare her. Harriet stared as the pathologist very carefully exposed part of the face. The limitation was for her benefit, of that she was sure. She could only imagine what terrors must lie beneath the rest of the sheet. Yet she knew the full extent of CJ lay there. Not moving. His once-handsome face bruised, scuffed, translucent gray. The world around her spun. More terrible memories flooded back. A violent end, to end all the violence.

A simple nod to acknowledge her husband, and Detective Fielding followed them back to the ward.

Patients, women on all sides, bored, now stimulated by police presence, could only speculate, nodding at one another, their eyes following with interest. With the curtains drawn around her bed, the nurse provided Harriet with pills, "To help you to relax," and left.

Detective Fielding remained and began with what sounded like an insincere apology. He wanted to close the matter as quickly as possible. First, he needed confirmation the body was indeed her husband. Then he softened his approach, once again apologizing before asking more difficult questions.

Harriet knew there was only so much she could share, but just how much? How would it benefit the police? Her husband was dead. She was embarrassed by her married life, ashamed of it. Yet, whatever she felt about CJ, she didn't want him dead, or the notebook in police hands. Harriet, eventually worn down, provided an account of her actions. Her reasons for running away elicited, her husband's unreasonable behaviors exposed. Even in her delirious state, the probing questions began to build a picture of something she had not considered. The detective's face betrayed his thoughts. And all the while he took notes.

Why Lady Sutcliffe? What was her involvement?

No, she didn't wish her husband dead.

Yes, Lady Sutcliffe was a friend to her husband. They were in business together.

No, she would not consider Lady Sutcliffe her friend.

Yes, she suspected there may have been relations between her husband and Lady Sutcliffe.

Yes, of course she was a terrible wife.

No, she had not told anyone she was running away.

Detective Fielding's questions were relentless, but his interrogation culminated in one simple suggestion. "You planned your husband's murder all along, didn't you?"

Dear God! The detective suspected she planned her husband's death? It was an accident! Exhausted, completely overwhelmed at the suggestion, Harriet stared in horror at Detective Fielding. How could he even think it?

Yes, she might be guilty of running away from her abusive husband. Yes, she was guilty of not making her husband happy. Yes, she prayed her husband would never find her. No, she didn't own a gun. No, she had not been behind the wheel of the car that killed him.

Why were they not looking to Margaux for answers? Harriet felt dread. The same dread and anxiety she'd experienced throughout her short but hateful marriage. So much for the miniscule belief that one day she might deserve to be happy, or at the very least might experience an existence again without CJ.

Now fear gripped Harriet's heart. Margaux had money, power, and the legal world at her fingertips. Harriet's fear for her own life had just about kept her alive during her miserable marriage. Now, one fear replaced another.

Harriet shook her head. She could never forgive CJ for his behavior, but she'd never wanted him dead. Only Margaux could truly help her prove her innocence. A rage began to build. How dare the detective make those assertions! How dare he press her for so many details when she had been victimized all along. No! She would not be bullied into submission. Never again!

Harriet raised her hand. Her words slurring, she could no longer think straight. At that moment she would have gladly closed her eyes never to wake. Matron was at her side in an instant, her savior, ushering the detective away. She lay back on her pillow, tears staining white cotton.

The next morning, Harriet woke to the clatter of a tea trolley. A new nurse was on duty, taking her temperature, marking notes on the chart. More medication, checking her wound, the agony still raw.

Harriet found she wore a hospital gown. When she moved, the back let a draught in where it hung loosely, and the ties had come adrift. She asked the nurse if she could borrow a dressing gown to maintain her dignity.

She also asked for pen and paper. Whilst her shoulder might be injured, she could still write. Her dominant hand remained strong, and her mind had to be supple. She would have to start fighting for her life now, but in an entirely different way.

With pen and paper in her dressing gown pocket, Harriet took her first tentative steps from bed and began to furniture-walk to the visitors' room. She wobbled, slightly woozy, but continued and acknowledged those who were awake, watching her progress, giving her encouragement. At the back end of the ward, the small visitors' lounge remained empty. Exhausted, but glad of her achievement, Harriet closed the door behind her. The room smelt of stale tobacco, but it was private, a place away from the distraction of sick women, rattling trolleys, and medical matters.

Her mind drifted. Shaking her head. Harriet began bullet-pointing her movements, starting from her first recollection of meeting CJ, Lady Sutcliffe, and Dorian Craddock. They were all strangely linked one way or another, even Kate. But Kate was the one person in all this whom she trusted implicitly. Harriet pondered the minutia of her marriage. Perhaps she could elicit some specific detail from her memory that would give her a clue how to sort this sorry mess out. Surely, somehow, if not Margaux Sutcliffe, then someone or something could prove her innocence? The notebook could not be used. It would tear too many lives apart. She had only kept it to protect herself from CJ. Then there was the life insurance policy, shredded along with the photographs.

Harriet rested, gulping, holding back tears. No two ways about it. Everything she wrote told a story that compounded one simple thing—she would be better off without CJ being alive. Just like the detective implied, she would look guilty to a room of jurors. If she even began to suggest her husband was drugging her, there would be no proof. It would make her sound paranoid, a liar, completely mad, or a combination of all three. There was no alternative. She asked to see Lady Margaux Sutcliffe.

Chapter 49

The following day, Detective Fielding returned with his interminable questions. He revisited her statement and gave nothing away. When he finally left, she felt shattered.

Harriet looked around, trying to recount in her head the days spent at the hospital. She eased herself to a more comfortable position just as the nurse arrived.

"Nurse, could you tell me what day it is?"

"It's Thursday, dear."

More than a week had passed already.

"You have another visitor. It's Lord Sutcliffe. He's requested a private room. But not before I've finished my duties, and only if you are up to it." She immediately popped a thermometer under Harriet's tongue. "You're doing surprisingly well. I bet you'll be glad when you can go home."

Harriet's eyes glazed over. The mere mention of home rang hollow. Where would she go? Not there. Not to the house where she and CJ had lived. The memories were too raw.

****

Lord Sutcliffe, QC, was nothing like she'd imagined. He was a much kinder version of his daughter, Margaux.

"I understand you saved my daughter's life. I can never thank you enough."

"I think, in the end, we saved one another, Lord Sutcliffe."

He placed his hands on hers, looking directly into her eyes. "And it seems you have saved mine." He paused, a shift of concern. I received your letter..."

"My word is my bond, Lord Sutcliffe."

"Very well." A heartfelt sigh. "I thank you from the bottom of my heart, but you must allow me in some small way to repay your kindness."

Harriet and Lord Sutcliffe spent the next hour going over the details of the case. She learned so much more than she could have thought possible. Margaux had confessed everything to her father. CJ was up to his neck in debt, gambling, had dealings with the underworld, even the insurance policy wasn't paid for—the list went on. Harriet slumped in her chair, drained. It was then Lord Sutcliffe offered to represent her, and insisted he take care of all legal matters without the financial burden, and with that offer, a true weight lifted.

Harriet had another visit from Detective Fielding. For the first time since their first meeting, he appeared relaxed, and his trusty notebook was nowhere to be seen. Harriet waited, wondering, watching him as he rolled his hat around in his hands before speaking.

"I've some good news, Mrs. Rutherford." Harriet held her breath. "I've received new evidence which puts you firmly in the clear." She could just hear his words over the clatter of a tea trolley. There would be nothing more for her to do other than give evidence. In any other circumstances she would have whooped for joy, danced down the ward, sung at the top of her voice. But life for her was not like that. Her marriage had been nothing more than a sham, her life a disaster, and her husband now dead. All she could do was sit on the edge of her bed and weep.

By early evening, Harriet knew one last thing needed to be managed quickly, and efficiently. Harriet asked for the hospital telephone. It was wheeled to her bedside and the curtain drawn around her. The nurse gave her two pennies. They needed to be used wisely. Slotting the money in, she dialed the number and prayed Kate would answer. A voice! She pushed button A. The money dropped. The conversation was brief and to the point.

The next afternoon Kate arrived with chocolates, sweets, and a huge bouquet of flowers. She managed to upset Matron by sitting on the bed, then immediately won her over with her personality and the chocolates meant for Harriet. Matron, a bit of a softy as it turned out, pulled the curtain around them, whispering, "Just don't let everyone see."

They laughed, they cried, they hugged. "It is true? I'm so sorry!" Kate began bombarding her with questions. "I asked about you so many times. CJ gave the impression that you wanted nothing to do with us, me, once you were married. I never really believed it! And then when I got the parcel and your note…"

Harriet shook her head. "Can we go to the visitors' room, Kate?"

"Can you? Are you strong enough?"

Harriet smiled. "Just try and stop me."

The afternoon autumnal light provided the room with a soft glow. If only she could open the window and breathe in the fresh sweet air, but Matron would have none of it. More tears, more hugs before Kate sat in one of the high-backed chairs whilst Harriet continued to pace the room. Eventually, she sat beside Kate and, without prompting, began to give a short, simple account of the reality.

"Bloody hell, Harriet. Why didn't you contact me?"

"I couldn't, Kate. I don't want to go into the details." Harriet paused, wringing her hands. "Truthfully, I didn't know if anyone would believe me anyway. Even I began to doubt my own sanity."

Kate hugged her. "I would have believed you, you bloody nitwit!" They laughed at that. Kate turned serious.

"The parcel." She pulled it out of her handbag, then studied her friend's expression closely. "It's all a little cloak-and-dagger, Harriet. What's it all about?" Harriet bit her bottom lip.

"All I can say is that I am about to make sure it never gets into the wrong hands."

Harriet told Kate exactly what she planned, then put the notebook in the pocket of her dressing gown. She pointed out the reporter from the *London Herald*. He was still hanging around like a bad smell on a hot day. Kate giggled naughtily.

"You want him gone? Easy. Watch and learn." Kate unbuttoned her blouse to expose a milk-white cleavage, then began strolling sexily back down the ward. Some of the husbands who were visiting gaped and were promptly given short shrift by their wives.

Kate easily had the reporter's attention. Whilst his back was turned, Harriet, wearing Kate's overcoat, slipped by unnoticed. If the journalist, or Matron for that matter, had been more vigilant, they would have spotted Harriet wearing slippers, and the game would have been up. The moment Harriet was out of sight, Kate smiled, kissed the journalist on the cheek, and thanked him for his help.

"Uh?"

"See you later, darling." She swung her slender hips, knowing she had him salivating with her every move.

"Can I have your number?"

"It's in your top pocket, darling," she called, glancing over her shoulder, giving him a cheeky smile. Kate knew he would check his pocket. Sure enough, as he did, she walked around the corner and moved quickly out of sight.

As discussed, Kate quickly headed for the exit at the back of the hospital and began searching for Harriet in the gardens.

"Harriet!"

Kate was nothing like discreet, Harriet thought, suppressing a nervous giggle. "Over here, and keep your voice down."

Kate found Harriet vainly striking a Swan Vesta. The match lit, and she put the flame to the book. It refused to burn.

"Here," said Kate, taking out a cheroot and lighting up. "Give me the bloody thing." She began tearing the pages out and, with the end of the burning cheroot, touched them until they began to catch alight. "Funny kind of ritual, Hattie."

Harriet didn't look up. Instead, her focus remained entirely on the matter in hand. Another edge caught. Harriet breathed a sigh of relief. As the pages turned from curling burnt umber into black ash and the evidence dropped to the ground, Harriet rubbed each page into the earth under her slipper with a look of defiance upon her face.

"Better?"

"Better."

"When are you being discharged?"

Harriet shrugged.

"Well, come on, then, let's find out, because you're staying with me for as long as you need."

Harriet, completely overwhelmed by the kind offer, burst into tears. She was always crying lately, but the thought of going back to that house frightened her more than she cared to admit. Kate proffered an arm and guided Harriet back into the hospital, past a bewildered and highly annoyed journalist—and Matron, who stepped in, blocking his way.

"Sorry, sir. Only one welcome visitor at a time." But it took Matron all of two seconds to admonish Harriet for not asking permission to leave and usher her straight back to bed. "And just look at the mess you've brought into my ward." One black footprint marked her passage all the way along the highly polished floor.

"Sorry, Matron. I just needed some air," said Harriet. Then she asked, "Matron, I wonder, when might I be allowed to go home?"

Chapter 50

The porter wheeled Harriet to the front of the hospital and the waiting taxi.

"Good to have you back, Harriet." Kate sat beside Harriet in the cavernous leathery interior of the taxi and held her hand. Harriet wound the window down and watched the hospital disappear entirely from view.

London. Home. Well, almost. It had been a lifetime ago, or so it seemed. The streets were teeming. How could she have forgotten so quickly? Hundreds of people wrapped up against the chill, in a weaving metropolis Maypole dance. Lines of traffic nosed end to end, hooting, honking, black sooty fumes filling lungs. She spluttered and coughed. It was nothing like the countryside and nothing like the starched, disinfected cleanliness of hospital.

Harriet, deep in thought remembering that last day she left Dingham's, wound the cab window back up. London was just the same. Nothing had changed. Not here. It had been so easy to feel alone, amongst so many. Yet it was Tom who saw her. Tom who saved her. Now she had been saved again, by the grace of good, kind people.

Someone crossed her grave, and she shivered.

"Are you cold, Hattie?" Kate asked worriedly. "Here, I've brought a blanket, just in case."

"How thoughtful." She warmed instantly as Kate

gently pulled it around her shoulders. She squeezed Kate's hand, returning to her private thoughts, not daring to think about her future. Soon Harriet realized they were not driving toward Soho where her friends lived. Instead they were traveling along unfamiliar streets, and the traffic was less busy. They were in a small suburb, cruising by a popular row of shops with names she recognized—Mitchell's, Bullen's, Perry's. The cabbie overtook a three-wheeled *Express Deliveries* van, different from the usual milk float, and Harriet wondered idly if any of the milk from Albert and Alice's farm ended up here.

"Where are we going, Kate? This isn't the way to your flat."

"Didn't I say?" Kate looked innocent. "We're staying at my Uncle Jack's for a bit. Our flat is being decorated. Besides, his place is much bigger."

"But—"

"Don't worry, he's expecting us. You'll love him. Promise."

Harriet turned to look out the cab window, hiding her concern, her heart racing. This wasn't the agreement. She'd expected to go somewhere familiar, somewhere safe. Not having to meet someone new.

The cabbie pulled into a road lined with an avenue of monkey trees and double-bay-fronted Victorian houses. A little like Mrs. Gaffney's house, she thought, but the area seemed somehow cleaner, smarter.

Kate paid the fare, then helped Harriet out of the taxi before whispering in her ear, "Before we go in, let me give you a tip. Whatever you do, don't gawk at my uncle. First time any women meet him, they gawk."

"What?"

Kate laughed. There was no need to press the bell, as the door immediately opened. Harriet gawked. For an older man he was very handsome, just like a Hollywood actor—and just like an actor, he gave her a comical smile, but as they were introduced she noted confusion spread across his face.

"Please, come in. Any friend of Kate's is a friend of mine," said Jack.

Harriet knew how random Kate could be, and her uncle's expression gave her to think he looked as if he'd had no idea she would be staying.

"Kate said you didn't mind me staying for a while? She has asked you, hasn't she? Please tell me if she hasn't. It's not a problem, honestly?"

"Of course, you're staying, and you are more than welcome. The rooms are all ready and waiting. In fact, I've been really looking forward to the company. Living alone is not all it's cracked up to be."

His timbre was warm, sincere, and hinted something else other than clipped British. He led her through the hallway and into the lounge. A fire burned brightly, and warm soft furnishings in pale yellows and gold enticed her in.

"Now, how about a cuppa, to get you settled? Kate's good at making tea, aren't you, Kate?" She was standing in the doorway and huffed.

"Fat chance."

"My house, my rules, chop, chop. Oh, and I've found the most wonderful cake shop. You'll find a selection in the kitchen."

"Now you're talking, Uncle Jack. Why didn't you say so in the first place?" He turned his attention to Harriet and winked.

"I knew that would do the trick." Already Jack's easy manner made Harriet feel comfortable, and soon they began chatting away as if they were old friends.

Kate had daintily layered a plate with a variety of little cakes and brought them through, and Jack rubbed his hands, looking purposefully at the delicacies.

"These look simply divine, Uncle Jack. Look, Harriet, aren't they sweet? So small they can't possibly put an ounce of weight on."

Harriet's heart skipped a beat the moment she saw the arrangement. Surely not? There were beautiful carrot cakes, coffee and walnut bites, lilac meringues, and the tiniest bite-sized eclairs.

"Looks like you've seen a ghost, Harriet. Is everything all right?" asked Kate.

Kate and Jack exchanged wary glances.

"I'll be Mum," said Harriet quickly. "It's the least I can do," and as she took over, she asked where the cakes came from. Jack was happy to provide the information, declaring the cakes, next to whiskey, were one of his favorite things in the whole world. He produced a pink broadsheet and, pointing to an article, proffered it toward her.

"Look, seems like the entrepreneurial spirit is alive and kicking." The *Financial Times* expanded too wide to hold sensibly, so Jack kindly folded it into quarter.

The picture, though grainy, was instantly recognizable. Tom looked just as she remembered, fringe flopping, that quirky lopsided smile. Daisy was right by his side. They were cutting a cake as if they were just getting married. The headline read "Grand Opening of The Daisy Bakery." The fifth, in a rapidly expanding empire, it said. The article gave aspects of how the business had grown and established itself amongst a wide range of clientele. Harriet smiled to herself reading the second from bottom line. Tom had his way. Two enterprises. The Tom & Daisy Bakery, the second arm of the chain, was not tea rooms but a simple bakery where pies, cakes, breads, and a specialist Italian range of products had been developed. Harriet sighed. All eyes were upon her.

"I know them," said Harriet simply, as if answering a question, and picked up her cup of tea. "I used to work for Daisy. I'm really pleased they're doing so well. They deserve it."

She stifled a yawn. "I'm so sorry. How rude. I'm really tired." She looked bashful. "May I go to my room?"

Chapter 51

Tom and Daisy had been trying to keep abreast of the developments from the newspapers and gleaned as much as possible about Harriet. Though Lady Sutcliffe and Harriet hadn't been charged with Rutherford's death, if the reports were to be believed, there appeared to be room for doubt. Tom had a friend, who had a friend, and after a lot of digging, he discovered the hospital where Harriet had been taken. He would go to her. She was a friend. A dear friend. He wanted her to know that he would be there for her. She might rebuff him, but he had to. For his own peace of mind, if nothing else.

Tom arrived at the hospital and instantly charmed the receptionist. She directed him to the ward, where he stood awkwardly outside, with a huge bouquet of flowers. He pondered what to say.

"Can I help you, sir?" A bubbly nurse smiled on her way out. She looked busy.

"Um… Yes, I wonder… May I see Miss Laws?"

"Miss Laws?" The nurse looked at him suspiciously.

"I mean, Mrs. Rutherford."

"And you are?"

"A friend."

"And who directed you here?"

"Uh. I kind of guessed?" He didn't want to get anyone into trouble.

"It was that receptionist, wasn't it. She had no

business. Wait there. Don't move a muscle. I'll get Matron." And as she dashed back inside, the doors closed behind her.

A few minutes passed, the nurse came out again, rolled her eyes at him, and told him to wait. Ten minutes passed, then ten more. A man in a gray coat turned up and gave him a nod.

"They're devils in there. Won't let me in. Won't tell me anything."

There was something about the man's demeanor. He couldn't possibly be visiting family. They wouldn't be that unkind. Would they?

"Are you a reporter, by any chance?"

"Yes." The reporter was about to elaborate when Matron came through the door. She glared at the reporter, then studied Tom.

"Too late, she's gone. Discharged, and before you ask," she glared at the reporter again, "I'm not going to tell you where."

"Is she all right, though, Matron?"

Matron smiled. "All I can say is she's fine, nothing more. Now move along!"

"Excuse me, before you go?" Tom offered her the flowers. "For you, for taking good care of her…" He had no use for them now. He was too late. Again.

Chapter 52

Two days later, Kate, full of ideas for a fashion show and all the work it entailed, was busily working in a large room specially set aside for the purpose. Jack, keen to give Harriet as much space as she needed, showed her his collection of books. He was going out and offered to get anything she wanted from the library.

When Jack came back from his walk, to his surprise he heard the Drifters on the radio and found Harriet in the kitchen humming along and doing arm exercises in time with the tune.

"I hope you don't mind." She looked shy. "I need to keep working on my arm to stop it going stiff."

"Like this?" Jack mimicked her movements, but badly, and laughed.

She liked his laugh; it was deep, warm, friendly.

"What's in the pot? It smells great!" Jack had already lifted the lid and dipped in a spoon.

"I hope you don't mind."

"Mind? You have to be kidding! I haven't had a decent homecooked meal in ages."

Harriet, blushing, shrugged.

"I don't know about you, but I'm starving." Jack was already getting bowls and spoons out and putting them on the kitchen table. "I'm ravenous. Are we going to eat, or just smell it?"

Harriet grinned, happily ladling some into his

bowl.

Within the first few days, Harriet came out of her shell, seemingly more relaxed and alive, and the little band of people in the house fell into an easy routine, Kate with her work. Jack and Harriet, reading. Harriet exercising and taking walks, then preparing their meals.

One afternoon Jack caught Harriet looking through his music collection. She was holding his favorite Miles Davis record. Then she hooked out Glenn Miller's "Tomorrow's Another Day" and asked if could listen to them. Then at lunch Harriet spoke about music and oddly linked jazz, rock and roll, and opera in the same breath, but he noticed a stray tear and wondered if the memory was good or bad. That same afternoon, Harriet surprised Jack by suggesting a game of chess. He quickly discovered Harriet was no pushover and wanted to know who taught her.

A wistful smile crossed her face as she spoke. "I never managed to beat my grandmother. Well, sometimes I did. When I was really little, just starting out. I guess she felt sorry for me."

Jack was touched by her manner. He noticed the way she held herself, so upright, so proud, yet so humble, but there was something else, something about her that he could not put a finger on.

"Your grandmother must have been really smart," he said when Harriet called checkmate. He leaned back and stretched his arms behind his head, then scrubbed his hands through his hair. "I'm going to have to watch you more carefully in future, little lady." When she smiled, he noticed the way she tilted her head to one side. Something pricked at a distant memory.

"It was fun, thank you. I needed to stretch my brain,

but I think now I also need to stretch my legs, and whilst food is good for the soul, so is exercise. I don't suppose you fancy a walk, Jack? I confess I'm beginning to feel a little stir crazy."

"Thought you'd never ask." He grinned and was on his feet in an instant, pulling on a warm coat.

Jack walked them to the closest park, which took around fifteen minutes at a brisk pace. Most of the iron fencing had been taken for the war, to make guns and ammunition. Now all that was left were the bushes around the perimeter, and a gate. They stepped up their pace, trying to beat the cold air, and by the end of one circuit Harriet's face glowed.

"Harriet, do you fancy a hot drink?" He did not say, but the cold was biting into his limbs and made his old war wound ache.

"Yes, that would be lovely. I confess I'm freezing!"

"Why didn't you say so before? It's brass monkeys, isn't it!" Jack laughed. "Come on, then, I've just the place in mind." And they headed in the direction of his now favored tearoom.

Harriet gazed at the pink-striped canopy over the front. Other than the name over the top, it virtually mirrored Daisy's bakery in Camden. Jack held the door open, and they stepped into a warm interior. The arrangement was delightful. Little tables were dressed in white linen with menus. A girl in a smart white-with-pink-trim uniform came to greet them and showed them to a table, then took their order. Jack watched Harriet's eyes travel keenly around, gathering detail.

"Does it bring back memories?"

"Yes, a little. Though of course I worked in the shop, not a tearoom." She smiled. "We had fantastic luck when Lady Carmichael placed a large order for a garden party. That really boosted business." She looked at him directly. "Tom said he wanted to create jobs, and he's done just that. Just look—I counted eleven waitresses, plus someone manning the till. Three covering the bakery area. Then of course there's what goes on behind the scenes." She was so passionate Jack could not help but grin.

"Seems you have a vested interest, Harriet?"

She shrugged. "I confess, I enjoyed working at Daisy's, and with Tom. He was always up for suggestions." She looked at Jack sideways, slightly embarrassed. "We were good friends, once."

"Well, they certainly have a winning product. Great food, good prices, and"—he took a sip of tea— "they know how to make a decent cuppa."

For the first time in quite a while, Jack felt comfortable in his bones. It was certainly not just the ambience of the café, but he felt sure it was having Harriet and Kate for company. Harriet, like Kate, had a way about her. She was easy to be with. Harriet also asked questions about his life without prying too deeply. She listened with an intellectual ear and posed questions that he'd never considered before. He was even surprised to find himself telling her about the South Africa debacle, Naidoo and his gang, and the children he'd seen working so hard. Harriet wanted to know more, and he agreed to show her photographs when they got back.

****

That night Jack had the recurring nightmare. There was no stopping it. The terror, the smoke, the unrelenting rat-tat of Luftwaffe guns raining down upon his comrades. "No!" Henry, his brother-in-law, was in trouble, and Ginger, the new recruit, was signaling an attack. "No!" Fire, pain, the burning Spitfire falling from the sky, the roar of the engine. "No!" It was then, in a rare moment of truce, as if the Luftwaffe had appreciated the skill and courage of the young pilot, that the enemy saluted, tipping their wings, and retreated.

Jack woke abruptly, bathed in sweat.

****

Harriet, woken by the sounds coming from Jack's room, lay sleepless, pondering what she should do as his shouts grew. He sounded terrified. She knew Kate could sleep like the dead, but really? Maybe she should go, check that he was all right. Then, with another unintelligible yell, she slipped on her dressing gown and padded out into the hall. She would get Kate—but all went quiet, so she went downstairs for a glass of water. A moment later, Jack arrived in the kitchen also. She squinted at him.

He looked surprised.

"I'm sorry. Did I wake you?"

Harriet swiftly turned the tables.

"The women I stayed with had their fair share of nightmares." Her eyebrows rose almost imperceptibly. "Why, they even told me I shouted out in my sleep."

It was the first time Harriet had come even close to talking about what had happened to her. Apart from the little Kate had shared, and the newspapers with their skewed view, the details were vague.

"Sometimes it helps to talk." She smiled, the gentle offer on her lips.

Jack accepted the offer of a glass of water and swallowed it in one gulp.

"I hope I don't sound presumptuous," she said, "but may I ask a question?"

Jack nodded, a little hesitant.

"It goes without saying the war has a profound effect on people's lives, not just physically but emotionally. And I know we Brits are reputed to have the stiff upper lip and all that, but I've always wondered if there was any kind of support for war veterans."

"The notion isn't without merit, Harriet. There is psychiatric help, but I think some of us feel it's an admission of failure."

Jack stood a while in limbo, then, saying good night, took himself off.

Harriet finished her water, thinking about her own need to be rid of demons...and the needs of other women like herself.

Chapter 53

"Uncle Jack!" Kate hollered up the stairs. "Get up, you lazy sausage!" Jack sauntered downstairs and ambled into the kitchen. "About time." She tapped her watch. "Harriet and I have been talking. I need women. Real women."

Jack's eyebrows raised in mock amusement. "What, there are fakes?"

Kate ignored the response.

"What I don't want are a full complement of professional models for my *special* collection, and Hattie-Cake's come up with a brilliant suggestion. Didn't you, Hattie."

Harriet pushed her glasses up her nose in amusement. Kate certainly knew how to work on her uncle. "We're going to visit Harriet's old friends and invite them to be the stars of my show. If they agree, they'll be my *natural* models. But what we need from you, Uncle Jack, is your car."

"You don't drive," he replied, falling straight into her trap.

"Exactly! Thank you for offering."

Jack threw his hands up in the air, defeated. Harriet handed him a cup of coffee, smiling broadly.

"You may need some sustenance." She guided him toward the table loaded with steaming porridge and hot buttered toast. "It's going to be a long day."

"If I didn't know better, you two could be sisters. You're always in cahoots with one another." Harriet and Kate looked at one another seriously for a full second.

"Nah!" They burst out laughing.

Chapter 54

Jack waited outside the house with Harriet, studying his shiny new Mini while he pondered his words. The girls appeared so in tune with each other, and so close, they really could be sisters. Why, he'd even discovered they were exactly the same age. At the very least he knew Kate had a great friend in Harriet, and she in Kate. He was distracted by Kate's arrival and carefully stowed her portfolio in the open boot.

"I've never known anyone with such poor timekeeping." He glanced at his new Rolex. It read ten fifteen. "Did you not specify we should be ready and in the car by ten a.m. pronto?"

"Keep your wig on. I had to make sure I have everything. Besides what's the rush?"

Harriet giggled, squeezing into the back seat of the tiny Mark 1. She knew just how infuriating Kate could be regarding timekeeping.

"Well, the salesman must have thought all his birthdays had come together when he saw you," exclaimed Kate, sitting next to her uncle. "Just look— your knees are almost touching your ears! This car is way too small for you. Look, it's going to be near on impossible double declutching. Why don't you let me drive?"

"Nice try, lady, but it's not going to happen, most probably not in my lifetime, anyway." Jack laughed.

"But if you're serious and you want lessons, I'll arrange them. So, until you pass your test, hands off!"

With Kate reading the map and giving Jack instructions, they set off. He liked the notion of being able to bomb around town and get in between tight spaces where larger cars could not, and soon the girls were screaming in delight at his racy driving.

Jack turned into Ham Street and pulled up right outside Rosa's door. He winked at Kate.

"I'll wait here and read my paper while you sort things out." He glanced around the street. The area was always known as a slum in his days, but what he saw surprised him. Clearly the council needed to make improvements—the pavements needed serious repair and potholes crazed the road—but it was clean. The fronts were well tended, and there was not a hint of flying debris or apparent disregard by its residents. Instead, he saw a woman come out of one of the houses, brush down her front step, and begin cleaning down the window ledge, and another woman walked down the road with a very-well-turned-out child holding her hand.

"I used to live over there with my Nana," Harriet explained to Kate, and pointed across the road to number nine as they clambered out of the car.

Jack observed the scene from a quiet distance. He watched Harriet's friend, Rosa, fling her arms about her so tightly he thought she would pass out. The woman's voice was clear with happiness as it rang out into the street. Then he listened in amusement to hear her admonish Harriet for not seeing her sooner.

Kate and Harriet were excited when they returned to the car. Apparently, Rosa was keen to be part of the show and loved the designs. Kate had explained she would need to go back and complete measurements and fittings, but for now, Calvert Street was next on the list.

"Give me a moment, will you, please?" Harriet asked anxiously as they pulled up outside. "I'd like to see Mrs. G first. I may need a little time to explain myself."

Jack and Kate watched as Harriet knocked the door. They laughed at the reaction of the woman who answered it. The older woman's cigarette, held in a long holder, fell straight out of her mouth, and then she threw her arms about Harriet and pulled her inside.

Kate murmured quietly to Jack how obvious it was that Harriet was loved by her friends, and he couldn't help but agree. Around ten minutes later, Harriet re-appeared.

"Sorry for making you wait," Harriet apologized. "Please, come in. Mrs. G will make you comfy while I go pay a visit to some of my other friends I spoke about. And don't be put off by Dotty. She speaks her mind, but she is an absolute wonder. Oh, and by the way, you'll need to keep an eye on little Charlie." And she left it at that, leaving Kate and Jack a little puzzled. Harriet introduced them to Mrs. Gaffney and quickly left them in her capable hands. Checking her watch, she hoped she had timed it right, as school would be over and they should be back. As luck would have it, Dotty was visiting Patience's, her first port of call. The women were surprised but very pleased to see her.

"Surely, this isn't baby Elizabeth, is it?' said Harriet. 'Why you're even prettier than I remember, and you're walking already. What a clever girl." Elizabeth caught hold of her mother's hem, looking very content with the compliment. Then Harriet feigned looking for someone else. "I was looking forward to seeing little Charlie. Is he about?" She held a tease in her voice. Charlie pushed himself in front of his mother, standing tall.

"I'm Charlie!"

"No, you can't possibly be! Why, the Charlie I knew was a little boy. Not a big strong young man like you." Charlie's chest puffed out, evidently chuffed. Harriet turned to the women. "I know this is short notice, but I've a friend I would like you to meet. Do you have a little time to spare?"

The women, curious, went with her to Mrs. G's. Little Elizabeth instantly took to Jack, tugging at his trousers. Mrs. Gaffney had made a up a toy box for the children, and Charlie was straight into it.

"I can catch a ball," said Charlie to Jack. Can you?" Charlie pulled out a bright yellow-and-red ball the size of a large onion and hurled it at Jack. Quick off the mark, he caught it.

"Charlie! Stop that you little..." Dotty clearly made a supreme effort to control her language.

"Perhaps I could take the children outside to play a while?" asked Jack tactfully. "What do you say?"

"Gordon Bennett! An 'an'some-lookin' man, offerin' to take my Charlie out to play, whatever next?" Dotty exclaimed. "What do you say, Charlie boy? Say, 'Yes, please,' that's a good boy." Dotty looked on as her son delivered the right answer. Patience, also in agreement that Elizabeth could join them, helped wrap up the children against the cold and showed Jack out to the yard. Once the children were out of sight, Harriet produced a licorice treat for Charlie and a farthing's worth of sweet candies for Elizabeth.

When Kate made her proposal, Dotty shrieked with delight. "Gawd knows what me 'usband would think, seeing me all dolled up like a dog's dinner, but what the heck? I'm up for it. And if I am, so are you, Mrs. G, and that includes you, Patience!"

A while later, when the children came in with Jack, another pot of tea was made, and the deal was sealed.

"One more thing, Harriet, before you go. I have something of yours." Mrs. Gaffney looked pensive as she left the room. Harriet knew that look. Mrs. Gaffney worried about all sorts, but when she reappeared with a shoebox in her hands, Harriet nearly burst into tears.

"My mother's ballet shoes! I thought they were lost forever." Harriet took the box from her. Old, battered, but still intact. She gingerly lifted the lid. She gasped as she pulled some of the tissue away to reveal its precious memory. A sliver of pink ribbon flicked between her fingers. "How can I ever thank you, Mrs. G?"

"I always knew they were precious and that someday you'd come back," said Mrs. Gaffney.

More tears, more explanations, and one more place left to visit. As they left, the women insisted Harriet return with Kate when taking measurements for the costumes.

Jack noticed Harriet was growing paler throughout the day, and Kate immediately took his hint and pressed her hand gently upon Harriet's arm while she suggested they visit Luigi's another time.

Harriet was adamant. She'd made a promise to Sofia and would not let her down.

"I'm fine, really, thank you. I confess my emotions have been all over the place, but I am so looking

289

forward to seeing her."

Luigi and his wife were at the door of the restaurant the moment Jack parked his Mini.

"Come, come," they both gushed, enveloping Harriet before she had a chance to introduce her friends. "We waiting for you," Luigi cried enthusiastically. "Come, come," already ushering everyone in. As Harriet stepped across the threshold "That's Amore" started up, played on a record player somewhere out of view.

"Surprise!" They were all there, Sofia, and little Carlo in her arms, and her husband. Sofia rushed over, squishing baby Carlo between them, his strong little arms fighting to get out as they hugged one another.

"I'm sorry, Harriet, but you know what my family are like. Family are everything, and we've all missed you so much." Jack and Kate exchanged glances. Their expression said it all.

Family. They were family. Harriet had already become part of theirs.

Luigi began singing to Dean Martin's recording, and in a natural, happy, response everyone else joined in. From the kitchen came more singing, and it was growing in volume. Then, just as Luigi raised his voice and began the chorus, his staff came pouring out through the swing doors laden with huge dishes of pasta fagioli and baskets of crusty bread, all perfectly timed to "That's Amore." And in that late October afternoon, in Luigi's trattoria, with raffia-covered Chianti bottles turned table lamps where once candles had licked spent wax down their sides, they all broke bread together. While it was cold outside, the warmth of family drew all their hearts together. They laughed, smiled, talked, and shared stories. And not once did anyone mention Harriet's marriage or the dreadful details being aired in the daily papers. It was clear to everyone Luigi and his family had imbedded Harriet into their hearts and family forever.

Chapter 55

Harriet, reading through the mail, found one letter that really didn't surprise her at all. Dorian Craddock requested her presence. Harriet made the call, and at precisely eleven o'clock, she was being shown into Dorian's lounge. The first thing that drew her eye was a tiger-skin rug, the poor animal stripped of his skin, his head bearing enormous snarling teeth.

A tower of a man stood up from his chair and limped toward her, beaming.

"I'd like you to meet my brother Davey."

He reached out. Their hands collided into an awkward handshake. Appreciating the effort, Harriet placed a hand gently over his.

"Pleased to meet you, Davey." Dorian seemed satisfied with Harriet's response.

"While I get us a drink, Davey, why don't you show Harriet some of your work?" Dorian's voice held an unusual sweetness when she spoke to him. To Harriet, she said, "I'm very proud of Davey. He's a fantastic artist, even after…" Dorian stopped mid-flow and looked embarrassed. "Sorry, Davey. I'll shut up." He shrugged.

Harriet suddenly remembered a hint about Dorian's brother from Kate, then the newspaper article about their father being indicted for murder and grievous bodily harm and now waiting for the gallows. She glanced at Davey, wondering. Maybe she was just adding one and one, and making three? Davey's eyes traveled to the rug in disgust. Harriet smiled. There was something kind about him, a gentleness she never saw in Dorian. He was showing her to a cream kid leather sofa. It was so soft, Harriet felt wicked sitting on it. It was then she saw the painting suspended above the mantelpiece, and her heart lurched. Just then Dorian returned with a tray of tea and biscuits.

"How are you? Better, I hope?" asked Dorian. Harriet's eyes were transfixed upon the painting, but she managed to compose herself.

"I'm doing well, thank you."

"Davey is very modest. I guess he didn't show you his artwork. He's been experimenting with a variety of mediums." Davey shot them a look.

"I'm here, Dorey."

"Well, if you won't show off, then I'm going to." Harriet followed her to the table heaped with pencil drawings, pastels, and watercolors. She lifted them one by one. "Davey's been painting in oils recently and has been relegated to the art studio in the garden. To be honest I can't stand the smell of fresh oils on canvas."

"These are stunning." Harriet turned to Davey, her eyes shining, and noticed he had already munched through the plate of biscuits.

"I should go now?"

"Yes, of course, darling." Davey got up and lumbered out through a door.

"Bye, Davey. It was lovely meeting you." Harriet called after the disappearing figure. "I can see why you are so proud—these sketches are fantastic and the watercolors amazing.'

Harriet pointed back toward the painting she had

been studying above the fireplace. "Is that his?" She waited for a reaction.

"No." A tiny spot above Dorian's right eye twitched. "Did you know your home, where you lived with CJ, was where I lived once?"

Harriet blinked in surprise.

"The stories I could tell." Dorian sighed, then swiftly changed the subject. "This is a bit awkward Harriet. My reason for you being here is not to discuss art. But we will get back to that later, if you wish. We should get to business."

"The notebook and photographs, I presume. I told you in my letter they have been destroyed."

"I'll pay handsomely for their return, of course."

Harriet shook her head, disappointed. Whilst Harriet understood Dorian's obvious concern, she felt insulted by the implication. "You're suggesting I'm lying, Dorian. Make no mistake, I'm disgusted and ashamed I married a man who could keep such an account. Do you honestly think I would allow *anyone* to use those things to hurt people?" Dorian colored at the insinuation.

"I wasn't going to…"

"You've nothing to fear, Dorian," said Harriet with finality. "As I said, it's gone. Dealt with."

"You read, you saw, you know? But you could…"

"What? Tell the world about you? Take over from CJ and blackmail everyone else on the list?"

Dorian pressed the heels of her hands into her eye sockets, mumbling. "How can I trust you?"

"How can you not?"

Dorian's right eye continued twitching.

"Look, Dorian, everyone deserves to love and live without fear, and that includes you. Think about Alan

Turin. The poor man. A prime example of bigotry and a misguided law. I shudder to think how terribly he suffered."

Dorian wriggled uncomfortably in her seat. "All that knowledge, and you won't tell?"

Harriet shook her head. "Never."

"How can I ever repay you?"

Harriet swallowed. She hadn't gone there expecting anything. But she'd wondered. Now she asked, "I would like to know how you came by that painting."

Dorian looked at her curiously. "You knew CJ taught me about fine art?"

Harriet said nothing. It would explain how he inveigled his way into her exclusive club.

"To begin with, CJ was my mentor." Dorian's voice took on a lighter note. She began describing how CJ took her to his shop, then his warehouse, then to private viewings, and then to auctions. Sometimes they would take Davey.

Dorian paused a beat, there had been pride in her voice, but also sadness etched into her face. She rubbed at the twitch, her mouth looping into a hopeful smile. "We planned to show some of Davey's work someday."

Harriet waited, listening, learning even more about CJ that she had not known before. Yes, she knew about the antiques shop, but not a warehouse. Neither CJ nor Margaux had ever mentioned that. Harriet placed her hands together on her lap. She needed to remain calm. She felt sure there would be a reason for telling her all this.

"I believe Margaux told you he was in debt?" Harriet nodded. "CJ arranged the delivery of the painting as part payment of that debt. He told me its worth and its future predicted value. Normally I would plan to sell, but Davey and I love it. I couldn't let it be hidden away in a sealed room."

Harriet remembered Margaux's story. It all tallied. CJ had arranged the burglary and had the painting stolen to pay his debts. The little codes in the diary she had not quite put together now began to make sense.

Dorian was frowning. All the time she spoke, Harriet's gaze had never left the painting. "Why do you ask?"

Harriet shot her a look. "It belonged to my grandmother." Finally she looked at her directly and steadily. "Have CJ's debts been covered?"

"Yes."

"Good. Then we are all square." Harriet wanted nothing more to do with Dorian or her dodgy dealings. She got up, said goodbye, and left, never turning back.

Chapter 56

One week later, Kate was in the study with "Mack the Knife" playing on the record deck, and as she sang along, she put the last of the invitations for her upcoming fashion show in February next year in a pile. Lucy and her parents, Treenie, the school. A multitude of fashion gurus she wanted to impress had already accepted. It was thrilling. Her own show! Jack had gone to get his daily newspaper. The decorators were finished. She could go home. Harriet was standing in the doorway, watching her.

"Hattie!" She slipped one final invitation on the heap.

"I've been thinking, Kate. It's time I went back." The word "home" stuck in her throat.

The front door opened, and Jack came whistling through the hallway.

"I wonder, would you mind coming with me? Just for an hour or two, just to air the ghosts?" The record ended with the repetitious clicking of needle on vinyl, and she lifted the arm back into its resting position.

"I could do better than that, Hattie. If you like, I could stay over the weekend and help you settle in."

"You're just too much. Are you sure? What about Sarah?"

"You know our Sarah. She's in love, and I know she would appreciate having the space to herself for a while longer. So you'd be doing us all favor."

"And Alexander? Won't he be missing you?"

"Haven't you heard absence makes the heart grow fonder?"

Kate's words had struck a note. Absence did make the heart grow fonder. She just needed to build herself up first. To pay a visit to Daisy's, and then maybe, with any luck, see Tom and try to explain.

The following day, Jack stowed their luggage in the tiny boot of his Mini and, knowing Primrose Hill well enough, navigated his own way there. As they journeyed, Jack filled awkward silences with childhood reminiscences.

He spoke about his love-hate relationship with London Zoo, trapping animals for showboating, versus the reasoning for conservation of rare breeds and educational value. He talked of his grandparents and his mother taking him and his twin sister to Regent's Park, with its wide-open spaces and picnics, and how Maury, his twin, started his love of photography with a tiny camera the size of a matchbox.

Jack spoke fondly of Lords, and cricket, and his father's evident passion for the game, but as they drew nearer to Primrose Hill, Harriet began fidgeting. Jack was about to cut short his dialogue when she pointed across his shoulder.

"We're here. If you can let me out, I'll open the gates," she offered in a tremulous voice. Before them, in the quiet residential setting of Wadham Gardens, stood an imposing, double-fronted, detached house. Jack followed Harriet into the driveway and parked.

"It's a great location, Harriet, and the house looks beautiful." Jack looked on appreciatively.

"Yes, the house might be beautiful, but sadly, not the memories." He and Kate exchanged wary looks as she stepped inside.

Harriet stood silently as if in contemplation, her gaze fixed on the wall at the far end. There was evidence of a painting hook suspended from the dado rail, but nothing hung on it.

"Are you all right, Hattie?" Kate touched her lightly on the arm.

"I will be." She turned to them. "Thank you for taking such good care of me, Jack. I don't know how I can ever repay your kindness, but please know that I am truly indebted."

Jack placed a hand gently on her shoulder. "It's been my pleasure. What do we say, Kate? All for one?"

Kate clapped her hands together. "And one for all!"

Harriet allowed the briefest of smiles, knowing a little of their pact, but her eyes traveled to a large bunch of keys resting on the hall table. A jailer would be proud. Memories flooded back. She picked them up. They weighed heavy in her hands. Seeing the study door, she flinched at another memory.

"Please, why don't you both look around while I prepare a light lunch, and perhaps you could choose which bedroom you would like, Kate? Mine's first on the right."

Whilst Jack and Kate meandered through the house, Harriet began unpacking the groceries, looking out the window and into the garden. She needed to get outside, to get some air. When she stepped into the garden, she couldn't believe how overgrown it was and began pulling at vine weed furiously, angry for everything that had happened. Angry and hurt that her husband could be so cold and calculating. Angry she could be so gullible.

As Kate peered out from the back window of one of the bedrooms and saw Harriet below, Jack came to her side.

"It looks like Harriet's having an argument with herself."

They were watching her flinging great clumps of vegetation attached to large clods of earth. "Maybe she needs a little more time. How about we sort lunch?"

Jack lit the fire just as Harriet came in through the kitchen, her hands muddied from her efforts. "I'm sorry. I'm not a great host, am I?"

"No, silly. Uncle Jack's sorted out the fire, and I've made lunch, so whenever you're ready…"

Chapter 57

Harriet and Kate stood on the porch watching Jack squeeze himself into his car. He raised his hands to the heavens with his comical smile upon his face. Then he was gone.

"Come on," said Kate, "let's get a hot toddy and blankets."

They huddled together on the floor in front of the fire, using the sofa as a back rest, and talked. Eventually Harriet, exhausted, fell asleep with her head resting on the cushioned sofa.

Kate wrapped her up in a blanket and stared into the flames as they flickered, lulling her to think. Harriet wasn't so different. Silly to suppose even at their age they considered themselves orphans. Harriet had told her about her mother. She'd showed her the ballet shoes, explaining she was a prima ballerina. It had been such a wonderful but sad story.

But like Harriet, who wondered about her father and what her grandmother was about to tell her before her untimely death, there remained questions unanswered for Kate, too.

Kate knew she'd had wonderful parents. If only they had been her real parents. If only she knew what happened to her natural mother and why she let her go. Had she been a bad child? Perhaps if she knew, she could move on with her life, try to put it behind her.

Early next morning, Harriet found herself on the floor with a cushion under her head, covered in an enormous blanket. She could only assume the arrangement, and the fire still burning, was Kate's doing.

Kate made tea and placed the tray on the small table by the side of the sofa.

"Don't tell me you slept here as well?" Harriet yawned and stretched.

"I can't say the floor is that comfy. I slept on the sofa." Kate grinned.

"Thanks for staying with me, Kate."

"All for one, eh?"

"And one for all." Harriet smiled, scooting up close. "Funny, witty, talented Kate, with a marvelous uncle who adores you."

Kate pressed herself against Harriet, a distant look on her face.

"What's up?"

Kate shrugged and looked at her palms. Harriet took her left one in hers.

"Let's see your lifeline." She traced it from the base of the thumb to just below her forefinger.

"Ah, a long life. And I see many children." Harriet hid a grin. "One, two, three, four, five—no, six!"

"Oh, bloody hell, Hattie, don't say that!"

"Don't you want children?"

"Yes, maybe, one day, but six?"

Harriet nudged her. "Come on. Tell me. What's going on? Let me in."

Kate's face plucked a dimple of doubt. "Maybe, another time." She looked at the palm of her hand, brooding. "Six children? You've got to be kidding!"

Chapter 58

The phone rang. In a fit of pique, Harriet had arranged to have the telephone moved from the study and into the hallway. It was one of those things she just had to do.

"Hello, Kate." Harriet smiled down the line. They had come to an agreement to speak to one another every night since Kate went back to her flat. It had been a wrench. Harriet found her moods would lift and soar, then other times as she cleaned the house or dug in the garden, terrible memories flooded back and brought her to earth with a solid thump.

"You okay?"

"Everything's fine, thanks, and you? How was your day?"

Harriet had been putting off going to see Daisy, and Kate was aware.

"Well, have you done it?"

Harriet sighed. Kate could be really bossy, but in the best possible way.

"I wrote. I decided it would give Daisy the chance to decline without embarrassing her."

"And Tom, did you write to him?"

"No," she said flatly. "Knowing Daisy, she would likely show the letter to Tom. It gives them both the out."

"Well, at least you've got this far."

Two days later, a letter dropped through the letterbox. Harriet picked it up and tore open the envelope. Daisy! She'd written back. So quick. Yes, she would love to see her. Then a moment of dejection. There was no mention of Tom. Harriet shrugged as she finished reading. She was pleased to visit Daisy, whatever.

****

Heart fluttering with nerves, Harriet got a taxi. What luxury! Having spent hours in front of the mirror practicing what she might say to Daisy, she chided herself. This was Daisy she was visiting, not the Queen. And if Tom by any slim chance should appear...

As the taxi drew alongside the little bakery, she stared as the memories came flooding back. Its canopy was still fresh and bright. A regular flow of customers went in and out, the windows shone, the sun sparkled, and as she stepped out of the cab, Harriet prayed Tom might show himself. Maybe it was more than a little presumptuous to think, but she could hope.

Harriet could see Mrs. Turpin behind the counter, bustling, busy, and chatting away. She grinned to herself, tempted to pop her head around the door and say hello, but decided she wouldn't disturb Mrs. Turpin, not just yet. Besides, she was here primarily to see Daisy.

Walking down the side of the building, she saw the back yard had changed. It no longer held a crumbling outhouse, or an old gravel yard. Instead, there was a new building connected to the bakery. The bungalow was pretty, adorned with pot plants and hanging baskets. There were net curtains in the windows and a shiny white front door.

Harriet pulled herself up to her full height, checked her hair in her compact, and knocked. "Come on in," a small voice called back.

Harriet tentatively called out. "It's Harriet, only me."

"Come on through, Harriet."

Harriet walked a short passage past a couple of closed doors on her left toward another door right at the end of the hall, slightly ajar.

"I'm in here, Harriet." Her little voice was clearer now. Harriet pushed the door open.

"Harriet, at last!" Daisy faced her. The familiar pearls at her neckline, her bright eyes, and her huge smile welcomed Harriet in. She flew to Daisy's side and hugged her where she sat. Tears fell. Sighs and phrases poured between them.

"It's been a long time. Too long, my girl," said Daisy when Harriet eventually extricated herself.

"Yes." Harriet wiped her tears. "I know. I'm sorry."

"No, dear. Don't be. I think we all knew there was something not quite right when you didn't come back. Not a word. Not turning up for a shift. It didn't make sense. It wasn't like you at all. We *all* worried."

"I am so sorry, Daisy. CJ..." She faltered. She believed CJ had handed her notice in. "It just happened." Daisy nodded.

"The paper—" Harriet exclaimed, capitalizing, not wanting to dwell on herself. "I saw you and Tom, the picture in the paper—five shops and growing. It's amazing." Harriet laughed now, pleased to change the subject, and offered her congratulations.

"Yes, work for Tom was always a passion, but

since…" She paused and stroked her pearls. "I think the business eventually became something of an obsession. To take his mind off…"

"Off what?" Harriet looked puzzled.

"Are those for me by any chance?" Daisy cut her short.

Harriet proffered the bouquet of flowers. "Yes, and something else, for you and Tom, maybe, to celebrate your achievements?" Harriet paused, just a moment longer than a heartbeat. "How is he, Daisy? How is he doing?"

"Maybe you could ask him yourself." Daisy smiled widely.

A slight cough from behind startled her. Harriet turned.

"Tom!" Her heart leapt into her throat.

"Harriet." And as Tom pushed his floppy fringe back, he gave her his lopsided smile.

All those old feelings rushed back. How she would love to be brave and give him a hug.

"Harriet."

Harriet took three paces toward him, then thought, to hell with convention, life is too short. She took the final step toward him, and as she threw her arms around his neck, she whispered, "It's oh, so good to see you again," and for the briefest of time, as he held her close, it felt wonderful.

"Harriet." His voice sounded gruff in her ear. He pulled away.

Harriet felt flattened. Hurt. But she recouped. She couldn't expect anything else. After all, she had been the one who left. Got married. Never spoke to them. They obviously never received her letters when she was with CJ. How could he, they, ever begin to understand? She could hardly understand it herself.

"I see you've brought champagne. Taittinger. No expense spared." Tom didn't take his eyes off her. Harriet, hot, embarrassed by her outpouring of emotions, flushed red. Then she remembered the glasses of champagne he had bought for them on that dreadful, wonderful, mixed-up night at the theatre. She cursed herself for her insensitivity.

"I'd wanted… It's a kind of, well, a part apology about…everything, but mostly to congratulate you both on your huge success. I've been following your progress in the papers."

"You have?" Tom looked surprised. He leaned against the door jamb, arms folded.

"Yes, I've even been a customer in one of your new tearooms. What you have created is nothing short of wonderful."

Tom looked pleased.

"I don't know about you, but I'm parched," put in Daisy. "How about we go mad and have that champagne?"

"Seriously?" Tom stared in surprise.

"Why not? I think we need to celebrate Harriet's return, don't you?"

Tom waved away Daisy's start to get up, saying, "Very well, but I'll do the honors."

Daisy glanced at Harriet, who quickly took the hint, offering to help, and followed behind. The kitchen was compact and well-ordered, and a chair had been placed at the worksurface. She remembered how Daisy needed to rest her poor legs.

"Daisy looks well. You look well, Tom…"

Words failed her as Tom put the kettle on to boil, but she said, "Shall I look out the glasses, Tom? I think Daisy's expecting champagne."

"Oh. Yes. Of course."

She remembered that dreadful day, the day when he saved her life. Then later, in the bakery, putting out the crates, making tea, and making her feel whole again.

"I've never forgotten you, Tom. Not once."

He pushed his hair off his forehead and sighed. "Sometimes life takes us on a path we could never dream of."

"You've done well, Tom." She was desperate to know if he were seeing anyone, or worse still, married. There was no ring, but how could she ask him such an intimate question?

Tom, distracted, began setting out the tray, kettle still on the boil, finding the cups and saucers. Harriet had so many burning questions, but how could she ask? How would he react? Then, with her eyes fixed on the milk jug, she said, "I remember seeing you in Pete's café, not long after you cut your finger…do you remember?" Harriet faltered. She remembered so much it hurt.

Tom turned to face her, his eyes distant for a second. "I've never been back there, not since that night. Not without you…" He sounded gruff. He bit down on his bottom lip.

Dare she say it? Then out it popped. "But I saw you, with a woman."

He looked puzzled, and then as if a hazy memory had been jogged, he replied, "Yes, you're right. I remember now. Most odd. A woman contacted me out of the blue. Said she knew Lady Carmichael and, off the back of the garden party success, had a business proposal. She suggested the time and place—I thought it strange at the time. After all, Pete's café is hardly a palace, or the place to conduct business. But she convinced me that she and her partner preferred casual, so I went along with it."

Harriet gasped at a flash of memory. Had CJ deliberately slowed the moment he drew alongside the café? It certainly gave her time to see Tom and his companion. Surely not?

Tom poured the hot water over the tea leaves and stirred thoughtfully. "He never turned up. The business partner, I mean, and I never saw her again. Most peculiar."

Harriet's heart lifted as he brushed past.

"I don't know what I've been thinking." Tom looked abashed at the tea tray. "Habit, I guess. I'll get the glasses, shall I?"

She nodded assent.

"Maybe…" His voice sounded gruff again. He lifted the tray.

"Yes, Tom?" Harriet trembled.

"Maybe…maybe we could…"

Harriet had been restricted far too long by CJ to allow Tom to slip through her fingers again. She had to try. She had to make amends. Even if they were only ever to be friends, she never wanted to lose him again. Dare she be that bold?

"Tom, how about we meet up, if you're not busy, or are you going out with someone?"

"I've not been a monk, if that's what you're getting at."

"No. Don't be silly." Her heart sank. Too late. Her

fault. But she wouldn't be put off. "Perhaps we could, though, get together some time, I mean when you're not too busy. I've some ideas I'd like to pass your way. If that's okay?"

"Really? Yes, all right." He laughed. "I'd like that. You and your plans, Harriet."

Harriet could have wept. It was more than she deserved. More than she could have hoped for. They walked back into the front room, where Daisy waited patiently.

"Harriet says she has some new ideas, Daisy." Tom shook his head, a light smile playing across his lips. "We thought it might be a good idea to catch up properly so I can hear these ideas of hers properly."

"Sounds like a sensible plan to me," agreed Daisy happily. "Now, Tom, are you going to pour the champagne or what?"

Daisy knew. It was obvious from their faces they were already back on track. She was pleased. Tom seemed so lonely, even with the business keeping him busy. Right from the very start she'd known they were right for each other. Now it was down to Tom to stop pussyfooting around. In fact, she would start working on him. In her own way.

Chapter 59

Harriet had been pacing the rooms, waiting, wondering, wishing she hadn't agreed he would pick her up here, at the house. The house of horror, as she had come to think of it. She foolishly hadn't thought about Tom seeing the home she'd shared with CJ as being a problem. Now she did, it was too late. How stupid!

Tom was outside her house, thinking about pushing the bell. He couldn't believe how swanky the place was. He pushed back his hair with a trickle of doubt. Perhaps his hope of them being together was a stupid idea. What was he thinking of?

After she heard a car pull up, she went to the door and glanced through the viewing pane. It was him! He was standing there looking oh, so awkward, but oh, so lovely.

She opened the door. "Dressed to impress, eh?" She sounded so cheerful, it instantly put him at ease.

"Harriet. Thank you. Yes, I've, uh, I've only got a van. Is that okay?"

Harriet giggled. "A man with a van, and a woman with a plan. Sounds good to me."

He grinned. She made life so easy. He opened the van door and ensured she was settled before closing it.

The memory of their journey back from Lady Carmichael's was in her head. That was when he first asked her to join him for a meal at Pete's café. They had gone Dutch because she insisted.

"I thought we might go for a walk in Hyde Park. There's a little tearoom there by the lakeside. Not sure if it's open. If it is, and if you don't mind, I'd like to check out the competition and look at ways to improve the business." He was pulling away out of the drive. "Will that be all right with you?"

"Absolutely, what a great idea." Harriet began to relax. A walk, no fancy restaurant that CJ would have insisted upon. It sounded perfect.

They came through Hyde Park by way of Marble Arch. Horses clopped by, and they walked on until they reached the Serpentine. It was an unusually glorious day, and everyone was making the most of it. Couples, families, friends, taking a stroll along the paths. Even with the chill in the air some took advantage of a picnic, wrapped up warm with blankets on the lawns. Normally, in the summer, the parks would be full of sun-worshipers, swimmers, boaters. They passed a serried line of bathing huts beside the water's edge. Children were standing on the jetty throwing breadcrumbs and screaming in delight as the ducks rushed toward them, pecking, quacking.

Harriet and Tom, standing side by side, laughed at the commotion. Harriet's nerves had settled. It was as if there had never been a time apart.

"Look, a table has become vacant." Harriet pointed, and Tom moved swiftly. She watched his broad back secure the two seats and wait for her to arrive.

"So, you have an idea, Harriet?" Tom looked at her quizzically. "I'm always up for suggestions."

"Straight to business. Perfect." She grinned as she pushed her glasses back up her nose and followed with a sigh.

"You're probably going to hate this idea, but I wonder...have you considered apprenticeships? Work is hard to come by, and learning a trade even harder..."

Tom sat upright with surprise.

"Goodness, Harriet, you don't come with half measures, do you?"

"No. Do you think it's something you might be able to work with?"

The notion wasn't without merit, he had to admit. Just then a young girl came and served them, but when she returned with dry buns and weak tea, he flinched.

"I don't think I'm going to learn much here, other than what not to do, but they've got a great location. I can't deny that. Maybe I can offer to supply my wares."

Harriet sat back amused.

"What?"

"It's so good to see you again, Tom."

He reached across and lightly touched her hand.

"Likewise, Harriet. We must do this again."

Chapter 60

Tom arranged to see Harriet as often as possible. He took her to open air concerts. They sat on stripey deckchairs in Ruskin Park and listened to the brass band in the bandstand. They walked for miles just talking and taking in London's often hidden vast green areas and missed treasures. It seemed so easy. They seemed so easy together. But he was worried. At times Harriet seemed distant, lost to her thoughts, pensive, withdrawn, pale, and on other days, she was bright and cheery and appeared not to have a care in the world.

Then one day, when he took her to Green Islands boating lake, Harriet began to open up.

They were walking through the trees and the half-light fell upon her face full of concern.

"Penny for your thoughts."

She looked startled.

"Nana used to say that." She pushed her glasses up her nose. "Seems like a lifetime ago."

"What's bothering you, Harriet? Would you prefer to go to a smart restaurant? You can tell me. I honestly don't mind. I can afford it now."

"No. You've got it wrong, Tom." She took a deep breath. "Everything we do together is perfect. I love our friendship. Walking, talking, just being together, I really cherish these moments. Fancy restaurants can do a hike over this any day."

Tom looked relieved but asked, "So, what's the problem?"

"I've got a meeting with Lord Sutcliffe." She looked contemplative. "He's managing the case over CJ's death. He's my lawyer." Her lip trembled a little.

"You don't have to tell me, not if you don't want to, Harriet."

"I would like to, Tom. I've not completely confided in anyone about the events that led up to his death, except Lord Sutcliffe, that is, and though I trust him, he's hardly you. I trust you, Tom, but some of the things that happened... I... Would that be all right? If I told you everything?"

Tom nodded thoughtfully. "How about you come back to mine? We could talk, or whatever suits you."

"I'd like that, Tom. I need to be honest—your views and friendship are incredibly important to me."

Friendship, he thought. Friends. Yes, he would make do with their friendship. But as they walked, she started to talk, and it seemed she couldn't stop. The words tumbled out in dashes, dots, and hiccups as the memories kept coming. Tom listened. How could that man be so evil, so cold, so calculating? Tom became angry at himself, blaming himself for letting her go, letting her be taken away.

He knew he would never tell her, but he would have killed the monster himself if he were not already dead.

Now, more than ever, he wanted Harriet by his side, to look after her. To comfort her. To love her. But Harriet's experiences were still raw, he hadn't got any younger, and how could he capitalize upon her vulnerability? That would make him almost bad as her husband had been. No, he would wait. And he would pray, and maybe dare to hope one day she would love him as much as he loved her.

Chapter 61

1960

It was nearing Christmas, and with the verdict of her husband's death settled by the courts as accidental, Harriet felt able to breathe again. Probate required a vast amount of painstaking detail, but with Lord Sutcliffe's help, she began with CJ's business.

Harriet gathered courage, found the key to his shop, and paid a visit.

Harriet's mouth puckered as she looked over the smart shop front with the name *CJ Rutherford Antiques* in gold lettering on a verdant green background. It looked classy. How ridiculous that this was the first she'd set eyes on it. Peering through the window, she saw the light on and Margaux acting like she owned the place, talking to a man. Harriet felt fury. She owed nothing to Margaux, even though her father had been amazing. Harriet took the plunge. A little bell above the door tinkled. Margaux gave her a look of sheer surprise, worry lines crossing her brow, but at a small gesture from Harriet she resumed her conversation with the client.

The shop interior was wonderfully arranged. Nothing ostentatious, but from what she could see, good quality items, in pristine condition. Just as she would have expected from CJ. Out the back was a room set up as an office-come-meeting-area, with a table and chair, and a comfortable sofa with a liquor cabinet filled with CJ's favored brandy. Off to the right, discreetly hidden behind a beautiful privacy screen, a filing cabinet. Harriet raised a brow, irritated, as she tried the drawers. She should have known. It was locked. Margaux arrived seconds later.

"I'd like the keys to this, please, Margaux." She held out her hand. Margaux drew a breath.

"Why don't I finish up, and we can talk?"

"No, Margaux, I'll have the key, and you can run along."

Margaux's mouth, set grim in matchstick red, reluctantly opened her bag and fished around until, at last, she retrieved the key.

"Your client is waiting. Don't mind me. I can manage perfectly." Harriet nodded toward a shadow outside, banishing Margaux from the office.

Harriet's flair for business, and previous tenacity at Dingham's Department Store, did her proud. She quickly scoured paperwork—meticulous, and the filing system a joy—and upon further inspection, beneath the suspended rails she found a ledger. Harriet sat at the desk and began reading the entries. There was another business, most likely hidden from the taxman. Stepping outside the office for a moment, she listened to Margaux discussing a possible sale. Once the customer left, unaware she was being watched, Margaux pressed a hand to her chest and rested against the door frame. Harriet stepped out from the shadow.

"I see you've taken it upon yourself to continue trading without my permission." Margaux's face became a picture of confusion.

"CJ and I had an understanding."

Harriet put her hand up. "Nothing formal, then."

Margaux flushed deep crimson; her eyes narrowed.

Harriet didn't skip a beat. "I can see the businesses are doing well."

"Business," Margaux corrected.

Harriet sighed. "Business-*es*. Though one may need a little explaining to the taxman. Unless, of course, you'd like to buy me out at a realistic price?"

"But?"

"I have a comprehensive list of the stock." She waved the ledger. "Thank you for your diligence. I would like the keys to the warehouse and the shop before you leave. All of them." Harriet smiled. "Oh, yes, and here is the name of my lawyer." She handed her a card.

Margaux almost fainted.

Chapter 62

It was nearing Christmas, and the verdict of her husband's death had been decreed accidental by the courts. Lady Sutcliffe's lawyer had done a brilliant job of getting her off the hook, which came as no surprise, as Margaux's father, Lord Sutcliffe QC, undoubtedly pulled many strings. Harriet sighed a breath of relief. It was over. No longer would she need to look over her shoulder. Or worry. She was financially sound. The life insurance CJ had taken out on her was nullified, and as per her agreement with Margaux, she never spoke of the woman's duplicitous hand in its preparation. Harriet was surprised to find CJ's business had been doing remarkably well under Margaux's careful eye, and the lies he'd told were just that, lies. His estate was worth far more than she could ever have imagined. Harriet could not believe all the time she'd scrimped and saved, with CJ berating her for being frivolous with the housekeeping, making her life a misery and trapping her at home—all that time he had been out enjoying life, carefree, and with a spend, spend, spend ethos. CJ had soundly played her. The painting that had once belonged to her grandmother—which had been "stolen" to cover his debt when he could easily have paid otherwise—remained with Dorian Craddock. At least, she consoled herself, it was loved and safe. Harriet could start her life over. No longer would CJ be able to torture her physically or mentally. In the new year she would sell up. The house would go to auction, and CJ's businesses would be sold. She would be able to afford something smart, small, and comfortable, maybe somewhere in the countryside. Then she would put her plans into action.

The phone rang in the hallway. Harriet took a deep breath and picked up the receiver.

"Hello, Kate." Harriet smiled down the line. Their agreement to speak to one another every night continued.

"You okay?"

"Everything's fine, thank you. How was your day?" Harriet decided not to share her dealing with Margaux. Instead, she asked about Alex, Kate's beau. They had been together for five months or more. It seemed Alex, an upcoming back bencher, was making a name for himself. Kate always breathed his name like a schoolgirl with a crush. It made Harriet smile. Alex seemed to be yin to Kate's yang. He was the calming influence when she got a little crazy. And she did get crazy at times. Harriet often thought it must be her creative genius that made her go off on one of her wild tangents, especially concerning her upcoming fashion show. But every time Kate spoke of Alex she sounded happy. Gloriously happy.

"I was thinking," said Harriet, the smile still on her lips.

"Oh, no, there you go again." Kate giggled.

Harriet sighed. "Can I speak? I wonder if you and Alex would like to stay over for Christmas. I love to cook, and I know Jack's off to South Africa in the new year. Do you think he might come as well? I hope so. It would be lovely to see him again." She couldn't stop talking. Like a child who ate too many sweets, she fizzed with the thrill of the idea. Just the thought of doing something nice for her friends already gave her pleasure. "Please say yes."

Kate, laughing, caught up with her enthusiasm, shouted down the line, "Yes, of course. You know how I hate cooking. Count us in."

Harriet was pleased, excited. A time to air the ghosts once and for all, and if Kate could come earlier to stay with her, all the better. If they were alone, it might even be the perfect time to talk about her plans to open a safe house for battered women.

Harriet replaced the receiver and made her next call. Mrs. Gaffney was in floods the moment she posed the question. A little holiday away? Time spent with lovely people? A Christmas meal? How could she possibly say no?

Next, she telephoned Jack. His deep timbre came across the line, polite, courteous, until his likeable comical tone caught Harriet's ear when he realized it was her. Jack's answer was a resounding yes. He loved her cooking. Couldn't get enough of it. *Yes, please, Thank you. What time shall I be there? Who else is coming? I can collect her. Just give me the nod.*

Harriet exhaled. Pleased. Happy. There were another couple of calls she would need to make. Daisy and Tom, her next priority—she prayed they would say yes. With her heart in her mouth, she made the call. When she put the phone down, she was bouncing with joy. They said yes! What to cook? Though Christmases with her Nana had always been wonderful, they were always a frugal affair. Now she wanted to splash the cash, be frivolous for a change, and make the holiday really special for her special guests. Harriet found Marguerite Patten's cookery book and began making a list, full of ideas new and traditional. She quickly got her order in with the butcher. Chicken was more expensive and much smaller. They would have turkey, and sausage meat stuffing, and cranberry sauce, and puddings. She would have to make a Christmas cake and puddings. Her mind flew over the list. She had never felt so happy and started singing Christmas carols. Turkey would allow for leftovers, but she ordered pork pies, and chutney, and cheese for the evening. She would make the bread, sausage rolls and mince pies herself, and she would make soup, like Nana's.

With the Christmas cards written, she dropped them into the postbox with a lift in her heart. Back home, she stirred, mixed, and baked the Christmas cake, and put a silver sixpence in the Christmas pudding for luck. She made the decorations and ordered a Christmas tree to be delivered.

Harriet bought small gifts for each of her guests. She freshened the bedrooms, beat the curtains, cleaned the windows, washed the floors, and put fresh linen on every bed. Even the garden looked neat and tidy again. She worked hard making everything welcoming and comfortable for her guests. It was a distraction, but a good one. A positive way of living in the house alone, without thinking too much about its history. Her history.

Chapter 63

Saturday morning, a week before Christmas Eve, with Kate sprawled out on the floor in Harriet's lounge with a heap of fashion magazines and a cup of coffee in front of her, the doorbell rang. Harriet was nowhere to be seen.

"Get that, Harriet, will you?" she yelled. There was no answer. Kate jumped up, hollering down the hallway, leaving the scent of chicory behind. A huge parcel had been left on the doorstep. Looking around, expecting see the Royal Mail, she caught sight of a black van pulling away down the road.

"Harriet!" Kate called out again.

She arrived looking flushed.

"About time, Missy!" Kate grinned.

"Where did that come from?" Harriet puzzled at the parcel.

"Bloody Father Christmas, who else? He couldn't get it down the chimney, so he thought, hey, why not drop it off early!" Kate, laughing at her own joke, turned serious for a second. "I guess you weren't expecting anything, by the look of you?"

Harriet shook her head.

"Well, it's got your name on the front. Are we going to bring it in, or leave it on the doorstep?"

Harriet's heart raced, checking the package over. She felt excited, but oddly afraid. Kate, impatient as always and unable to contain herself, found scissors and a sharp knife and handed them over. Three layers in, Harriet came across a large cotton covering constructed like a pillow. As its contents were slowly revealed, Harriet gasped. She'd guessed already, she was right, it was her Nana's painting! She found a small envelope hooked into the back and tore it open. She read the brief note, signed DC, and everything slotted into place. The burglary. Dorian.

Kate watched Harriet's every expression but said nothing as she helped lift the painting off the table and prop it against the couch.

"I never thought to have this, ever again." Harriet suddenly looked crestfallen.

Kate blinked, puzzled. "What do you mean? No! Is this the painting, the one you told me about?"

"Yes."

"But how... I don't understand. It was stolen?" Kate stepped back, still admiring it. "It's beautiful, Harriet. Funny thing, I feel I know this place. Yes, I'm sure I do. I can't believe it—it's just like the place where I grew up."

"Really? How wonderful..."

Instead of wanting to know more about Kate's home, Harriet could only feel anxiety.

"I have a problem, Kate. I need to do the right thing and notify the police and the insurers. They're sure to take it off my hands while they decide what to do." Her eyes flicked from the painting to Kate. Her chin jutted out. This was stupid. She had nothing to fear.

"I'm not telling the authorities until after Christmas. It's mine, and its going in my bedroom until the experts can decide who it belongs to."

"Okaaay," said Kate slowly.

Harriet pondered a moment or two. She could see the open door to the study. Her eyes narrowed. One thing that puzzled her was how neither the police nor the insurers had found the priest hole. She caught Kate's hand.

"I want to show you something."

Kate, curious, followed Harriet into the study.

"Have you ever seen a priest hole, Kate?"

Harriet, not waiting for a response, walked her straight over to the huge wall of books.

"I don't think I could do this without someone else being here," she whispered, running fingers along the lower half of one of the shelves until she found it—*Tail of Two Cities*.

Kate spotted the misspelt cover as Harriet lifted the base of the book. The door to the priest hole silently swung open.

"Bloody hell, Hattie!" exclaimed Kate. "No way!" They stepped inside. Even in the gloom Harriet could see the paintings were no longer there. Harriet privately thought no doubt once CJ discovered the notebook and photographs were missing, he would have moved the paintings somewhere else. Maybe even sold one to Dorian.

Tentatively, Harriet switched the light on, the memory of that day still raw, vivid in her mind. The fear, the sheer terror of feeling trapped inside and being found by CJ. The door swung closed.

Kate gave a low groan. "I hope you know how to get us out of here."

"It's all right. Just bear with me." Harriet felt terrified, like a trapped animal, all over again. How stupid to even enter. What the hell was she thinking?

Seconds later, the light went out. Kate groaned again.

Harriet, shaking, fumbled along the wall until the memory flooded back and calm took over.

"Before I switch on the light, Kate, allow your eyes to adjust to the dark." She could feel Kate's warm breath on her neck. "Can you see through into the study?"

"Well, I bloody never!"

Harriet laughed despite everything. She flicked on the light, and the door slid open.

"Phew! I was beginning to think we might miss Christmas Day altogether!" Kate grinned with relief.

Maybe, just maybe, Kate would understand. Harriet lifted her eyes. "I'd like to tell you everything, but I don't know where to begin."

Kate slipped her arm about her. "Uncle Jack always says the best place to start is from the beginning."

That day, Harriet and Kate opened their hearts like never before. They divulged their innermost feelings, their views on the world, and how they felt they were viewed.

Harriet spoke fondly of her grandmother and the mother she never knew. How proud she was of her grandmother taking care of her from birth, and also of her mother, who had been a prima ballerina until pregnancy determined otherwise, right up until her untimely death. Harriet lightly touched on the ignorance of people, and how she was bullied at school once they found out her mother was unmarried. Harriet then recalled that fateful day when her grandmother passed. She had hinted at the possibility her father was out there, somewhere.

Kate admitted she'd never told anyone she had been adopted, even though her adoptive parents were wonderful and so easily could have been her own. She always felt there was something missing, and though she felt deep shame for thinking like that, the doubts, the questions were still there. Why was she abandoned? Had she been a bad child? Was her natural mother still alive?

Harriet listened carefully and digested everything. They held hands, shared their hopes, their dreams, and their aspirations. She was surprised to find Kate's desire to know more about her family matched her own, and they came to an agreement. February next year they would be twenty-one. After Kate's fashion show was over, they would invest time to search for family members, or at least attempt to find the truth, once and for all.

Chapter 64

Christmas Day 1960

Waking to a cold Christmas morning, Jack read over the last communication from Africa. Naidoo had a contract delivering for a worldwide soft drink company, and his business was growing. What pleased Jack more was that the gang had stuck together. He knew the boy would make good and was proud of him. Jack jotted some notes down and decided to make the journey to see Naidoo while he was in the country and make sure he would be back in time for Kate's birthday and her show. If he missed either, he would never live it down. But today, he was looking forward to sharing Christmas at Harriet's with family and friends.

Collecting Mrs. Gaffney as promised, he drove them over to Harriet's. Kate would already be there, as she'd promised to help with the preparations, and Jack was keen to meet Alex, the man Kate was clearly besotted with. He would have to give the man the onceover and give his approval. Not that Kate would take any notice of what his views were—she would do what Kate always did and please herself.

Alex answered the door when they arrived, and when he introduced himself it was clear from the start that he and Jack would hit it off. Whilst Alex relieved them of their coats, Mrs. G was beside herself looking around. "My goodness, this place is as huge as it is beautiful, Harriet," she said, kissing her on the cheek. "And the tree, spectacular!" Harriet thanked her warmly, having spent hours trying to make it look at least acceptable.

"I agree, but without Kate's addition of the bowed ribbons, I don't think it would be half as good, Mrs. G."

As Mrs. Gaffney was led through to the lounge, Alex and Jack put their overnight bags in their rooms. Kate had been on the sofa, her legs folded under her, but she jumped up as Mrs. Gaffney arrived.

"What perfect timing, Mrs. G," she greeted her, having adopted the same abbreviation Harriet used. "I was just about to pour a sherry. Do you fancy one?" Kate smiled broadly, having remembering Harriet's comment about her former landlady's love of it—with her regular reasoning "for medicinal purposes."

Mrs. G had brought her best cigarette holder for the occasion and now pulled it from her handbag with a flourish. "I think that would be marvelous." She smiled, planting a cigarette securely in the holder's end and selecting a comfy chair in which to settle down.

While Kate busied herself making sure they were comfy, Jack took charge of the fire, adding more coal, and Alex helped stack logs, bringing them from outside and putting them into the basket by the hearth. Kate joined Mrs. G in having a glass of sherry and happily talked to her about her latest beau and plans. Kate as usual was funny, entertaining, and Mrs. G was in stitches with the stories she exaggerated to great effect. "You modern girls, if only I were young again," she sighed, wiping away tears of laughter.

Harriet nervously paced the kitchen, deliberately

putting tea towels at jaunty angles. She could do that now. Tom and Daisy had yet to arrive. She needn't have worried—they arrived not five minutes later. Harriet was first to the door. Her heart leapt right into her throat. Tom was here! She was so excited to see him, she almost forgot to ask them in.

"Where are my manners? Please come on in." Harriet helped Daisy into the lounge, and Jack, with his easygoing manner, quickly made the introductions and helped them get settled.

Harriet went into the kitchen again, though she would have much rather stayed with Tom and forgotten about the food. Deep down, she agonized it wouldn't be to a good enough standard. She needn't have worried. They were all seated, with crackers popped, glasses raised, and wearing the obligatory paper hats, and the meal was demolished with rounds of approval and contentment. Harriet caught Tom looking at her more than once throughout the meal, and it made her heart race. Afterward, Kate insisted they play Treenie's party game after the meal was finished, and she directed each person to think of someone famous. Jack smiled. It was kind of Chaz and Treenie to take them under their wing that first Christmas without their own family. Maybe Kate thought the same.

Jack was charming and attentive as always, and Mrs. G was smitten. Once Harriet began clearing the dishes, Tom insisted he help do the washing up. At three o'clock it was agreed they would listen to the Queen's speech, and they settled down for that.

"My granny always thought you had to stand up when the Queen was on the television," said Alex. "She was convinced the Queen could see her, so she would always mind her p's and q's when she was on."

"She can't see us, can she?" questioned Mrs. G, quickly checking her face in her powder compact mirror. Kate nudged Harriet in amusement.

Silence fell as the Queen wished everyone "a Happy Christmas and a prosperous New Year" and thanked the people around the world and the commonwealth, delighted to receive so many kind messages earlier in the year when her second son was born. A murmur touched the room as she eloquently stated that to achieve and make improvements in life here and across the commonwealth could only be done with the determined effort of men and women everywhere. After her speech, Harriet switched the television off, and Kate enthused about the CND movement and the proposal to demonstrate.

"It's Christmas!" Harriet sang loudly in Kate's ear. "We'll have no talk of politics today, thank you, missy! Besides what would Alex do? Him being a back bencher, you could ruin any chance of his promotion."

"He would say…"—Kate raised her glass, and winked at Alex—" 'Have a drink and enjoy yourself.' Therefore, I propose we dance instead," and she pulled several black vinyl discs from their sleeves and stacked them one on top of the other and set the record player into motion. As the needle hit the deck, Bill Haley and the Comets blasted out with "Rock Around the Clock" and Jack immediately grabbed Mrs. Gaffney's hand, insisting she dance with him. Mrs. Gaffney laughed as he spun her around. Tom caught Harriet's waist and whisked her into the dance, and next, Alex and Kate joined in, and when "Shake, Rattle, and Roll" dropped as the next tune, an exhausted Mrs. Gaffney declined to continue dancing, so Jack took to spinning Harriet and Kate around the room, giving Tom and Alex short breaks.

Thirsty from all the revelry, they rested a while. Kate and Harriet topped everyone up with drinks, and Jack set about organizing silly games they could all get involved in, including Daisy. It brought a delighted whoop from Kate, recalling some of them from her childhood. Charades were first, followed by Spin-the-Bottle, and then Black Magic—in which Jack and Kate clearly took pleasure in astounding everyone with their ability to mind read.

Harriet watched the scene with pleasure. This house, a place that had never felt like home, was filled with laughter and joy. She glanced at Tom. He looked well. He caught her eye and smiled. This short time of having people around had already started the healing process. By late evening Mrs. G was nodding off, and as Harriet gently removed her cigarette holder from her fingers she came to with an embarrassed start. "I didn't drop off, did I?"

Jack chuckled, "You're not alone, Mrs. G. I think I might have been snoring."

Kate did a quick impersonation for him.

"I actually sound like a grizzly bear, do I?" Jack chuckled again and yawned.

With the suggestion that the day had come to a natural close, Daisy prepared to leave. Harriet was in the kitchen sorting out the remainders of the evening's supper when the remnants of Tom's cologne drifted her way.

"I think Daisy is almost ready to go, but I thought you could do with a hand first." He smiled. "It has been really lovely to see you again, Harriet, and you've made Christmas so special, for everyone. I've had the best time."

She turned off the tap. "I'm glad you came."

This Christmas for Harriet was like no other before. Friends, all sharing friendship and love under one roof. So much food and drinks, and the loads of silly games that Jack insisted they play. How she wished Nana were here to share it with her, with them. Kate was such a good friend... No, Kate was far more than just a friend. She caught him watching her. She smiled.

And Tom...Tom was more than a friend. He was a solid and permanent part of her life. She followed him out of the kitchen to say good night to Daisy.

"Harriet?" Tom, outside in the driveway, had just helped Daisy into the taxi, where she was now settling herself. Harriet and Kate were by the door. Mrs. Gaffney had already said good night and gone to bed in one of the spare bedrooms, and Jack and Alex were chatting outside. Tom had his usual shy smile on his lips and pushed his hair back as he stepped up to her.

"Life is so strange." He looked thoughtful as his eyes searched hers.

"It is, Tom. Who would have guessed you would be here with me right now. It's been lovely, hasn't it, Christmas?"

"More than lovely, Harriet. Far more than that. Thank you. I really mean it. I'm just sorry I have to go, but Daisy..."

"Of course. I know."

He turned to go and then came back.

"You know, I've been wanting to do this all day." He caught Harriet by the shoulders and gently pulled

334

her toward him and kissed her fully on the lips, warmly, deliciously, and—dare she think it—full of desire.

Harriet pulled away and looked him in the eye.

"I'm sorry." Tom looked mortified. "I shouldn't have done that. It was inappropriate."

Harriet immediately moved back to him.

"Yes, you should have, you idiot, but you should have done it a very long time ago." She kissed him right back, and the sensation of being able to do that after all this time made it all the sweeter.

"Call me tomorrow?"

Tom's expression was replaced by a glow of realization. He turned to Kate, who was wolf-whistling them. He laughed, elated. He leaned forward and kissed Kate on the cheek, and she promptly kissed him back.

"Don't be a stranger," she said, "and take care of Harriet, or I'll have to come and knock your bloody block off!"

Tom turned to Harriet and kissed her again.

"Tomorrow?"

And in that moment Harriet knew. His face said it all. She knew Tom would be back and that life was going on a far better path than she could ever have hoped for.

There is a sequel to this book. Here's a glimpse:

The Twenty-One-Year Contract

Chapter 1

February 11, 1954

Pops winked at Kathleen in the rearview mirror as he reversed their brand new Morris Minor into the Latimers' drive. Excited, Kathleen wriggled impatiently around on the blue leather back seat. Beside her she had a small overnight bag, and a bunch of delphiniums, cut fresh this morning from their garden.

"Now, Kathleen Gray…" Her mother turned around in the front seat, with baby Bobby sitting on his mother's lap, gurgling. The words drifted over her and out the window. She'd heard it all before. Great Aunt Jane was ill. They would bring her home to look after her. York was a long drive. All Kathleen could think about was staying over with her best friend, Lucy.

"Please stop worrying, Mum. I'll be fine, really."

Lily Latimer, Lucy's mother, waited at the front door, and Kathleen handed her the flowers.

"They're divine, Kathleen, thank you," said Mrs. Latimer, sniffing their scent. "Now, remember to call me Aunty Lily. It would never do being called Mrs. Latimer. It makes me feel so very old."

Kathleen smiled, and, remembering her manners, waited whilst Mr. Latimer came through the hallway. He looked every inch the newly elected local MP, so very proper. So proper, in fact, Kathleen had to resist the urge to curtsey.

"Kathleen." Mr. Latimer offered a polite, reserved nod as he walked past to join the group at the door. Kathleen listened to Pops speaking with Mr. Latimer, thanking them for their help. She loved Pops' voice, deep, gentle, easygoing, just like him.

"They could be hours and hours droning on," Lucy whispered, and dragged her upstairs to her room, grinning. "You can wave goodbye when they leave."

Kathleen half smiled. Once upon a time her shy little friend would never have said boo to a goose. At last she was coming out of her shell.

"Well, what do you think?" Kathleen studied Lucy's bedroom with a keen eye. She knew all about her friend's room, having helped her own mother to make the curtains and swags.

"Groovy." She used their most recently learned word, something Lucy's mother had heard in one of the latest films from America.

Aunty Lily poked her head around the door. "Kathleen, your parents are going."

Kathleen trailed back downstairs after Aunty Lily.

"Look after Mummy and Pops, won't you, Bobby dear?" Kathleen tickled her little baby brother's soft chubby cheek and kissed him fondly.

Bobby babbled happily with his little fist in his mouth, drool dribbling down around fat creamy white knuckles. Kathleen loved everything about Bobby, right down to his soft curls tumbling around his ears. A beautiful little miracle. Especially as her adoptive parents had been told they could never have children of their own.

"Now be good, won't you?" said her mother, hugging her goodbye.

"Bye, Mum." She sighed but laughed as her father bear-hugged her one last time. Just one last kiss, for Bobby, and they were off.

That night the girls were treated to supper in Lucy's bedroom. Napkins were prettily arranged in neat triangles on filigree plates with cold milk in fluted glasses. Kathleen looked at the plates of ham, tongue, and one cherry tomato nestled inside a crisp cupped lettuce leaf, amazed Mr. Latimer allowed such decadence, and in the bedroom of all places.

"Look," hushed Kathleen once Aunty Lily left. She locked the door. "I've brought us something a tad better than milk," and she produced a jam jar filled with red liquid.

"What's that?"

"Cherry juice." Kathleen giggled, draining the milk and rinsing their glasses in the bedroom sink.

"Chin-chin!" Kathleen grinned widely, sharing the contents between them. "Down the hatch in…three, two, ONE!"

Lucy swallowed the contents whole—and gagged.

"Cherry juice?" Lucy shuddered.

Kathleen laughed. "Now, how about a ciggie, dahling?"

Lucy's eyes popped as her friend produced a packet of cigarettes and matches.

"Come on!" They opened the bedroom window, letting the freezing air in, and Kathleen leaned out and lit the cigarette. She took a deep drag, spluttered, and said, "Here."

338

"What if Mummy or Daddy…"

"Just stick your head out the window." The tobacco made Kathleen feel lightheaded, and she didn't like the sensation at all.

Lucy took a quick puff and coughed all over the place.

"What are you trying to do, kill me?"

"It's *so grooovy* staying over, darling." Kathleen laughed.

Lucy waved a forty-five vinyl in the air, forgetting the cigarette in her hand.

"I have Bill Haley and the Comets." She took the black gem from its sleeve.

"Oops-a-daisy," said Lucy as the needle scratched the surface. Seconds later, the music burst into the room. Kathleen clapped her hands in delight and started swinging her hips. Lucy joined her, wheeling Kathleen under her arm and spinning her around.

The girls danced to virtual exhaustion, playing the record over and over, and by the time Lucy's mother collected their trays, they were so excited it took all her effort to contain them. Aunty Lily raised a brow. "It's cold in here." Her eyes narrowed as she sniffed the air. Lucy held her breath.

"Now, girls, it's time for bed. Remember to clean your teeth, and then lights out."

"Yes, Mother," said Lucy.

"Remember, Lucy, Father would be very unhappy to have his sleep disturbed." Raising her brow and glancing at Kathleen, she added, "No more noise, or music, or anything else!"

As the door closed, the girls, stifling their laughter, threw themselves onto their beds. As the evening wore on, they settled into whispered hushes. Kathleen having secretly borrowed torches from her father's garage, they lay in their beds, searchlights crisscrossing the ceiling as if hunting for wartime doodle bugs, until eventually sleep won.

****

Six forty-one a.m.

Propping herself on her elbow, Kathleen peered into the breaking light and exhaled, "Groovy."

Lucy was curled into a tight ball, blankets tucked right up around her chin, sound asleep. Pulling on her dressing gown and tiptoeing to the window, she inched the curtain open and peered out. Her eyes popped. Scattered across the ledge, ash had stuck in the frost. There would be hell to pay if Lucy's parents found out.

Lucy snuffled and turned, mumbling something, while Kathleen scraped the incriminating evidence away.

"Groovy." Kathleen's breathing returned to normal as she gazed out the window. The frosted road sparkled, the avenue of brand new houses spelling wealth. She stood a while watching a bird flit between manicured bushes, acknowledging this must be the perfect home for Lucy's father, though she doubted he understood the lowly constituents of his borough. After all, he didn't seem completely in tune even with his own family, not at all like her wonderful Pops. She shivered. Someone walked over her grave. She decided to snuggle back under her covers until Lucy woke.

****

Seven fifty-six

"Wake up lazy bones!" Lucy bounced up and down on her bed, tugging at her blankets. Kathleen dragged them back.

"I don't want to, thank you very much, Luce!"

"Come see. There's a police car outside the house. Come on!" She dragged Kathleen out of bed, and they poked their heads through the gap in the curtain. Sure enough, there was a police car parked in the same spot where Kathleen's father parked only yesterday.

"Groovy."

"You don't think anyone saw us smoking, do you?" Lucy's eyes were fearful and wide. "Or found out about the sherry?"

"Don't be stupid."

At a knock on the front door, they fell silent. There was talking. To their dismay, a female began to cry.

****

Seven fifty-eight

"Mummy?" Lucy moved toward the bedroom door, listening, hesitating. Kathleen instinctively reached out a hand. Moments later, a door closed. The sounds disappeared. The girls flung on their dressing gowns, shoved feet into slippers, and crept downstairs. Even though the study door was tightly shut, they could hear muffled voices, and intermittent sobbing. Without warning, the door opened. Light flooded into the hallway. Two gargantuan uniformed policemen stepped from the study, followed by Mr. Latimer. The girls looked guilty, as if caught in the act of stealing.

"Mummy?"

"Lucy, you are to come with me." said Mr. Latimer, taking charge. Kathleen noticed Lucy's father voice held a warmer edge than his usual formally clipped British.

"But...Mummy?" Lucy's eyes were wide and round.

"Your mother is fine," Mr. Latimer said with finality, nervously smoothing down his moustache. "It's Kathleen they have come to see."

The girls gasped. Kathleen released Lucy's hand, shrinking against the wall. Three men filled the hallway, eyeing one another awkwardly. Mr. Latimer nodded toward his wife, propelling Lucy toward the kitchen. From along the hallway, over the radio airwaves, came the familiar voice of the newsreader delivering the eight o'clock news.

"No! Don't leave me, Lucy!" cried Kathleen, watching her friend disappear. Aunty Lily tenderly placed her arm about her and gently encouraged her into Mr. Latimer's study.

The room smelt of stale tobacco and old leather. A large desk, almost central to the room, held piles of neatly arranged paperwork. To Kathleen, it looked how a judge's court room might be. The sherry? Cigarettes? Aunty Lily asked Kathleen to sit. The door closed behind them. The adults stood uneasily.

Kathleen, scared half to death, wondered if maybe they really did find out about the sherry. Maybe they'd found her stash of cigarettes.

Aunty Lily crouched beside her, eyes red, swollen with tears. When she spoke, her words came choking out in tiny pieces, unravelling themselves like a horror story.

Kathleen sat in rigid disbelief.

"Kathleen?" Aunty Lily's voice came from a distant planet. "Kathleen, I'm so sorry."

The room pressed in on her. Judgment day. Her beautiful parents were dead? Her gorgeous little baby brother Bobby, dead? Great Aunt Jane, dead?

"No! Never. Liar!" Kathleen screamed, furious

Aunty Lily could say such things, oblivious her arms were flailing, striking everything and everyone. One of the policemen held her tight, armor wrapped around her, until she could fight no more.

Aunty Lily collapsed to the floor. Kathleen folded, sobbing, weeping, disbelieving, in a heap. Eventually, using her last ounce of energy, she threw herself at Aunty Lily, crying, "Make it better, please, please, make it better."

And together they hugged one another on the floor of that office, in wretched misery.

A word about the author...

L. B. Griffin was born, raised, and married in the City of Bath, UK. Between being a College Lecturer, bringing up a family, and writing, her passions are travel, art, reading, sport, and socializing with friends. Her writing has always been inspired by stories of courage and survival. This is her debut novel, *Secrets, Shame, and a Shoebox*, and is entirely a work of historical fiction. She is happily married and surrounded by her family in Wiltshire.

~*~

www.facebook.com/lynngriffinauthor
www.instagram.com/lynngriffinauthoruk/
www.WifeInTheWest.com
www://twitter.com/LBGriffinAuthor/

Thank you for purchasing
this publication of The Wild Rose Press, Inc.

For questions or more information
contact us at
info@thewildrosepress.com.

The Wild Rose Press, Inc.
www.thewildrosepress.com